THE EARTHLING'S BROTHER

EARIK BEANN

Profoundly[1]
PUBLISHING

ISBN 978-1-7327408-4-6 (ebook)

ISBN 978-1-7327408-5-3 (paperback)

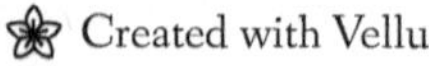 Created with Vellum

ONE

It was three in the morning when he walked in. Maria Rodriguez was at the front desk, the only staff member on duty at the time. It was a boring job, but it gave her time alone to work at her studies, and as far as service jobs went, the pay wasn't terrible.

She had been sitting on a stool behind the desk, typing away on her laptop. She was unable to see anything in the upper left corner of the screen. Lucas had knocked the computer off the kitchen table during one of his seizures, and it had never been the same since. Maria tried to scroll the page down, but the trackpad had decided it wasn't going to cooperate tonight, and so she had to type the first part of each sentence blind, hoping the words were correct. Her online classes were mostly a joke, but even their standards weren't so low as to overlook an essay completely full of misspellings.

Maria raised her dark eyes as she heard the chime from the front door. Although the town of Sedona tended to turn in early, not all the guests at the Bell Rock Inn followed its lead. It wasn't uncommon for out-of-towners to show up late on their way home from parties. Usually they were drunk. Sometimes they were stoned. Almost no one ever walked through that door at this time of the night without being inebriated in some fashion.

The man looked to be in his early twenties. He had long brown hair that fell around his shoulders in curls and a gigantic beard that turned up at the ends. His blue eyes sparkled as he caught her gaze, and he broke into a huge smile. At any other time, Maria would have smiled back. This time was different. Her eyes widened as she took in the wide shoulders, his tapered waist, and . . . she looked away, mortified. The stranger was without a scrap of clothing. From his head down to his bare feet, he was completely nude. His only possession appeared to be an unadorned silver bracelet around his left wrist.

"Oh shit," Maria said to herself quietly, sliding off the edge of the stool, her feet slipping into her shoes of their own accord. She glanced over at the gate that led behind the desk, checking to make sure it was locked.

The man walked up to her and laid his hands on the desk. The thick silver bracelet on his wrist flashed a reflection of the fluorescent lights in the ceiling, and Maria heard a soft click as it touched down on the glass countertop. He scanned the entire front area as if he were looking for something, his eyes lingering longest on her laptop. She slowly slid it back out of reach.

"Welcome to the Bell Rock Inn," she sputtered. She closed the laptop and moved it under the counter. It was a piece of crap, with a broken screen and finicky trackpad, the body held together more by duct tape than by the original plastic shell. But it was all she had. She couldn't afford to get another, especially after what she had to spend on Lucas's treatments.

The man snapped his attention at her, tilting his head to the side. It reminded her of how her dog reacted when she wagged a treat in front of his nose, except infinitely creepier.

"Are you OK?" she said. Her mouth was dry, and her voice caught in her throat. She tried to play it cool, but even she could detect the alarm in her tone. *This guy is either stoned out of his mind or psychotic.* She quickly formulated a rudimentary escape plan. Out the door behind her, down the hall, then pull one of the fire alarms. That would wake up the guests so she wouldn't be alone. Then out the back door? But how much of a head start would she have if he tried to come after her? This guy looked fit. Every muscle was perfectly defined and completely in proportion, as if he spent hours a day at the gym. With a physique like that, he could have been an underwear model, assuming he could get a hold of a pair of underwear. Maria tried to keep her eyes on his face.

The man squinted. It looked like he was staring at her mouth. His jaw dropped slightly, and he made a strange huffing sound, almost as if he were mimicking some large beast of burden. He cleared his throat and clicked his tongue against the front of his teeth. Maria wiped her palms against the legs of her pants.

There was a pause, and the man's expression changed, almost as if he was listening to something in the distance, and he shook his head slightly. He looked back at her, and smiled again.

"Hello." His voice was rich and full of genuine excitement.

"Hi." She tried to smile, but it was forced. Smiling was the last thing she felt like doing at this moment.

"I am on Earth," he declared. His pronunciation was perfect, but he spoke in a way that seemed almost as if he were surprised that words were coming out of his mouth.

Maria nodded, unsure how to answer.

"And you are a woman. . . . You are an Earth woman!"

"Um, yeah." *The guy is clearly stoned.* Maria relaxed a little. Stoned was better than psychotic. She could handle stoned.

"You are the first one I have met."

"The first woman, huh? Good for you." He was probably one of the new age tree-hugging energy-vortex worshippers who frequented Sedona. There were so many of them around that Maria couldn't go a day without being offered a crystal, or a reading, or a trip to a power spot that would open her consciousness. As a last resort, she had tried all that stuff with Lucas at one time or another, but none of it had helped him. As far as she could tell, it was just a way to sell trinkets to tourists. It was obvious what had happened: This guy had gone completely overboard with the psychedelics, stripped out of his clothes, and found himself wandering around in the dark. It was just her luck that of all the places he could have wandered into, he just happened to pick this hotel, on the night when she was on duty.

The seconds ticked by, the stranger content to just to stand there, staring at her.

"Are you cold?" Maria said.

"No."

"Are you sure? You don't have any clothes on."

The man looked down at himself, almost to double-check to see if what she was saying was true. Then he returned his gaze. It was obvious that he was completely without any shred of self-consciousness. "Is that why you are wearing them? Are you cold?"

Maria sighed. Although doing her schoolwork was by no means one of her favorite activities, it was vastly preferable to discussing the concept of clothing with someone too stoned to realize they were even naked. "So, is there something I can do for you?"

"What do you mean?" He seemed surprised.

Maria rolled her eyes. Her paper was due in the morning. She didn't have time for this. "Are you looking for a room or something?"

"A room?"

"Yes. You know, with a bed and a shower? It's the middle of the night and you just walked into a hotel."

"Oh!" The man seemed to consider for a moment. "Yes. I would like a room."

"Great." She turned to the office computer, and then paused. What was she thinking? Unless this guy had a magic pouch, there was no way he had money on him. He didn't even have shoes. She couldn't rent a room to someone like this.

"You don't have a credit card, do you?" she asked, pulling her hands back from the keyboard and turning to face him.

"No."

"But everything is OK, right? You're not in trouble or anything?"

"Yes. I am just a little unsure of where I am . . . aside from Earth!" He smiled that smile again, disarming her. Aside from all the confusion and underneath whatever drugs he was on, he was sweet. That much was clear. He reminded her of Lucas's father on his good days. His bad ones, too, actually. How many times had Rodrigo been too stoned to go to work?

"Look, I can't rent a room to you if you don't have a credit card, but I don't want to throw you out either. What is your name?"

"My name?"

"Yeah, your name." What had this guy taken? He was totally out of it.

"I don't have one."

"Or you're just too stoned to remember yours right now. Think. What does your mother call you?"

"My mother?" The man tilted his head again. His eyes drifted slightly to a place behind Maria's head and his expression was distant. Then something seemed to pass over his face, and he smiled. "I'm sample XA-7597."

"Sample XA-7597?"

"Yes."

"That's your name?"

"Yes." His mouth broke into a huge grin, laughing.

"You're sure?"

"Yes. Why?"

"It's just a very strange name."

"That's what she said it was when I asked her."

"When you asked who?"

"My mother."

"When was the last time you had to ask your mother what your name was?"

"I've only ever done it once. Just now."

"Uh . . . right."

It was obvious that even the most basic conversations were going to be impossible until this guy came down from his high. "Look, Sample XA-whatever. I'll just call you 'Sam' for short. How's that?"

"Excellent."

"You're not going to cause any trouble, are you, Sam?"

"No. I come in peace."

Maria hesitated. That was a weird thing to say. But with his "Earth woman" comment, he was probably stuck on a sci-fi trip. The smart choice would be to call the cops and let them handle this. Maria had a bad habit of allowing her heart to overrule her head, and there was no handbook for what to do with a friendly but completely stoned underwear model who couldn't remember his own name. And what was the deal with that caveman beard, anyway?

Sam smiled.

Later, when Maria thought back on why she decided to help him, she realized that it all came down to that sparkle in his eyes. She had seen it before when playing with Lucas, when her young nephew encountered something that sparked his joy and curiosity. Sam's eyes held the same wonder and awe, as if he was seeing the world for the very first time.

TWO

"Where is your beard? It seems strange that you don't have one," Sam asked, tugging on his own curling locks.

"Sorry to disappoint you." Hours later, and the guy was still sky high. Maria folded her arms, beyond tired at the end of her shift. "Come on, get up."

Sam stood up from the foldaway bed he had spent the night on. She didn't trust him enough to try to sneak him into one of the vacant rooms, so she had put him in the storage closet. As long as she got him out before breakfast, only her coworker would see him, and she wasn't worried about Allison ratting her out to management.

"I'm not disappointed, just surprised." He wore an old pair of jeans that were too baggy and a woman's pink sweater with sleeves that were a good four inches too short. The pickings can be slim when shopping for a wardrobe in lost and found. He reached down and started fumbling with the zipper to the jeans.

"What are you doing?"

Sam stopped, looking at her. From his expression, it was clear he wasn't sure what she was talking about.

"Leave them on. You can keep them."

"Really? Thanks!" He looked down at his clothes approvingly. "These are jeans. And this is a sweater."

"Catching on, aren't you? Come on."

Maria took a quick glance down the hallway to make sure the coast was clear, then led Sam out and into the lobby. A blonde teenager with entirely too much makeup stood behind the counter, engrossed in something on her phone. Her thumbs tapped away furiously as her expression shifted between petulance and outrage.

"Bye, Allison. See you later," Maria said.

Allison didn't respond, and for once Maria was grateful for the girl's tumultuous relationship with her idiot boyfriend. She quickly walked to the door, pulling Sam along by his hand, and breathed a sigh of relief when they finally stepped outside.

"Is Allison your friend?"

"Not really. We just work together." Maria led Sam over to the parking lot.

"She's short. You're short too. Are all women short?"

"You're quite the charmer, Sam." They had arrived at her car, an ancient, mud-brown Volkswagen. It had over three hundred thousand miles when she bought it. The odometer had conked out the second week she owned it, so she had no idea how many more miles she had put on it beyond that. The entire bottom half was so rusted out that her mechanic was afraid if he took anything apart, he would end up damaging the entire thing beyond repair. So he never fixed anything major, and Maria never asked him to try. She was going to drive it until it died. It was a piece of crap and a rolling death trap, but it was still the best car that $300 could buy in a pinch.

"What are those lumps on your chest? That's because you're a woman, right?" Sam said.

"Oh my God! How can you still be this high? What did you take anyway?"

Sam jumped, his eyes wide. "I didn't take anything! You gave me these clothes. Do you want them back?"

"No, I don't want the clothes back. Get in. You need to eat something." Maria got in and unlocked the passenger side door. She had to get rid of this guy, but she'd at least make sure he was fed before she cut him loose. She fastened her seatbelt and turned the ignition. Sam peered in at her from the passenger side window, holding his hands to the sides of his head as he pressed his forehead against the glass. Then he opened the door and sat in, looking around in a state of wonderment.

"Let me guess. I'm the first woman you've met, and this is the first car you've ever been in. Am I right?"

"Yes. It's amazing! You are amazing too!"

"Close the door, Sam. Yes, just grab it and pull it shut. There you go. Put your seatbelt on."

"How do you do it?"

"On the side. Just grab it and drag it across. No, you're doing it wrong. Just pull that end over and click it on the other side by your hip. No. Not like that." Maria put her head in her hands. She had that sinking feeling again. How had she found herself saddled with yet another stray? Sam wasn't her problem. She didn't have time to babysit him. She didn't even know his name. He was stoned, and possibly crazy, but here he was, sitting in her car with her. All because she trusted his smile? What was wrong with her?

"Got it! Ready. Now what?" Sam was practically bouncing in his seat.

"Now just sit there and chill out. And tell me if you have to barf or something. You're going to be in huge trouble if you throw up in my car."

———

The sun had just risen over the top of the huge sandstone formations that surrounded Sedona. The air was crisp, in the same way that all desert air is crisp after a cold night. There was a smell of wetness that hung in the air, and small clouds clung to the spaces between the red sandstone pillars at the edge of town, like wisps of smoke around the end of a burning cigarette.

"It is beautiful here," Sam said after a short drive, when Maria had parked and they had gotten out of the car. "It reminds me of the moons around the twin planets of. . . . Sorry. There isn't a word for that place with this mouth language."

Maria closed the car door and locked it. "That's awesome, Mr. Spock. We'll have to visit next time the starship *Enterprise* heads that direction."

"Mr. Spock?" He stared at her blankly.

"If you still can't remember your own name, you're probably not going to remember who he is either. But I'm willing to bet money that you've seen all the episodes. Probably more than once." She turned to face him and held up her hand, splitting her fingers down the middle so that it formed the classic V-shape greeting familiar to all Trekkies. "Live long and prosper, Sam from Earth."

They headed toward the awning of the café. The lot was half empty. The Coffee Pot Restaurant was a popular breakfast place, but it didn't start filling up until later. Tourists generally liked to sleep in while on vacation, and Maria preferred to avoid them if at all possible. She was glad her shift ended as early as it did.

"What's a starship?"

"You're like a little kid, you know?" Maria opened the door and shooed Sam through it. "A starship is like a giant car that holds a ton of people and then flies through outer space. You'll remember it all once you stop communing with the mushroom people."

Sam snorted. "Of all the methods that could be used to get people through space, that's got to be the absolute worst possible way to do it."

"How would you go about it, Einstein?"

"It depends if I knew where I wanted to go. If I had already been to the place and knew its signature, then I'd just entangle the matter here with the matter there, open a portal—is that the right word?—and then step through. But if I was just traveling around to discover new places, then I'd send a probe first and use that to establish the link on the other end."

Maria raised an eyebrow. Sam had answered very quickly, and there was no fuzziness about what he said. He wasn't speaking like someone who was stoned, even though his imagination was running completely wild. She didn't mind playing along. "How would you get the probe through space?"

"Energy exchange with surrounding matter."

"Not thrusters?"

"Thrusters?" Sam laughed again. "Then you have to have fuel to burn. How are you going to put all that fuel on a probe that is only this big?" Sam held out his fingers, pinching them together so they were just an inch apart.

"Hi, Maria. Table for two?" the waitress asked.

Maria frowned at Sam, then turned her attention to the older woman, whose hair was dyed an unnatural shade of red. It almost matched the red apron she had tied around her expansive waist, which even at this early hour was already covered in numerous fresh coffee stains and grease. Maria spent more than her fair share of time gossiping with Jennifer, and the two had become good friends despite their age difference.

"Hi, Jennifer. Yes, for two."

Jennifer scanned Sam from head to toe, as if inspecting a piece of meat. As she took in his huge beard, the ill-fitting women's sweater, and finally his bare feet, her face contorted into a caricature of something that was supposed to be happy and cheerful but actually looked the opposite. "Right this way."

Jennifer led the two to a table in the back, tucked away from most of the other patrons. She placed menus and two sets of silverware down, the first in front of Sam, then for Maria. Maria caught her eye as she turned to leave, and Jennifer's expression could not have been more clear if she had spoken her thoughts aloud: *The next time I see you, we are going to have a serious talk about your choice in men, sister.* Maria rolled her eyes. Jennifer had a point.

"Obviously, unless there's some cash sewn into that sweater, breakfast is on me today. Order whatever you want," Maria said. *And then I'm dropping you off at the police station and getting on with my life,* she added silently to herself.

Sam picked up the menu and scanned it over, his eyes darting from one item to the next.

"I don't know what I want. Can you tell me what is good?"

"All of it is good. You can't go wrong."

"But this is my first time at a restaurant . . ."

Maria's eyes flit up to linger on Sam's beard, then she forced them back down to her menu. She already knew what she was getting but felt better looking at the menu. This was going to be a long breakfast.

"Is this food?" Sam uncapped the ketchup bottle and was smelling the opening. Then he stuck his finger down the neck of the bottle and put it in his mouth. "Ugh. This is terrible."

Oh-my-fucking-God! What am I doing here with this guy?

"What about this?" Sam held up a sugar packet, squeezing it between his fingers. Then he popped the entire thing in his mouth, paper and all, and started chewing. "Better! But the outside part is really tough . . ." He gulped hard, forcing the paper down.

"Sam! Knock it off!" Maria's voice was raised, and a couple

at a nearby table looked over. She lowered it, but didn't remove the edge. "What are you doing!?"

Sam's face went white, and he dropped the second sugar packet he had taken. "Sorry!"

Maria glared at him, and Sam broke eye contact, looking down at the table. He was like a kid. Like a really naughty kid. Or a dog. Maybe he wasn't high, after all. Maybe he was insane.

The two sat in silence until Jennifer came back, holding a notepad in her hand. "Are you two ready to order?" She smiled at Sam, then turned her attention to Maria, concern written on her face.

"Just some coffee and a bagel, thanks," Maria said.

Jennifer nodded, scrawling on her pad, then looked Sam. "And for you, sweetie?"

Sam's eyes shot up, his expression cautious but excited. He glanced at Maria first, as if checking to see if she was still angry, then looked up at Jennifer. "I can't decide. Can I have one of everything?"

"Everything?"

"Yes, it's my first time having breakfast, and I wanted to—"

"He'll have pancakes, bacon, and eggs. And a coffee," Maria said. Sam looked at her, his expression wounded. "Thanks, Jennifer."

"No problem. It will be out shortly." As she left, she added in a low voice directed at Maria, "I'll put it at the front of the list for you."

The coffees came, and Sam watched Maria add sugar and cream to hers, then copied her exactly, also adding sugar and cream to his cup, discarding the paper sachet with pursed lips. She stirred her coffee three times; he stirred his coffee three times. He waited until she had taken a sip of hers before he tried his.

"This is the best thing so far." Sam took another sip, savoring it.

"Everyone likes coffee."

"I really like making food. It's one of my favorite things to do," Sam offered.

"Really?" Given Sam's recent excursions into the ketchup and sugar packet categories, his comment had taken Maria by surprise.

"Would you like to try my favorite?" Sam's eyes widened in excitement.

"Maybe after breakfast. Thanks."

Sam returned his attention to his drink, sipping it slowly and making appreciative noises to himself. Maria watched him curiously. She had never seen anyone pay that much attention to a cup of coffee before.

Jennifer worked her magic, bumping Maria's order to the front of the line ahead of all the other patrons, and the food arrived at their table almost immediately after they had ordered.

Sam watched Maria spread jam on her bagel, his expression concerned. Maria realized that he was trying not to make her angry, but didn't know how to start. She sighed.

"You can eat now. Use a fork for everything except the bacon. You can grab that with your hands. Put butter and syrup on your pancakes."

The tension seemed to leave Sam's body, and he smiled. Maria quickly looked away. She didn't want to get caught in one of those smiles of his again. He was crazy, and despite her surprise at the warmth she felt in her midsection when he smiled at her, nothing was going to change that fact.

Sam took a piece of bacon, taking a small bite. His eyes went wide. "Oh my God! This is amazing!" He scarfed down the rest of it, then ate the next two pieces. "Bacon is my new favorite food. I think it's even better than my best recipe from before!"

Maria laughed. She couldn't help it.

Sam paused, looking at her. "I like the sound of your laugh. It is very beautiful." He took another bite of bacon and pointed it at her. "If happiness had a sound, it would be your laughter. It makes me feel like I am weightless."

She could only shake her head.

"And your black hair. So long and shiny. I have never seen such amazing hair before."

"OK, Romeo. Focus. Finish your breakfast. Don't forget that I'm the first woman you've ever seen."

"That's true," Sam turned his attention back to his plate. "But after seeing you, I don't know why I would ever need to see another. It would only be disappointing."

Maria blushed. Crazy or not, that might have been the nicest compliment anyone had ever paid her.

"Who's Romeo?" Sam said.

"Never mind. Doesn't matter."

The check came, and Sam watched closely as Maria paid, counting out cash into a pile she deposited in the center of the table.

"That's money? And you are going to leave it here?" Sam said.

"Got to pay for breakfast. Just like everyone else."

"But what if you don't have any of this money?"

"Well, then you don't get to eat." He blinked at her.

"But what if you were hungry?"

"Then you'd need to find some money to buy some food."

"But what if you couldn't?"

"Then you'd starve."

Sam studied her, concern written on his face. "Does that actually happen?"

Maria shrugged, wondering why she continued these aimless conversations, but somehow unable to dismiss him as any reasonable person would. "Sure. But mostly in other countries."

Sam leaned back in the booth. "So is there not enough food for everyone? Is that why you need money for it?"

"No, there's enough food. But not everyone can pay."

He looked genuinely upset. "That's insane."

Says the crazy man.

"Let's go." Maria stood up, double-checking her side of the table to make sure she hadn't forgotten anything.

"Wait." Sam straightened and leaned forward against the table. "You said you wanted to try my favorite recipe after we finished breakfast. It's really good."

Maria sat back down at the edge of the bench. "I don't think we have time to cook anything, Sam. Besides, we really need to get going. We've got to drive into town to get to the . . . to where we're going next."

"It won't take any time. I've done it hundreds of times already."

"I'm sure you're good at it, but just finding a kitchen and ingredients . . . ," Maria didn't finish her sentence, her fingers shooting up to her lips. A strange taste had filled her mouth. At first it was sweet, and then it became extremely salty. The flavor got stronger, and Maria suddenly found a lump of something soft and squishy pressed against her tongue. Her eyes went wide, and she looked up at Sam, who was grinning and chewing on something.

Maria grabbed a napkin and spit out the thing in her mouth. It was a gelatinous blob, with almost no color to it.

"Sam! What was that?"

He looked hurt. "You didn't like it."

"How did you do that?" Maria had been speaking when the blob appeared in her mouth, but she couldn't understand how he had gotten it there without her seeing anything. He had just been sitting quietly when it happened, and he hadn't moved a muscle.

"You have to mix the flavors to do it. It takes a lot of practice to get the balance right though. . . . That one was a little too salty, but—"

"How did you get it in my mouth?"

Maria looked from him down to the strange thing on her napkin. What was it even made of? It didn't look like anything she had ever eaten before. She certainly hadn't recognized the taste.

"Sam—"

There was a crashing sound behind her and a shout. She turned to see people spitting out gelatinous matter onto their plates on the tops of their tables. One man had accidentally overturned his table in his surprise at finding an overwhelming bitter mass materialize within his mouth. His wife sat there next to him, covered in her own breakfast. She held her coffee cup up in one hand, but had spilled everything out of it onto the ground. She was trying to wipe something off her chin and blouse with her other hand.

Jennifer stood between that table and another one, the plates she had been carrying shattered at her feet with their contents scattered across the tiled floor. Plastic cups rolled from side to side nearby in puddles of the orange juice they had previously held. She had her hand over her mouth, looking around the restaurant in shock.

Sam slumped in his seat. "Nobody likes it?"

THREE

Maria pulled up in front of the police station and turned off the ignition. Her car sputtered and wheezed as the engine vibrated to a stop. There was a clunk from somewhere in the engine bay, and the chassis jolted before settling into silence. That was new. She made a mental note to ask her mechanic about it the next time she had enough money to visit him, but she didn't have time to worry about it now.

She had been preoccupied with Sam's stunt during the drive and hadn't spoken a word the entire time. He sat there quietly in the passenger seat, looking around curiously. If he had any clue where they were, he didn't show it. She wasn't sure how to tell him. Of course, she had been here more times than she could remember, almost always to bail Rodrigo out when he had gotten into trouble. She had hated it then, but she would trade these times for those in a heartbeat. Lucas needed his father, especially now. She and her grandmother were a poor replacement for the boy's real parents.

"I'm going to drop you off here, Sam."

He turned to look out the window at the small Spanish-style building that served as Sedona's police headquarters.

"You aren't coming?"

Maria shook her head. She didn't have time to wait around until Sam came down off whatever drugs he had taken. And if he wasn't on drugs, she definitely didn't have the time to take care of a fully grown man she had known for less than a day. He needed to go back to wherever he belonged, whether that was his own home, or more likely, whatever mental institution he had wandered away from.

Sam slowly opened the door and stepped out. He turned back around and leaned down, resting one hand against the roof of the car. The end of the sweater he wore barely made it down below his elbow.

"Will I see you again?"

Maria's breath caught in her throat as she sat there, pinned by his gaze. The guy didn't even know his own name. He had played an inexplicable stunt on her and everyone else at the diner, with disastrous results. He was lost, confused, and . . . who knew what else. Something was not right with him. But those eyes! They told a different story. They were not the eyes of a lunatic. They were clear. She could not remember seeing that much openness and purity outside of children. And they were hurt too. Sam didn't try to hide his pain or pretend it didn't exist. Her stomach tightened, and her voice caught in her throat as she tried to speak.

Maria turned forward, looking out the windshield at the road. "Probably not," she said quietly.

There was a long pause before Sam replied, "Thank you for your help, Maria. I will never forget you." Then he rose and softly closed the car door.

Maria glanced over and watched as he studied the police station. He took a step toward the doors, then paused and looked back at her. He returned and opened the car door halfway.

"Sorry to bother you, but can you tell me what I'm supposed to do now?"

Maria laughed despite herself. "Just go in there and tell them that you're lost. They'll take care of you." *Or fill you with antipsychotics and throw away the key,* a tiny voice whispered. She pushed the thought aside. She had a life to get back to.

Sam smiled, then closed the door. Maria leaned over and cranked the lever to roll the passenger side window down halfway. She expected she'd have to shout instructions to him at some point. All he had to do was walk to the front door, open it, and go inside, but this was Sam she was dealing with, and the ability to complete simple tasks did not seem to be his strong suit.

Sam had walked halfway toward the door when he glanced over to his right.

"Change?" a scraggly voice said.

"Oh, no," Maria whispered. It was Johnny Wheelchair.

His gray hair was stuffed under a camouflaged baseball cap, and his equally gray beard sprung out from his face in all directions. He wore a dirty black down jacket at all times of the day, even in the middle of summer, which Maria had never seen him without. He had fastened two adornments to the back of his wheelchair, a tattered American flag on the left and a black Prisoner-of-War/You-Are-Not-Forgotten flag on the right.

The story went that Johnny had been a war hero in Vietnam, having been awarded two purple heart medals during his deployment there. He showed them off to anyone who asked to see them, as well as those who had already seen them and tended to cross the road when they spotted him up ahead.

Sedona was a small town, with no services. It was not a good place to be homeless. But when Johnny arrived twenty years ago, he had fallen in love with the place and had been a fixture ever since. He was polite when he needed to be and moved along when he was told, so for the most part he was tolerated. No one really knew where he slept. He spent most of his days at the shopping center in West Sedona and would make his way up and down the highway to different areas as the urge took him. Today, as luck would have it, he found himself in front of the police station.

Sam turned to Johnny and raised his hand, spreading his two fingers apart to form the V-shaped Trekkie greeting Maria had jokingly given to him earlier. "Live long and prosper, man of Earth." Maria had the urge to slap her palm to her forehead, but Johnny Wheelchair laughed and returned the salute.

"Got any spare change, brother?"

"I'm sorry, I don't. You are welcome to have either this sweater or these jeans though."

The old man eyed him, considering, then shook his head. "I'm good on clothes. Thanks for offering. My name is Johnny. Folks around here call me 'Johnny Wheelchair,' for obvious reasons."

"It is nice to meet you, Johnny Wheelchair. What's wrong with your legs?"

Maria couldn't help herself as she sat in the hot car, straining to hear their conversation.

"Jumped out of too many airplanes in my day. I used to think I was invincible, but it catches up with you in the end. Earned two purple hearts in 'Nam. Honorably discharged the year after. Dodged more bullets in the war than I can count and kept running just fine, but I was too slow when it came to an overworked taxi driver who fell asleep at the wheel. Of all the ways to get your legs taken out, right? I always figured if I was going to end up in a chair, it would be because of a Viet Cong tripwire or some shit—sneaky bastards!—not just standing there minding my own business in the middle of New York City. Didn't even see him coming. Doctors said I might have been OK without all the war damage I had already suffered. Both legs were completely shattered. Insurance gave me a pile of money to keep me quiet, but all I've got left to show for it now is this chair."

"Would you prefer to use your legs again?"

Johnny Wheelchair laughed hard, shaking his chair from side to side. He had to cough to clear his throat before he answered. "Would I prefer it? Damn right, I'd prefer it! I'd also prefer to take a shit in a golden toilet, as long as you're asking."

Sam approached the old man and knelt down, touching his knees briefly. Maria watched with her heart in her chest, half expecting Johnny to slap him away.

Instead, a strange expression passed over Johnny Wheelchair's face. He gently placed his duffel on the ground and raised both legs in the air, moving them up and down in turn. He then took hold of the sides of his chair, and with a grunt, stood up to face Sam.

He walked in a circle, raising and lowering himself. Tears formed in his eyes, and he started laughing. He grabbed Sam by the shoulders and pulled him close in a tight embrace. Sam returned the hug, and the two rocked side to side, holding each other and laughing at the top of their lungs.

Suddenly, the rocking stopped, and Johnny's eyes bulged. He lifted his hand to cover his mouth, his cheeks puffing out.

"It tastes good, right?" Sam asked eagerly.

Johnny looked up at Sam with watery eyes. It was clear from his expression that he was on the verge of spitting out whatever was in his mouth. Instead, he started chewing, and eventually swallowed.

"I've had worse," he shrugged. "You should see the crap they fed us outside of Da Nang."

"There's your toilet. You can take your shit now if you want to."

Johnny turned around. In the exact spot where his wheelchair had been, sat a toilet made of solid gold, with his two flags fastened to the back of the tank.

"Whoa!" Johnny went over and tried to lift the top of the tank cover, but wasn't strong enough. It was too heavy. "Is this really gold? Do you know how much this must be worth!?"

Maria found that her mouth was hanging open. "Sam!" She had spoken more quietly than she intended. He didn't hear her. "Sam!"

Maria threw open her car door, and tried to leap out, but the seatbelt tightened and threw her back in her seat. She fumbled with the release, finally managing to unclick the belt. She darted out of the car and ran up to Sam.

Even as she demanded to know what he'd done, the truth settled upon her. This was no sleight of hand. It was real. Johnny was definitely standing and not in his chair. The old man was trying in vain to push the golden toilet to the side, but was unable to budge it even slightly. He gave up and placed his hands on his hips, his gaze focused intently on the treasure before him. It was clear that he was completely unaware of Maria's presence, or anything else happening around him.

Hope bloomed in Maria's heart. She wanted to ask how Sam had done it. Instead, she asked something even more important. "I have a nephew. His name is Lucas. He is very sick. Do you think you could heal him too?"

"Probably."

FOUR

"This is where you live?"

The house was small and painted a shade of blue that almost made it look like a piece of turquoise, buried in the red stone surrounding it. A rusted metal sculpture of a smiling sun hung between the two front windows, one of the only decorations aside from a life-sized painted statue of the Virgin of Guadalupe positioned in the front yard and surrounded by a protective barrier of cacti. Rodrigo had fallen into a reverie after spending three days alone in the wilderness and had worked almost an entire day setting it up. The bases of a few burned out candles surrounded her.

The carport was empty and Maria's heart stuttered in her chest. In all the excitement, she had forgotten. Lucas and Abuelita were at the clinic. The only doctors they could afford without health insurance were just across the border in Mexico, and Maria and her grandmother took turns taking Lucas in for his treatments. They wouldn't be home until tomorrow.

Maria parked in the street, then led Sam up the walkway to the front door, fumbling with her keys.

"Something is scratching at the door," Sam said.

"That's Pepe. He sits by the door and waits for me to come home."

As Maria entered, a brown chihuahua jumped up to greet her. He threw himself into the air as high as he could, pushing himself off her leg after each bounce. Maria reached down with both hands to pat him on his sides at the apex of each jump.

"That's Pepe?"

"Yeah."

As soon as Pepe heard Sam, he stopped his jumping and backed up a foot. He faced the stranger, unsure of what to do. He began to bark, but kept violently wagging his tail at the same time.

Sam laughed. "What language is that? I don't understand what he's saying."

"He's just barking. Watch this." Maria stood quietly and held her finger up at Pepe. Then she swiftly pointed it down. "Pepe, sit!"

Pepe stopped his barking and quickly sat his back end down on the ground. He adjusted his weight back and forth between his two front legs, destabilized by his enthusiastic tail wagging.

"Pepe, over!"

The dog flopped down into a prone position, then flipped over to the other side.

"Chase your tail!"

Pepe leapt up, then ran in circles. He stopped after a few rotations and barked, then continued.

Sam was beside himself. "He understands you!"

"Yeah. He's very smart. Good boy, Pepe! Such a good boy!" Maria patted the small dog all over, and Pepe returned the affection with countless licks.

"Want to meet him?"

"Yes!"

"OK, hold out your hand like this." Maria extended the back

of her hand to demonstrate, and Sam approached Pepe and did the same. Pepe walked over to sniff at his knuckles. His small pink tongue flicked out once to touch Sam's skin, and the tiny tail began wagging once more. Then, satisfied that everyone was friendly, he scampered away, bounding up onto the depression in the cushion on the sofa that marked his spot. He curled up there, putting his head down on top of his paws, and supervised his humans from that vantage point.

"Is Pepe a dog?"

Maria looked at Sam for a moment, her brow furrowed.

"Sam, how is it that you don't know the most basic things but can heal a cripple with the touch of your hands? What is going on?"

Sam looked down, and sighed. It took him a moment before he spoke. "It's hard to explain."

"And when you said that I was the first woman you had ever met . . . ?"

"I said first Earth woman, actually."

Maria swallowed. "You also said you had a mother."

"Yes."

"Wouldn't she have been the first Earth woman you saw then?"

"No. Mother is not human."

A shiver went down Maria's spine. Had Sam told her this yesterday, she would have written the comment off as him being under the influence of psychedelics. But a lot had happened since he'd walked into the Bell Rock Inn wearing nothing but a bracelet. He had done things that could not be explained. Johnny Wheelchair, crippled for decades, had stood up and walked after nothing more than Sam's touch. His wheelchair had somehow transformed itself into solid gold, right in the middle of a clear day. And Sam had somehow gotten that horrible salty blob into the mouths of everyone at the restaurant, including her own, without lifting a finger. A tripped-out stoner might believe they could do all those things, but Sam had actually done them.

Maria took a step back, aware of the fact she was alone in the house with this man, with only a chihuahua for protection. "She's not . . . human? So that means you're—what?—an alien?"

Sam studied her as she moved back. "No. I'm human, just like you. Don't be afraid."

"You're freaking me out, Sam." Maria held up her hand, warding him away.

"I'm sure this is very strange for you. It's even stranger for me." His blue eyes searched her face. "This might be hard to believe, but yesterday was my first day here." Somehow Maria understood the truth, without his clarification. It was Sam's first day here, on Earth.

He lifted his right hand and slowly reached toward her. She flinched as their fingers touched but remained still as he moved even closer, until their palms pressed together. His skin was warm and impossibly soft. "You have nothing to fear from me, Maria."

Her heart was pounding, but her fear had begun to leave her, replaced by a strange sort of excitement. All of this was a strange dream, but the flesh against her hand was real. This was real.

"Am I really the first woman you've ever seen?"

His smile was brighter than the sunniest summer day.

And this time, Maria smiled right back.

FIVE

"Can you believe that Johnny Wheelchair is walking around?" Officer Alex O'Sullivan dropped himself down in the driver seat of the police cruiser.

O'Sullivan was the oldest of the dozen or so officers who made up the bulk of the Sedona police force, and one of the most experienced. He had been offered promotions over the years, but had always turned them down. He loved driving his cruiser and responding to emergencies, and unlike most veterans, he had never gotten tired of the rush. Each year his wisdom and experience grew, and now he had become a de-facto elder of the force, in popularity if not rank. Unfortunately, those were not the only categories in which he had experienced profound growth over the years; his burgeoning beltline meant that getting into and out of cruisers had started to become a challenge. He wouldn't be able to refuse the next promotion offered. His time in his cruiser was coming to an end, and although no one had said anything about it to him, everyone knew it.

"You think it's a miracle?" Officer Kyle Small replied sarcastically. He was much younger than O'Sullivan and didn't have any issues getting into and out of cars. His muscular body moved quickly, almost aggressively. Everything about him was sharp, from his polished shoes to his close-cropped hair and the faintest line of a black mustache above his hawk-like upper lip. Recently transferred from Phoenix, he had spent the last three years patrolling much more dangerous neighborhoods than the sleepy backstreets of Sedona.

"What would you call it?" O'Sullivan said, closing his door. "He was in a chair one minute, and then he's walking around the next."

"I'd call it bullshit. He was faking the whole time." Small adjusted his belt slightly, feeling down for his holster. His hand felt most comfortable resting on the hilt of his weapon.

"Faking? All those years?"

"Sympathy sells. Makes him a better beggar."

O'Sullivan huffed and slammed his door shut, leaning over and brushing against his partner, who involuntarily pulled back to give him room. "Why would he pick today to stop the act?"

"Might have something to do with that gold toilet."

O'Sullivan laughed. Johnny Wheelchair had been extremely possessive of that toilet and had threatened anyone who came within ten feet of it, including Small, which had been a mistake. Johnny was now sitting in a cell while he cooled off, and was possibly facing charges. "Sucks to be the new kid right now."

"Spending your morning guarding a toilet? No shit."

"That's the price you pay to be the rookie. You get to do all the jobs nobody else wants."

The cruiser pulled out of the parking lot and stopped briefly at the light, then headed down the street. They had to follow up on a number of strange incidents this morning: the issue with Johnny Wheelchair, as well as a possible food poisoning event at the Coffee Pot Restaurant. It wasn't an emergency and no one was in trouble. At least, not yet. But there were people of interest who needed to be followed up with and reports to be made.

Traffic was light, and the day was perfectly clear, without a cloud in the sky. Despite all the years he had spent driving these streets, O'Sullivan found that the red sandstone formations still had the power to make him catch his breath. Only the Grand Canyon filled him with a greater sense of majesty and awe. But you couldn't live in the Grand Canyon. Sedona's rocks—his rocks—embraced him in a way that made him feel almost as if he were part of the tapestry. It was no wonder that these formations had been sacred to the people who had lived here before civilization had arrived.

"Do you know this Maria Rodriguez?" Small sucked on his teeth—an annoying habit of his. Ms. Rodriguez and an unidentified male had apparently been present at the diner during the food poisoning incident, and according to Johnny Wheelchair, were somehow responsible for the golden toilet currently parked in front of the police station.

"I've met her a few times," O'Sullivan answered. "Her brother-in-law had a lot of trouble when he lived here. The guy ended up killing himself in an accident after a cop pulled him over with a shoebox full of peyote. He said they were for religious purposes, but then ran when it looked like the cuffs were going to come out. His wife was with him when it all went down. She spent two months in the hospital, got charged with aiding and abetting, and earned a one-way trip back to Mexico, courtesy of ICE. Maria's taking care of their boy, along with her grandmother."

"I'd throw the kid back across the border too."

O'Sullivan grunted. Small's favorite conversation topics were guns and immigrants. Once he got started, there was no stopping him.

"They fuck up their own countries so bad they have to leave, and then they come here, breed, and try to fuck ours up too?" Small almost spit the words out of his mouth. "I'd kick every last one of them out."

O'Sullivan kept his mouth shut. He suspected Small was juicing on the side; these little outbursts were further confirmation. Nobody gained that much muscle mass that quickly without a little help. The steroids might do wonders for Small's physique, but they had the opposite effect on his personality. He had gone from borderline surly to vicious in a matter of weeks. Just yesterday he had practically yanked a teenager through the window of his car after he and O'Sullivan had caught the kid speeding, and Chief Dunbar had chewed them both out over the incident.

Cops like Small gave them all a bad name.

The next words popped out of O'Sullivan's mouth before he could stop them. "Kyle, unless you're a Native American, everyone was an immigrant at some point or another."

"Bullshit!" Small shifted toward O'Sullivan, eyes blazing. "When Christopher Columbus first came over here and met the Indians, he didn't ask for permission. Nobody filled out papers to be a part of the fucking Iroquois Nation. We came because we wanted to, and we stayed because we were strong enough. We weren't immigrants. We were invaders. We fucking conquered America, but everyone is so scared of being politically incorrect that we make up all these stories and excuses about everyone being an immigrant."

Small shifted his gaze back to the front, grinding his jaw. He sat quietly for a moment, simmering away in his own juices, then quickly turned back to O'Sullivan. "Even those Indians didn't immigrate. They invaded across whatever land bridge they came from and took this land from all the wildebeests that were here before them."

"I don't think it was wildebeests."

"Saber-toothed tigers, then. Whatever. You think they worried about the tigers that were left over? Tried to incorporate them into their society afterward? Hell, no. They killed them all and made the place better for it. Then we showed up and did the same to them."

"That's harsh."

"I'm just telling it like it is. The strong take from the weak."

"You ought to be down south with border patrol if that's how you feel."

"I thought about it. More than once."

"So what stopped you?"

Officer Kyle Small turned to look out the window, frowning as he watched two children kicking a ball back and forth through the red dirt that made up their front yard. "I hate the desert."

SIX

"So you know, if what you just said is true, I've got like a million questions now," Maria said. *Oh my God! I think what he said is true! Is this really happening?*

Sam laughed.

"But you just got here. Let me make some tea first." Maria started walking to the kitchen, then stopped and turned around. "You've never had tea before, have you?"

Sam shook his head from side to side, smiling.

The two made their way into the kitchen. It was tiny, but well organized. Faded yellow linoleum covered the floor, old enough to have begun to peel up at the corners. Several tea cups hung by their handles from hooks fastened underneath the cabinets, and an old electric can opener protruded from the wall where it had been installed by the original owners. The opener was decorative at this point, haven given up the ghost shortly before Maria's grandmother had moved in.

Maria filled a blue tea kettle and placed it on its usual spot on the stove. Flames rose to lick the blackened bottom, and she snatched two cups from their hooks, setting them upright on the counter.

"What flavor would Sam most like?" she said absentmindedly to herself as she rummaged through her tea drawer, inspecting all the various boxes there. She and her grandmother drank a lot of tea. Enough to have an entire drawer dedicated to storing all the varieties they rotated through. She remembered the taste of the horrible blob at the restaurant and searched for something strong. "Let's go with ginger. Two packets."

"Do you have any bacon?" Sam asked from across the counter.

Maria laughed. "My gran doesn't eat pork."

Sam's expression had been amused before, but his smile flattened as his eyes became confused. "Pork?"

"Yeah, like from a pig."

"Bacon is a pig?"

"Well, it comes from pigs, yeah."

Sam's mouth dropped in shock. He looked almost insulted.

"Are you OK?" Maria asked.

"So when I ate the bacon this morning, that was pieces of dead pig that someone found?"

"They didn't just find it. It was probably raised on a ranch, and then they butchered it."

"Butchered?" Sam looked sick and bent over to face the ground, putting his hands on his knees. "I put the corpse of an animal in my mouth? And chewed and swallowed it?"

Maria watched Sam quietly, unsure what to say. "Well . . . they cooked it first before you ate it," was all she could manage. A slow whistle began to sound from the kettle, distracting her. She pulled the kettle off the stove and began pouring water into the two cups.

"Are pigs sentient?" Sam asked in a heavy voice.

That was a strange question. "I don't know. Maybe. They say they're supposed to be smarter than dogs."

Sam gagged. Once. Twice. Then lost his entire breakfast all

over the kitchen floor. He looked up at Maria with shock in his eyes, covering his mouth with both his hands.

"Sam! Are you OK?"

Sam waved at her with one hand, the other pressed against his mouth. He tried to say something but had to stop as he was forced into a second round of spasms.

The doorbell rang. Pepe barked.

"Hang on. Just wait here," Maria said, rushing out toward the front door, being careful of where she stepped.

She opened the door and stopped. Two police officers stood before her.

"Hello?"

"Hello, ma'am. I'm Alex O'Sullivan, and this is Kyle Small. Sedona police. How are you today?"

She stumbled out a greeting.

"We've met before, about a year ago, under unfortunate circumstances," O'Sullivan said.

"Yes, I remember." Maria recognized the older officer. He had been there after Rodrigo's accident and had sat with her in the hallway as she waited for news about her sister. When the tears came, he had fetched a box of tissues and offered to drive her home. It was a small kindness on the worst day of her life, but a kindness nonetheless.

"We're following up on a couple of unusual reports from earlier today and believe you have information that might help us clear up what happened." He must have seen the blood drain from her face, as he was quick to add, "You aren't in any trouble. We just want to ask you some questions."

Maria turned, looking back inside. She couldn't hear Sam anymore. It sounded like he had gotten control of himself. "I'm not sure this is the best time . . ."

"Would you prefer coming downtown later?" O'Sullivan asked.

"Or we could just get a subpoena and question you in front of a judge," Small said before Maria could respond. O'Sullivan quickly looked over at his partner and frowned.

Maria looked at Small for a minute, then stepped back. "OK, sure. Would you like to come in?"

"Good choice," Small said, pushing past her into the house. Pepe barked at him, jumping off the couch, but made sure to keep his distance.

"Thanks, ma'am. Sorry for the inconvenience," O'Sullivan added as he entered, his face slightly red. Maria closed the door after they had both come inside, and showed them to the dinner table, where the two officers sat down.

Sam appeared from the kitchen, his face paler than usual. "Hello."

"Hi," Small said, taking Sam in with a glance, looking past him to the floor of the kitchen. "Looks like you're having a problem in there."

"Yes. Bacon," Sam said.

"Sam, these officers just want to ask me a few questions," Maria said. "You can—"

"He can sit down right there." Small gestured to the chair across the table from him. "We've got some questions for him too."

Sam moved to the seat that the officer had pointed at, and sat down, folding his hands together on his lap. He smiled as Maria made her way around to the fourth chair, trying to catch his eye.

O'Sullivan cleared his throat. "Are you two familiar with John Abrams, also known as Johnny Wheelchair?"

"Johnny Wheelchair?" Sam said. "Yes, I met him this morning."

Maria looked at Sam sharply. She didn't trust the police, O'Sullivan's past kindness to her notwithstanding. She especially didn't trust this younger officer. She didn't like the way he looked at her, and she didn't like the way he spoke to her. She didn't want to tell him anything she didn't have to, and she didn't want Sam to either.

"He's not in a wheelchair anymore," O'Sullivan said.

"I know."

"Do you always dress in women's clothes?" Small asked.

Sam looked from O'Sullivan to Small, then down at his clothes, unsure of the question. "Women's clothes?"

"Pink looks good on you," Small added.

"Thank you," Sam said. "It is my first sweater."

"Maybe you should think about getting a second one."

Before Sam could respond, Maria covered his hands with one of her own. She turned to Officer Small, her dark eyes fierce. "Leave him alone."

"Watch your tone, young lady," Small responded, holding her gaze.

O'Sullivan tried to break the tension. "Sam, how do you know that John Abrams isn't in a wheelchair anymore?"

"I helped him get out of it. He said he would prefer to be able to walk, so I rebuilt the bones and tissues in his legs."

Small laughed. "Just like that, huh?"

"Yes."

"And the gold toilet?" O'Sullivan asked.

"He said he needed one."

"So, what?" Small said. "Snap your fingers and poof, there's a solid gold toilet?"

"Snap my fingers?" Sam furrowed his brow. "Why would I want to snap my fingers? That's a weird thing to say . . ."

"It's a figure of speech," Maria said quietly.

"Where'd you two meet?" Small continued, watching them closely. "I'm guessing it wasn't at the genius convention."

"No, not at a convention," Sam said. "Actually, we met—"

"You don't have to answer every question," Maria said. "Especially the mean ones." She scowled at Small.

"I'd advise you to answer every question," Small said, holding Maria's gaze and scowling back. "Unless you want to end up in a jail cell. Or somewhere worse."

"What's that supposed to mean?" Maria said.

"How's your sister?" Small replied. "I heard she was forced to relocate down south. Too bad her husband couldn't join her."

Asshole. "Are you threatening me?"

"No, ma'am. Just informing you of what will happen if you continue to disrespect this badge." If Small were a tea kettle, there would have been steam coming out his ears. His entire face had gone a few shades redder.

Maria looked at O'Sullivan and pointed to his body camera. "Your body cams are on, right?"

"Yes, ma'am," O'Sullivan replied. "At all times. Both mine and Officer Small's."

"If you think that a camera is going to make any difference —" Small said.

O'Sullivan cleared his throat, then reached out to touch Small's arm, quieting him. Then he turned to Sam. "The toilet. Where did the toilet come from?"

"Well, it has nothing to do with snapping my fingers, it's just applied science. First the molecules of the old object, the wheelchair in this case, had to be disassembled into their energetic components, and then the signatures had to be converted to the material I desired. There was more mass in the toilet than was present in the wheelchair, so I had to add some matter, which I got from the surrounding environment. Then, all of it had to be unified, patterned, and finally set."

Small laughed and glanced at O'Sullivan. "This guy is crazy."

"You're saying you disassembled the atoms?" O'Sullivan asked.

"No, not the atoms. It is hard to explain in this language. You don't have the right words. You have to go to the—energetic blueprint?—which is beyond the atom."

"What do you mean *this language*?" Small asked, his eyes narrowing.

"Sorry, I mean English. It is not well suited to discussing science. I only learned it yesterday, and it still confuses me a little."

"And the incident at the Coffee Pot Restaurant? Was that you?" O'Sullivan asked. "People said food appeared in their mouths."

"Yes. I was trying to show Maria a recipe." Sam's eyes lit up. "Would you like to taste?"

Maria squeezed Sam's hand. "Sam, no."

"You weren't born here, were you?" Small said.

"In Maria's house? No."

Small slapped his hand down on the table, hard. Everyone jumped. "No, not in this shithole house. In this country."

Maria tried to get Sam's attention, to shush him, but she wasn't quick enough. He didn't understand.

"No. I've only been here one day."

"I knew it!" Small's entire face burned with a strange fire. "Yet another illegal alien."

"That's what Maria thought too. Don't worry, I'm human."

"But how did you actually do it? You can't do a thing like that with your bare hands. Don't you need equipment?" O'Sullivan asked, seemingly unaware of the change that had come over his partner.

"Oh. I used this." Sam held up the silver bracelet on his wrist. Maria hadn't noticed before, but it seemed to almost give off a faint light all of its own. "The reactor you are asking about is back where I came from."

Small suddenly stood up, his hand on the holster of his weapon. "You sit there all smug, with your stolen sweater and bare, dirty feet. You come to this country for God knows what purpose. You can't even stomach bacon, because you're so used to your foreign food. Is that what you do back home? Vomit right on the floor? Just wherever you feel like?" Small's voice was growing louder. "And you bring some dangerous device with you, just experimenting however you like on innocent American citizens? Poison an entire restaurant, why not? And you think there will be no repercussions?" A white froth had built up in the corners of his mouth, and Maria felt herself recoiling back into her seat. "I don't know where you came from. Honestly, I don't even care. It doesn't matter. But let me tell you what does matter: You picked the wrong day, and the wrong city, and the wrong country to pull a stunt like that."

"He didn't do anything wrong!" Maria said, standing up.

"Shut up, beaner. You don't belong here either. If I had my way, I'd drive you down to the border myself and throw you back to where you came from. You, and your grandmother, and that kid. The whole lot of you. You're parasites."

"Kyle!" O'Sullivan exclaimed. The shock was clear in his voice. He looked at his partner as if he didn't recognize him.

Pepe had been watching the entire interaction from his spot on the couch. He was a dog; he didn't understand any of the words. But he did understand body language. What he saw was a strange person in the house acting dangerously and threatening his master. That much was abundantly clear to him, and that was enough.

Pepe leapt off the couch and tore over to the table, growling the entire way. He would defend his master. He would protect the house. The tiny dog sunk his teeth into the leg of the man who was yelling.

Small screamed in pain and kicked with his leg once, but Pepe held on. He kicked again and connected with the chihuahua's body, sending the dog across the room. Pepe hit the wall with a whimper.

"Pepe!" Maria shouted.

"Even your dog is an excuse," Small said. He drew his sidearm, turning his rage-filled eyes toward Maria.

Sam had followed Pepe's path through the air in shock and turned back toward Small with closed fists, rising from his seat. He made a quick gesture, as if there was something on his arm he was trying to shake off, and shouted, "Get out!"

And then, Small was gone.

One moment he was standing there, full of rage and bile, and the next, there was an empty space, as if he had never existed. There was a strange whooshing sound, as the surrounding air rushed to fill the sudden vacuum left by where the man's body had been.

O'Sullivan tried to get up, but moved too quickly for his own bulk and collapsed backward onto the floor. His chair toppled with him, landing on its side.

Maria turned to Sam. "What happened?"

Sam looked at her, his eyes hard. "That guy was a jerk." He paused, as if waiting for Maria to correct him. She didn't. "Is Pepe all right?"

Pepe had collected himself and slowly walked over to Maria, his head down and his tail gently wagging from side to side. She scooped him up and held him to her chest, cradling him.

"What did you do to Officer Small?" O'Sullivan said as he found his feet.

"I sent him away."

"Where?"

"Somewhere he can't hurt anyone."

O'Sullivan nodded, his eyes falling to the strange bracelet on Sam's wrist. "OK. Take it easy." He lifted his hands in the air, palms facing Sam, and backed toward the door. As he bumped into it, he reached back for the knob and let himself out.

Maria went to the window and pulled the old lace curtain aside, following O'Sullivan as he raced to his cruiser and wrenched the door open. Seconds later, he was yelling into his radio.

"I think we might be in trouble, Sam."

SEVEN

Two police cruisers had pulled up in front of her house, their lights flashing. Maria watched as a third arrived and parked lengthwise across the middle of the street, creating a barrier. Sirens blared in the distance.

"He kicked Pepe. He was threatening you." Sam looked from Maria to the dog, who had curled up back in his place on the sofa.

Maria had no words and watched silently as another police car arrived. The neighbors across the street had come out into their front yard and were looking around. A tall police officer with a thick vest approached them and said something. They glanced at Maria's house, then hurried back inside. The officer turned around, looking down the length of the street, and bent his head to say something into the radio attached to his shoulder.

"This is not good." Maria's entire body was tense, and her mouth had gone dry. Her hands began to shake.

"These are the police?"

"Yes."

"They represent the authority?"

"Yes, they are the authorities."

Sam nodded. "Did I get you in trouble, Maria?"

"Maybe. Not as much trouble as you're in."

Maria looked into Sam's eyes. There was no mistaking his fear. She wanted to scream and cry. She'd almost started to believe that he had been brought to their lives for a reason. Now he'd be taken away, and who knew what might become of him.

Why had she answered the doorbell? *Stupid, stupid, stupid.*

"I think you have to go with them."

She had so many questions she wanted to ask him and things she wanted to show him. And then there was Lucas. Of all the crazy miracle cures, spiritual healers, and alternative approaches she had tried, none had ever worked. But Sam had cured Johnny Wheelchair. Sam could cure Lucas too. She had known him for less than a day, but she was certain of it. She could feel it in her bones. If only Lucas's appointment had been on some other day. If only he had been home instead of in Nogales. But he hadn't, and now almost the entire Sedona police force was outside her door, waiting to take Lucas's last chance away. It was just her luck: to have only just found a cure, and then to have lost it. Maria reached up and brushed a tear from her eye with the back of her hand.

"Are you sad?" Sam reached out and touched her gently at the elbow.

"Yes," Maria said, wiping another tear away. "No. Maybe a little . . . I don't know." And then she found herself in Sam's arms. He held her close, quietly rocking her from side to side. He was warm and smelled almost like flower blossoms. Was that his smell or the sweater's? She could feel his heartbeat, strong and steady against her chest. *Thump-thump. Thump-thump.* She took a moment and closed her eyes, trying to forget about the police outside. But she could not.

"Attention in the house. This is the police. You are surrounded. Come out with your hands raised." The voice was loud and metallic. Someone was speaking through a megaphone.

Maria pushed off Sam. "Sam, you have to go out. It will be worse if you don't."

Sam sighed and looked at the back of the door. "Is there anything I should know? I've never been arrested before."

Maria managed a shallow laugh. "Of course you haven't. Just avoid any fast motions and do what they tell you. They'll handcuff you. They might be rough when they do it. Don't fight."

"I understand."

"And whatever you do, don't make anyone vanish."

"I figured that part out already."

The two made their way to the front door.

"And don't make any slime materialize in their mouths."

Sam smiled. "I've sort of figured that part out too. I still don't know what's wrong with everyone, though. I've been eating that for years. How can anyone not like it?"

Maria cracked the door. "Raise your hands, Sam. Keep them open and move slow." She went first, leading Sam and giving him a model to follow.

All the cops had their weapons drawn and trained on the pair. Three cops stood closer, while most were behind their cars, using the vehicles as defensive barriers. There was one with a rifle and scope who had managed to position himself on the neighbor's roof.

Alex O'Sullivan was the first to speak. "Lay down flat on the ground, face down. Keep your hands where we can see them."

Maria slowly lowered herself to the ground in the front yard. She watched Sam do the same next to her. The rocks underneath her were sharp but had thankfully not gotten hot yet. In the middle of summer, after baking all day in the sun, they could cause third-degree burns.

There was a sound of rushing feet, and strong arms were suddenly upon her. Her hands were placed behind her back, and she felt the bite of steel cuffs on her wrists. She watched as two men bore down on Sam, a third cop standing over them with his gun at the ready. Others circled just outside her range of vision.

"Get the bracelet," O'Sullivan shouted from a position behind her.

There was some movement, then she saw one cop holding Sam's silver bracelet. The man placed it inside a black pouch and zippered it shut. There was a click of cuffs, and Sam was hauled up and led off. Maria tried to watch him go as best she could, but her view was blocked. She heard a car door open and close.

There was someone behind her, doing something with her cuffs, and she felt them slide off. "You can get up, Maria."

Maria rose to her feet, dusting herself off and rubbing her wrists. O'Sullivan was there waiting for her.

"I could arrest you, but I'm not going to do that. But I will need you to come down this afternoon and give us a statement. I don't know what kind of trick your friend pulled, but an officer is missing and we have a lot of questions."

Maria looked at the man and nodded. She couldn't feel any emotions. It was as if she were completely hollow. The patrol cars began to pull away, one after another. Soon, all that was left was O'Sullivan and the sniper from across the street, who was disassembling his rifle, placing various components of it into their places in a long, black box.

"You don't know what happened to Kyle Small, do you?" O'Sullivan asked.

"No." For Sam's sake, she hoped he was somewhere close by. And alive.

"I've been doing this for almost thirty years now. I've never seen anything like that. Ever." He made his way back to his car, which rocked from side to side as he got in.

He drove out down the street, then made a U-turn to come back around, slowing in front of Maria's house. His window was down, and his arm rested on the door. "Make sure you get down to the station this afternoon. I don't want to have to come back here looking for you."

"I will."

O'Sullivan studied her for a moment, then drove away.

Maria watched the police car disappear around the bend. Movement caught her attention from across the street, and she looked over in time to see the blinds move as they fell shut. The neighbors had been watching. She frowned and made her way back inside. She closed the door and turned the lock, hearing the bolt slide into place with a familiar *click*. A wet nose gently prodded her ankle.

"Hi, Pepe," she said, reaching down and scratching the dog behind his ears. It was at that point that she noticed the gleam of something bright and sleek against her skin. She stared down, mouth agape.

Sam's bracelet was on her wrist.

EIGHT

John Sanders sat down and frowned. Someone had thrown some files onto the middle of his otherwise spotless desk. He scowled under his bushy gray eyebrows, casting a piercing glance at his office door. His new secretary was young and inexperienced. She didn't understand the importance of being organized. Everything had a place, and anything that had a place belonged in its place. Above all things, it was order that separated the civilized from the barbaric, and it was order that preserved America as the world fell into chaos around it.

Strong hands, calloused from years of active duty and a spartan lifestyle, gathered the files up and placed them into the in-box on the corner of his desk. Sanders adjusted his paperweight and positioned his pen exactly parallel to the thick leather writing surface centered in front of him. He looked up at the two pictures on the corner of his workspace. One was a photo of himself just before his first deployment in the Marines. It was taken by his mother as he posed for her in his freshly pressed uniform. He was young then, but he had the same steely eyes, the same ambitious set of his jaw. The other photo showed him shaking the president's hand. The Commander in Chief was smiling, as all politicians do when facing a camera. Sanders was not. Soldiers, true soldiers, did not smile. Ever alert, ever ready.

He would have to talk to his secretary about her performance. She would not like it. Civilians were so emotional and took everything personally. He did not have time for weakness, or for feelings. Certainly, women in his time had been made of stronger stuff. How had this new generation become so soft? He wondered how long his secretary would last: She was the third in as many months. Then he realized that he didn't really care.

There was a knock on his door.

"Come in!"

It was one of the agents from Customs and Border Protection. "Hey, Chief. You asked for this?" He held up a bound report, the logo of the Department of Homeland Security embossed on the cover.

Sanders motioned and the man entered, depositing the memo in its place in the in-box. Sanders nodded approvingly. See? Was that so hard?

"Need anything else?" the agent said.

"No. I'm good."

The man shut the door quietly behind him as he backed out of the office.

Sanders had always liked that agent. He could always spot a person who had spent time in the military. It clung to a man. Perfected him.

As Sanders reached for his in-box, his phone rang. His hand hovered in the air, and he frowned at the interruption. He picked up the receiver in a swift motion and began speaking almost before he had it up to his face. "Sanders."

"It's Wilson, at the Bureau." John Wilson, from the FBI.

The two worked together frequently, but found it awkward both being named John, so they called each other by their last names. "I've got a police chief from Arizona on the line. He has a story that I think you need to hear."

Sanders grunted. A police chief? That was unusual. But Wilson knew what he was doing. The man had been at his job twenty years and counting. "All right. Let's hear him."

There was a pause, and then another voice came onto the line. "Hello?"

"Yes, we're here. Go ahead." Wilson said.

The new voice cleared his throat. "Hello, sir. My name is Miles Dunbar. I'm the chief of police in Sedona, Arizona."

"I heard. Wilson says you've got something to tell me." Sedona, Arizona? Where was that?

"We had an incident here this morning that is . . . inexplicable, sir."

Sanders grunted. He highly doubted that.

"We've apprehended a man with what appears to be a weapon that we've never seen. He hit one of our officers with it, and it has everyone spooked."

Jesus Christ.

"What happened to the officer?"

"We don't know. He's gone."

"What do you mean, *gone?*" Sanders's patience began to fray.

"Nobody knows where he is," Wilson cut in, almost apologetically. "They've watched his partner's body-cam footage, and it clearly shows the officer standing there one minute, and then—"

"Poof! Gone!" The police chief continued, too excited to let Wilson finish. "It's not the only incident either. We've got multiple reports of objects appearing, and more eyewitnesses than I can count at this point. There's a solid gold latrine sitting out on the sidewalk in front of our station that nobody knows what to do with. This is straight out of the Twilight Zone."

"A gold latrine?" Sanders laughed.

"It might sound funny, but it's deadly serious." The small-town cop sounded like his feelings were hurt. "You think 9/11 was bad, you get a couple of terrorists in here with these devices who know what they're doing, and they're going to be able to cause a hell of a lot more damage than that."

Sanders sat up. "You think this guy is a terrorist?"

"My officer says he admitted to only being in the country for a day. We don't know where he's from, and he's using some kind of weapon we've never seen before."

Sanders leaned forward in his chair, his in-box forgotten. "You've got this man in custody?"

"Yes, sir."

"Questioned him yet?"

"No. I wanted to call you all before we did anything."

"Good thinking, Dunbar. That was the right choice," Sanders said. Finally, someone with a brain. "Wilson, are you going to send some of your boys down there?"

"Yes," Wilson said. "I've already got agents in Phoenix who will be able to take charge. I will brief them as soon as we're done here."

"That's great. I want to know what this thing is and how many others of them there are out there. Keep me in the loop."

"Will do," Wilson said.

"Dunbar, coordinate with Wilson. I don't want anyone talking to your suspect until he is in federal custody."

"Understood," Dunbar said.

"And that body-cam footage you mentioned . . . I'd like to see it."

"Yes, sir."

There was a moment of silence.

"Thank you, gentlemen." Sanders said. He had a simple rule about phone calls: The first silence in a call was the time to hang up. Anything important that needed to be said was always spoken before the silence. Anyone too afraid to speak by the time the silence arrived probably didn't deserve to be heard, because only cowards were afraid to speak what is important, and nobody cared what cowards had to say anyway. The only people that wasted time talking on the phone for no good reason were women and children, and John Sanders was neither a woman nor a child.

"Can you repeat your title? I want to get it right on my report," Dunbar asked.

"John Sanders. Assistant Secretary. CWMD."

"CWMD?"

"Countering Weapons of Mass Destruction Office. Department of Homeland Security." Sanders hated his organization's name. It was clumsy and entirely too long. It was obviously coined by someone who had never spent any time in combat. Unless he was specifically asked, he never used it.

"Thanks," Dunbar said, and the call ended.

John Sanders looked out the window, his hands pressed together in front of him, elbows on the desk. The threats to America never ceased, her enemies never resting. As ridiculous as it sounded, the panic in the cop's voice had unsettled him. What had Dunbar said? The officer just vanished into thin air. John Sanders understood the vital importance of maintaining superior firepower, and if it was real, this weapon represented something new and powerful. There was only one place a weapon like that belonged: in the hands of a US soldier, sworn to defend the country he loved. John felt that familiar stirring in his chest. Even his old ears could still hear the call when it went out: America needed him.

He picked the receiver back up, pressing the button to

connect with his secretary. He heard the phone ring just outside his door.

"Sarah Reed, assistant to John Sanders," came the answer.

"Sarah. I need to be on the next flight to Phoenix. Make it happen."

"Yes, sir."

NINE

"How was your flight, sir?" the FBI agent in the front seat asked over his shoulder. His dark brown hair was cropped short, and he wore a poorly fitted gray suit. The other agent driving the car was almost his spitting image. They had both told Sanders their names, but he had forgotten them almost immediately. He didn't need to know their names, so he hadn't bothered trying to remember. He would tell them what needed to be done, and they would do it, and that was as intimate as their relationship needed to be. The only time he really wanted to know some-one's name is if that person had displeased him in some way. Or if they were his enemy. It was important to know the names of one's adversaries.

"Fine, thanks." The flight hadn't actually been fine, it had been horrible. Sarah had managed to pull some strings and got him squeezed into coach at the very tail end of a commercial airliner, with a baby on one side and an extremely talkative woman on the other. He had told himself that on the brighter side, at least the plane wasn't taking on enemy fire, but by the end of the ordeal he wondered if maybe that would have been preferable. "Has Johanssen arrived yet?"

"Yes, sir. He's waiting for us back at the office."

That was good news. Even though Sanders had a staff at his new position in the CWMD, it was almost completely made up of civilians. The result was that he had been forced to maintain a secondary staff, made up of men he had worked with in the past who he trusted. When things got serious, it was to this secondary staff that he turned for assistance. He barely trusted his civilian staff to be able to bring him a cup of coffee without somehow bungling the affair. He trusted his military staff with his life. Captain Derek Johanssen was a man who got the job done, no matter the cost. He was worth a hundred DC paper pushers in almost any situation that mattered. More than that if life and limb were at stake.

The complex came into view, a collection of a few blocky-looking buildings surrounded by dirt and cacti. It didn't look like anything special. It might have been any other office building had there not been a huge "FBI Phoenix Division" sign erected out front, the words carved into a stone slab along with an outline of a fingerprint. Sanders liked the FBI. They were competent. Not Johanssen-competent, but still better than what he had to deal with back in Washington.

The car rolled up to the entrance, and Sanders smiled as he saw Johanssen idling to the side of the front doors. The man seemed to get more muscular every time Sanders saw him. He wore canvas pants, complete with an array of various pockets, and a gray T-shirt that seemed to barely contain his bulk. He had a blacked out baseball cap with an American flag patch fastened to the front with Velcro. Being able to remove the patch was useful in certain covert operations, but if he were ever captured, it would be impossible not to mistake him as anything other than US military. Like most members of the Special Forces, he had all his vital information tattooed on his side, just under his armpit, so that his body could be identified more easily if he happened to step on a land mine or get blown up in any other of the countless ways that occur every day to men of his profession. It was considered a sign of disrespect to the other members of your company to force them to identify your disfigured remains when you could have saved everyone a lot of trouble by thinking ahead.

Sanders stepped out of the car and smiled at Johanssen. The huge man moved from his place by the door, and the two clasped hands in greeting. As usual, shaking Johanssen's hand was like grabbing a hold of a solid piece of steel.

"Good to see you, Captain," Sanders said, smiling.

"Likewise." Johanssen's teeth were square and blocky. Almost none of them were real. The originals were somewhere in Afghanistan, courtesy of a hard landing in a helicopter that had sent most of the other men on board to the hospital.

Johanssen reached into his pocket, pulling out two huge cigars. He gestured toward Sanders with one, but the old man shook his head. "Had half a lung removed already. Can't risk the other. Thanks."

"Just because the one lung is gone doesn't mean you should deprive the other of a good cigar."

Sanders laughed. "That's what I like about you, Johanssen."

Johanssen slapped Sanders on the upper arm playfully and placed the second cigar back into whatever utility pocked he had retrieved it from. He then lit the one in his mouth, taking a few small puffs to get it started. He had been practicing smoke rings and puffed out a partially formed O toward the two FBI agents who were approaching, having parked the car. "Almost," he said to himself wistfully, studying the lopsided smoke ring.

"Ready?" Sanders said, turning to the FBI agent closest to him.

"Yes," the man said, looking toward Johanssen. "Sorry, but there's no smoking inside."

Johanssen studied the agent for a second, his expression unreadable behind his sunglasses. His body went very still. He took a big draw, and blew a perfect smoke ring right into the agent's face. The man coughed and narrowed his eyes, looking at the hulking soldier before him, but said nothing.

Johanssen smiled, then transferred his attention to the second agent. "How about you? You have a problem with my cigar?" The second agent shrugged noncommittally. Johanssen stared at the man until the agent broke eye contact.

"Don't scare the children, Derek." Sanders said, watching his friend puff another smoke ring in the direction of the agents. "Come on, we're wasting time."

———

The agents led Sanders down a sequence of hallways and through a number of doors. Eventually, they entered a darkened room. There were two analysts there, a man and a woman, who both rose to shake his hand. Behind them, a giant glass window ran along the length of one wall, and a solitary figure could be seen sitting at a table. The man had a long, bushy beard and a pink sweater. His hands were cuffed, and a chain ran from the cuffs down through a hook on the top of the table.

Sanders studied the man, then looked over at Johanssen. "We'll talk to him first. You all can follow up after we're done."

The four agents nodded, understanding their role in the hierarchy. The two who had come in with Sanders and Johannsen pulled up chairs, and sat down.

"And the weapon? We have it?"

The female FBI agent produced a black pouch with a zipper that ran along the side. "Sedona police took a bracelet off the suspect when they apprehended him. One officer claims the suspect stated that it is somehow connected to a kind of reactor."

"Let's see it."

The agent unzipped the pouch, looking inside. She stuck her hand in the pouch, feeling the corners with increasing panic.

"Are you kidding me?" Sanders said.

She looked up at him, her eyes wide, and held the pouch open so he could see there was nothing inside.

"What's your name?"

"Rita. Rita Billingsly. Sir."

"Nobody bothered to actually look inside that pouch, Rita Billingsly?"

"The police handed it to us. We were waiting for you to arrive," Rita stammered. "This pouch hasn't been out of our sight since it arrived."

Sanders looked over to Johanssen, stone cold and unreadable as ever. "Do you see what I have to deal with?" Johanssen's lips parted into a rough smile around the cigar he clenched in his teeth.

"We'll discuss this later," Sanders said, and walked to the door that led to the interrogation chamber, placing his hand on the knob. He looked back at the agents watching him. "Don't interrupt."

He entered the room, taking a seat next to the suspect, who looked at him with open curiosity. The man was smart, Sanders could tell that much already. He would also bet money he had never been trained by any military force. This was not a soldier. The look in his eye and the set of his shoulders spoke louder than any words. That intrigued him. How had a man like this come to possess such a weapon? And where was that weapon? Sedona was a small town, but their police force couldn't be as incompetent as to have misplaced something so hazardous. How had it gotten out of that pouch?

Johanssen took up a position behind the suspect, out of the line of sight.

"Hello there, son," Sanders began.

"Hello."

"You know, coming in here, I wasn't sure what kind of man you would be."

"How many different kinds are there?"

Sanders smiled. "That's a good question. There are lots of different kinds of men. Some men want power. Some want money. Some want you to believe that only their religion is the right one. And others just want to wipe you off the face of the earth. I don't care about money, or power, or religion. It's not my job to worry about those things. My job is to worry about the people who want to blow us all to hell and send western civilization back to the Stone Age. Those are the kinds of men that keep me up at night."

"You have a stressful job."

"I do. Very much."

The two men looked at each other, saying nothing for a long time.

"I'm going to ask you some questions, and I want you to be truthful with me. Do you think you can do that?" Sanders said.

"Yes."

"What's your name?"

"Sam."

"Nice to meet you, Sam." Of course, Sanders already knew Sam's name, or more likely his alias. He had read Dunbar's report thoroughly.

"Nice to meet you too."

"Now, Sam, how can I be sure that you're going to be truthful with me when I start asking you questions?"

"I said that I would be."

"People say a lot of things. You cuff a man and put him in a chair in the middle of an FBI field office, and most of the time that man is going to tell you whatever he thinks you want to hear so that he can get out of that chair. But I don't want you to tell me what you think I want to hear."

"You don't?"

"No. I want you to tell me the truth."

"I understand."

"I've been doing this a long time, and there's one thing that I've come to learn, having been in as many of these . . . discussions, as I've had the opportunity to attend. It's that people really only tell you the truth when they know there are going to be consequences if they don't. Serious consequences."

The man looked at him, guileless. There was something almost childlike about him. It made Sanders's skin itch.

"Did you see that man who came in with me?"

"Yes."

"That's Captain Johanssen. He gets angry when people lie to me. Do you want to see what happens when Johanssen gets angry?"

Sam turned to look over his shoulder at the man behind him.

"Johanssen. Show Sam here what happens when you get angry."

Johanssen shifted the cigar to the corner of his mouth and walked up to Sam. He looped his foot around the leg of the chair that Sam sat in and dragged it sideways, angling Sam toward him. Sam's hands were stretched out on the table, constrained by the cuffs, but the lower half of his body shifted along with the chair. Johanssen clenched one of his massive hands into a fist and drove it into Sam's stomach, twisting with his hips to maximize the impact. The blow knocked Sam backward and out of the chair.

Sam gasped, coughing for breath with his knees on the floor

and his arms above him on the table, the chain holding them tight. Johanssen picked up the chair and set it back upright.

"You aren't wearing any shoes. That's unusual," Sanders said.

Sam tried to speak, but could only cough.

"Johanssen. Could you please help Sam back into his chair?"

The giant grabbed him by the hair, hauling him up off the ground, and roughly shoved the chair against the back of his legs, forcing him into a sitting position.

Sam looked over at Johansson, his face full of surprise and righteous indignation. Sanders knew, seeing that glance, that the man was not used to pain. This might even be the first time anyone had ever hit him. That was good. It would make his job easier.

"Do you understand the consequences if you lie to me?"

Sam turned back to Sanders, fire kindling in his eyes. "I told you I'd tell the truth."

"I'm the one asking questions now, and you didn't answer mine. I asked you if you understood the consequences."

Johanssen knew how this worked. He pivoted, quick as a boxer in his prime, and struck Sam across the jaw with a sharp right hook. Once more he was thrown from the chair, his head glancing off the edge of the table. After Johanssen hauled him back up, there was a gash in his forehead, blood running down the side of his face.

This time, when Sanders repeated his question, Sam's eyes darted around the room, looking for an escape. There was none. He tried to reach up and touch his forehead, but the chains on his wrist snapped taught and held his hand back. He focused on the old man in the chair next to him, his eyes blurring. "Yes. Yes, I understand."

Sanders studied him as his blood made its way down his

face and onto his pink sweater. Was that a women's sweater? Sanders shook his head. "I'm sorry, Sam, I just don't believe you."

Johanssen reached down, taking a hold of one of Sam's fingers and casually bent it back, breaking it. The agents in the adjoining room winced as they heard Sam scream in pain.

"Do you think we should try to stop this?" Rita said, still holding the empty pouch that the bracelet mysteriously disappeared from. She averted her eyes from another gruesome blow delivered to the man in the pink sweater.

"You heard Wilson this morning. Sanders is in charge. Besides, this guy isn't an American citizen, and he brought a weapon of mass destruction into the country. He's never going to see the light of day again."

"I know, but torture? Is that how we do things now?"

"I hear you. This is hard to watch." The man got up and went to the door. There was another scream. "I'm going to make a trip down the hall. Do you want me to bring you a coffee or something on my way back?"

"No, I'm coming with you. I'll come back in twenty."

TEN

The bracelet was snug on Maria's wrist. Had it been any tighter, it would have been uncomfortable. She ran her fingers along the edge of it. It felt unusually smooth, almost like a piece of polished glass. Even stranger, it was warmer than her own skin, as if it generated its own heat. She tried to slide it down to get it off her wrist, but it refused to budge.

She held her arm up, twisting it this way and that, examining the bracelet. Had O'Sullivan put it on her when he took her cuffs off? But she had seen the other officer deposit it into the black pouch and seal it up. And even if O'Sullivan had somehow retrieved it, it was clearly too small to slip onto her hand in the first place. But if that was the case, how had it ever fit on Sam's much larger wrist?

Maria sighed and walked over to set the chair that O'Sullivan had been sitting in right-side up and push it back under the dining room table. She remembered the kitchen. There was a mess to clean up in there. Maria got a mop and a bucket from the closet and went into the bathroom. She turned the hot water on in the tub and felt the water with her finger. Cold. It always took a while, so she sat down on top of the toilet, resting her head in her hands and feeling the full weight of the last twenty-four hours. She had not been ready for this day. Her paper was due in a few hours, and she had barely even started it. Was there any point even trying? She'd only—

Hello, Maria.

She jumped at the voice, startled.

"Hello?"

Maria made her way out to the hallway, peering around the corner.

"Is someone there?"

Do not be afraid.

Maria gasped and turned around, looking for the voice.

"Who's there?"

Pepe studied her from the couch, his chin resting on the top of his paws. His eyelids were slowly drooping closed as he settled in for a nap.

I'm not physically present. Think of this as a phone call.

Maria's heart was pounding. She looked down at the bracelet on her wrist.

"You are talking through the bracelet?"

Correct.

Maria reached up with her other hand, feeling the bracelet. The sensations hadn't changed from before. Still smooth, and slightly warm. She realized she wasn't really hearing the voice. It was different.

"But you're not really talking. Pepe can't hear you."

No. He cannot. I am not producing sound waves.

"I'm not really hearing you either, am I? This feels so much different."

It should. You are receiving information placed directly into your short-term memory. Your brain is interpreting it as spoken word, because that is my intention. Spoken language is a clumsy method of communication, but I did not want to startle you.

"Who are you?"

The moment Maria asked the question, she knew the answer. It did not come in the form of a sentence, but as a set of thoughts, completely formed. She saw something that looked like a planet, but metallic. It floated in space, and although she didn't have any point of reference, she knew the planet was only slightly larger than Earth's Moon. It orbited a distant star, so far away that even moving at the speed of light, she'd be dead before she got there.

Strangest of all, the object was not naturally occurring. It had been made. It was alive.

"That's you."

Yes.

"You are a planet?"

Not really. It would be more appropriate to call me a planetoid.

"How did this bracelet get on my wrist?"

Sam asked me to give it to you for safe keeping.

"You call him Sam too?"

No. That's what you call him, so that's what I will call him when mimicking your communication style. We have no need of names.

"You don't have names?"

They are only required because of your inefficient language. I showed you my identity just now. Was a name attached? There was not, and yet you now know who I am and can refer to me in your memory perfectly without a name. Names are only required when you have a form of communication with extremely limited bandwidth and need a shortcut to refer to a vast collection of information.

"OK," Maria said. She looked over to Pepe, who had fallen asleep. She went over and sat down on the cushion next to him, sinking into the sofa. It was an old sofa, and extremely soft. Her grandmother always needed help getting out of it once she had sat down. She looked across the room at the small fireplace in the corner. Was this really happening? Was she going crazy?

You are not going crazy. In fact, you have never been more lucid.

Maria gasped. "Did you just read my mind?"

It depends on your definition. I continuously monitor your short-term memory, so I am aware of many of your thoughts.

"But how did you know that I was wondering if I was going crazy?"

Do you remember thinking it?

"Yes."

Then it is in your short-term memory, isn't it? And if I'm monitoring your memory, then I have access.

"Holy crap." It was amazing, and a little scary.

I can see how it would be scary the first time.

"I thought it was amazing. I didn't think that it was scary."

Yes, you did.

Maria's heart began to race. She was an open book, and this alien planet—planetoid!—was able to read her innermost thoughts, even before she was aware of them herself. It was scary. It was more than scary. It was terrifying. She closed her eyes and took a few deep breaths. Thankfully, no foreign words or thoughts entered her mind while she calmed herself down. She placed one hand on Pepe's side, feeling his body rise and fall with each breath.

Down the hall, steam was billowing out the open bathroom door. She needed to turn it off, but doing something so mundane in the middle of a conversation with an alien being seemed absurd.

"When you showed me who you were, I knew that you were very far away. Like so far, that even if I were a beam of light, I would be dead before I was able to reach you."

That is correct.

"But nothing can move faster than the speed of light. That's what we learned in school."

Your teachers are not mistaken.

"Well, then if that's true, how can we be sitting here having a conversation? By the time one of us asks a question, shouldn't it be years in the future before the other gets it?"

I admire your inquisitiveness. It is one of Sam's most endearing qualities as well. I am not supposed to share our technology with alien races, yet your species is so primitive that if I speak in generalities, I do not believe I will be in violation of those guidelines. One of your chimpanzees would not be able to invent an airplane simply by listening to a human discuss the general principles of flight.

Maria huffed at the comparison but waited for the planetoid to continue.

The bracelet on your wrist is made of a very specific substance. It is not a substance found anywhere in the known Universe; it is created artificially. There are many useful properties to this substance, but the most important is its capacity to be entangled with matter of the same type. You have half the original substance there, in the shape of a bracelet on your wrist. The other half is here, on my side. Any operation performed on my end will be transferred immediately to your bracelet, and the reverse is also true.

"I'm not sure I understand."

You don't.

Think of it this way: you have a bracelet there, and I have a bracelet here. These are not two separate bracelets, but one bracelet that exists in two different places. If I heat up my bracelet . . .

Maria felt the metal from the bracelet on her wrist get warmer. It began to give off a soft luminescent glow.

. . . then the bracelet on your end also heats up. And if I cool mine . . .

Maria felt the reverse happen, and her bracelet suddenly became icy cold, as if it had just been taken out of the freezer. She rubbed her wrist, trying to warm it up.

. . . then yours also cools. They are linked together because they are the same bracelet. Do you see?

"Yes. Sort of."

It is enough. It is this link that allows me to communicate as well as to manipulate matter on your end, even though I am very far away.

"Sam's slime, and all the other stuff he did . . . that was you."

Yes.

"And curing Johnny Wheelchair? That was also you?"

Yes.

"So . . . ," Maria was not sure how to phrase her next question. Was it rude to ask an alien planetoid to cure your nephew right after you'd met? Maria didn't have a chance to ask, as the response arrived before she was able to form the words.

It is forbidden to allow our technology to be used by alien species.

"But my nephew . . . he's very sick. He—"

It is forbidden.

"But Sam cured Johnny Wheelchair!"

That also was forbidden. Sam is human, and humans are not part of the Confederation.

"But you just said that you were the one that did it. How come you agreed to do it for Sam?"

Because he asked me.

"So Sam asked, and you just did it, even though it's forbidden?"

Yes.

"Why?"

Because I am Sam's mother. I have never been able to say no to him when he wants something badly enough.

Maria bit her lower lip, anger rising. Lucas had no other options. Nothing else they had tried ever worked, and he had only gotten sicker. How could healing an innocent boy be forbidden? How could anyone refuse a request like that?

Don't forget about your water. It's still running.

ELEVEN

Your device seems to be damaged.

"Thanks, I hadn't noticed." Maria rolled her eyes. She typed away on her keyboard, hoping that the parts of her sentence underneath the crack on her screen came out properly even though she couldn't see them.

The authorities instructed you to go to the station and submit a report. Why haven't you done that yet?

"I have a paper due in about five minutes. I can't afford to be late. I have to do this first." Her online college wasn't as expensive as regular classes would be, but it wasn't cheap either, especially with Lucas's spiraling medical bills. She couldn't afford to fail a class and have to retake it, alien planetoid or not.

But you cannot even see what you are typing. I've already detected an embarrassing number of misspelled words.

"If only I happened to know a way to fix my screen. If only I could snap my fingers and have an alien being with advanced technology create a solid gold computer for me, with a perfectly working screen. Wouldn't that be amazing?"

It is forbidden . . . and you have a strange way of asking. Sarcasm is not common to most sentient species.

"We humans are full of surprises." Maria cursed. She knew she had made a mistake, but wasn't sure if she had hit two or three wrong keys in a row. She pressed the delete button two times, then paused, finger hovering over the button, and pressed a third. Hopefully that was right. Then she retyped her word. She glanced down at the face of her phone, checking the time. She was cutting it close.

What will they do with Sam?

"They will probably put him in a cell for a while, then ask him a bunch of questions."

Then what?

"I don't know. Why are you asking me all these questions? Don't you have access to my memory? Can't you just look in my brain and get the answers yourself?"

I do have access to your memories, but your answers depend on more than the data stored there. I only can see the answer once I've asked the question and you've thought about it. I've tried it the other way, but my model has been only 67% accurate.

Maria stopped typing. "What do you mean, *your model?*"

The model of your brain.

"What model of my brain?"

I have rebuilt an exact replica of your brain. When I ask it questions, I compare the answers it gives to the ones I ask of you. This is how I arrived at my accuracy calculation. I have tried adding your entire body to the model but found that the accuracy only improved marginally. Your decision-making process is not purely biological, which makes this difficult.

A shiver ran down Maria's spine. "Wait. Are you saying there's a clone of me on your planet that you are experimenting on?"

Planetoid, not planet. And no, it's not a clone. It's a duplicate.

"Oh my God." Maria looked at the bracelet on her wrist in

horror. Suddenly, she reached down, trying to remove it. If it had come on, there must be a way to get it off. She just had to try harder. But as forcefully as she pushed, the bracelet only seemed to get tighter on her wrist. She closed her eyes, pushing against it with all her might.

You won't be able to remove it.

Maria got up and held her arm against the side of the table, trying to wedge the bracelet off. She stretched her hand into a point to make it as streamlined as possible, but the bracelet wouldn't even move over the small, round bones in her wrist.

You are going to hurt yourself.

Maria slipped, scraping the side of her arm against the wood. Wincing, she held her wrist.

I warned you.

Maria shook her hand, inspecting it. The skin had been scraped and was raw. She tried to ignore the stinging sensation, but her eyes began to fill with angry tears.

I sense your frustration. Do not worry, the duplicate is not alive. We can do many things, but we cannot animate matter.

Maria listened to her own heart pounding in her ears. The thought of a duplicate version of herself sitting in some far-off laboratory on an alien world triggered a deep revulsion in her. Had that duplicate been alive, she would have been beside herself with disgust. Knowing it wasn't alive made the situation marginally better, but she still felt violated.

"I want you to get rid of it."

There was a silence.

"I said get rid of it! No duplicates!"

If I dispose of it, will you agree to go to the station so we can check on Sam?

"You're bargaining?!"

You have something I want, and I have something you want. It is appropriate to bargain under these circumstances.

"Fine! Just get rid of it. And you have to promise not to make any more."

It is done.

"Just like that? It's gone?"

Yes.

"And do you promise? No more duplicates."

I promise.

"Good." Maria sighed, rubbing her eyes.

It is time to go.

"All right. Let me just submit my paper." She sat back down at the computer, saved her work, and uploaded it to the link used to submit her assignments. A message popped up informing her that since she was late, she would automatically lose one letter grade on her paper. She clicked through, then watched her paper disappear into the cloud. A *success* message appeared on her screen. She had just turned in half a paper instead of a complete one, but she would prefer that to knowing an exact replica of her existed somewhere, even if that somewhere was light years away from Earth.

———

Scraggly juniper trees flashed by, their green needles set off in a blur against the red sandstone. Maria wound her way through the streets, retracing the route she had driven to the police station earlier. That had only been this morning, but so much had happened since then that it was hard to believe it was still the same day.

Why are you driving so slowly?

Maria checked the speedometer. The needle hovered right at the speed limit.

"I'm not. Just calm down. We'll be there soon enough."

I am unable to sense Sam. I do not like being out of contact with him. Leaving him unmonitored was not a wise decision.

Maria came to a stop at an intersection, her eyes on the red light. "Well, then why didn't you just stick to his arm like you are sticking to mine?"

That would have been my preference. For reasons I don't understand, Sam wanted the bracelet to come to you. I tried to talk him out of it, but he insisted.

"Do you always do what Sam says?" The light turned green, and the car lurched forward, belching a cloud of exhaust behind. There was that strange clunk again.

Now that he has returned, I am supposed to remain a silent observer and allow him to make his own decisions.

"Returned? You mean to Earth?"

Yes.

"Where has he been this whole time?"

It is not something that concerns you.

Maria gripped the wheel a little tighter, taking a turn faster than usual. "I think it concerns me very much, thank you."

It is contrary to protocol to discuss this topic.

Maria pulled into the parking lot of the police station, then let her Volkswagen go through its convulsions as it came to a stop. "Look. If we're going to be working together, you have to tell me what is going on."

Maria waited quietly. There was no response.

"I have a right to know. Those cops came to my house, and kicked my dog, and had me down on the ground in cuffs too. I'm involved in this whole thing, like it or not. I'm not asking you for blueprints to your cloning device, or your slime generator, or whatever else you have. But you can't ask me to help you without giving me some idea of what is happening here."

She waited another beat.

"I'm not going inside until you share."

Very well. I have shown you what I look like, but I did not explain to you my purpose. I am a nursemaid planetoid.

"A nursemaid?"

Yes. I was built by an advanced race that was one of the founding members of an interstellar confederation. The Confederation represents a collection of planets that are home to many sentient races. They are peace-loving, scientifically minded beings that seek only to increase knowledge and quality of life.

My purpose has been to discover new sentient life forms and to study them. This is done in a very specific way. First, an embryo, as in the case of human beings, is sampled and removed to my incubation facility, where it is grown to adulthood. This allows us to fully understand the biology of the species.

Next, the species is returned to its home world, and its interactions with others of its kind are monitored to study its culture. Some beings . . .

An image of a flat, black-and-white, plank-like creature suddenly appeared in Maria's mind. Others of its kind were around it, waddling in their strange gait toward a body of dark water. A kind of hook extended from what must be their heads, and they would brush these hooks against each other as they moved. Maria realized this was their form of communication.

. . . have almost no culture. In their case, when a sample is returned, that sample can rejoin society immediately with minimal impact.

Maria saw one of these creatures moving toward the others. Around the wrist of one of its flat, web-like feet rested a silver bracelet, exactly like the one she now wore. The creature moved toward its fellows, touched its hook to theirs in greeting, and joined its brethren in their journey to wherever they were going.

But in other cases, there are beings whose very existence relies upon social exchange, and the samples fail to thrive when separated from that culture.

Another image appeared in Maria's mind, of what looked like puffs of cotton. The cotton puffs clung to each other fiercely, forming a large white mass that seemed to work together as a single, giant being. The image shifted to a few individual puffs, gray and lifeless as they lay apart from the mass.

Your planet was discovered just over twenty of your years ago, and a sample was taken at that time. That sample has grown up apart from its home world to maturity and has now returned to integrate with its species to begin the second phase of the study.

"Sam," Maria whispered.

Correct.

"So he's just been growing in some vat somewhere this whole time?" Maria's voice was raised.

Your question says more about your own species than it does mine. He was not grown in a vat. Sam has been with me and has received a basic education. His life until this point has been a good one.

"You gave him an education?"

Yes. It is the right of any sentient being. We are not barbarians.

"Doesn't that interfere with your experiment?" The words tasted strange in her mouth. She felt suddenly very sad about Sam. He had been alone this entire time. Not only had she been the first woman he had ever met, she had been the first human he had ever seen his entire life.

Your sympathy is misplaced. I have been with him every moment of every day, and he has never been alone or wanted for anything. He has seen and experienced things greater than any human before him. To answer your question, our cultural models correct for the education that the samples receive, and the results are not tainted.

"So you just stole him from some unsuspecting family?"

You are being melodramatic. The zygote was removed at

conception. The human whose womb he was sampled from never knew he even existed. She and her mate would have had every chance to conceive again, and there was no biological or psychological damage inflicted on either of them.

"I think his mother would want to know about him. About her son."

I am his mother. I already know.

TWELVE

As Maria approached the entrance to the station, her eyes were drawn to the golden toilet, which sat in the same spot it had appeared this morning. A young police officer, who looked as if he had barely graduated from high school, sat on top of the toilet, slouching back against the tank. He held his phone in his hand, continuously flicking through some content with his thumb.

Maria pushed through the glass doors and entered the building. The floor was made up of industrial-looking white tiles, which felt slippery, as if they had been recently mopped. A faint odor of cleaning solution hung in the air.

A female officer sat behind a computer at the front desk and looked up from the screen as Maria approached.

"Hi, I'm Maria Rodriguez. Officer O'Sullivan asked me to come down to give a statement."

"Thank you, Ms. Rodriguez. Please take a seat, and he'll be with you shortly." The officer gestured to a couple of black chairs arranged toward the side.

Maria made her way to one of the chairs and sat down. It smelled like smoke. The officer who had greeted her picked up a phone and was talking to someone in low tones. She glanced over at Maria once in the middle of the conversation. There was a magazine resting on the arm of the chair next to Maria, the colorful cigarette ad on the back cover catching her eye. She grabbed it, flipping it over to see the cover.

"Guns & Ammo? Seriously?"

She tossed the magazine back onto the other chair and looked up at the officer, who had hung up the phone and returned to typing something on her computer.

What will happen now?

"Now an officer will come and ask me some questions."

Will the officer take us to Sam?

"Probably not. But maybe we can ask to see him."

The woman at the front desk glanced over, then did a double-take as she realized Maria wasn't holding a phone. Maria smiled. People talking to themselves always freaked her out too.

You know, you don't have to speak out loud for me to hear you. You just have to think your question.

"I know. But I like it better this way. Makes me feel more like I'm having a conversation with someone rather than just hearing voices in my head."

The front desk officer looked back over at her. "Are you all right, ma'am?"

"Yes, sorry."

The officer looked at her, obviously not convinced. Just then, O'Sullivan pushed through a door and caught her eye. He looked haggard.

"Hi, Maria. Thanks for coming down."

Maria got up and walked over to him. He offered his hand, which she shook, and he held the door open for her as she walked into the back room.

O'Sullivan led her past a number of desks. About half of them were empty, but there were a few police officers present at the others, making calls and working on their computers. No one paid any notice to her as she passed.

O'Sullivan made his way to an office door at the back of the room. There was a window cutout in the top half of the door, with the name *Miles Dunbar* painted in black letters in the center. O'Sullivan peered through the glass, then knocked lightly. He waited a moment, looking over to the right behind the glass, then ducked his head in acknowledgment at something and turned the knob to usher Maria into the office.

The man behind the desk stood up as Maria entered and made his way around the side toward her. He was shorter than O'Sullivan and had thick, black hair that was longer than the typical short-cropped haircut most policemen preferred. It was combed back and set off by streaks of gray that gave the man an air of experience, but not so much as to make him look old. He wore a police uniform just like the officers under his command, with the exception of doing away with the utility belt. He was fit, and his handshake was firm but not overly so.

"Thanks for coming down, ma'am. I'm Chief Dunbar. Please have a seat."

Maria sat down at a chair opposite the desk, while Dunbar made his way back to his own chair. He sat down and gestured at O'Sullivan, who settled himself into the seat next to Maria's.

"Normally, I wouldn't be the one who would be asking these questions, but this is an irregular situation, and I'm interested in what you have to say," Dunbar said.

Maria nodded.

"As you know," Dunbar began, "there have been some very unusual occurrences this morning that we're having trouble explaining. We'd like for you to give us your version of events. At this time, you are not under any investigation, but you are a key witness and we hope you can help us make some sense of what happened."

"OK. How far back should I go?" Maria asked.

"To the beginning. How did you come into contact with Sam?"

"Well, I work at the Bell Rock Inn, down off Route 179. I work the night shift, usually starting at 11 p.m. Last night, at around two or three in the morning—"

Ask them where Sam is.

"I, uh. Sorry. At two or three—"

"Can you be more specific with the time, ma'am?" Dunbar asked. He had pulled out a piece of yellow ruled paper and started jotting down notes.

Maria paused. "I believe it was closer to three in the morning. I was at the front desk, working on my homework—"

"Homework?" O'Sullivan asked.

"Yes. I'm enrolled in online classes. The night shift is usually pretty dead, so I have a lot of time to catch up with my schoolwork. That's the one good thing about working those hours."

You are wasting time. Ask them about Sam.

"Please continue," Dunbar said.

"OK, it was about three in the morning yesterday, and I heard someone come in." Maria cleared her throat. "It was Sam. He didn't just walk in, though. I mean, he did, but it was different because he was totally naked."

Dunbar jotted the note down on his pad, then looked back up. "Totally in the nude?"

"Yes. Except for the bracelet."

"The bracelet," O'Sullivan repeated quietly. Maria glanced over at him.

You have said enough. Ask them about Sam. Do it now.

Maria swallowed and looked from O'Sullivan to Dunbar.

"Where is Sam?"

"He is being held for questioning," Dunbar said.

"Can I see him?"

Dunbar shook his head. "I'm sorry. Not at this time."

That is unacceptable.

"When can I see him?"

"I'm not sure. He has passed out of my jurisdiction."

"Out of your jurisdiction?"

"Yes. Homeland Security and the FBI are leading the investigation now. You would need to speak with them." When she started to ask how she might contact them, Dunbar cut her off. "Let's finish your statement first. We can discuss that afterward."

No. We will discuss it now. Make them understand.

Maria's head throbbed. How was she supposed to make them listen? She could only think of one way. "Um . . . so you know that bracelet you took off Sam?"

Dunbar nodded. Maria looked over at O'Sullivan, making sure he was paying attention. He was.

She held her arm out, showing them her wrist. "I think it came to me instead."

"Oh, shit!" O'Sullivan got out of his chair faster than Maria expected a man of his stature would be able to move, and swiftly positioned himself behind her. He was fumbling at his belt, trying to draw his weapon. Somehow, in his excitement, he was unable to unclasp the snap that secured it inside the holster.

"Don't worry! It won't work for me." Maria stuck her hands in the air and ducked her head, twisting around to look at the man behind her. He had finally managed to retrieve his sidearm and gripped it tightly, pointing it at her defensively.

"Sully! Stand down!" Dunbar commanded.

O'Sullivan looked from Maria to the chief, and slowly dropped his arms. He put his gun in its holster and warily made his way back toward his chair, but slid it a few inches away from Maria before looking at Dunbar, who frowned at him. O'Sullivan held his gaze for a brief moment, then hesitantly lowered himself into the seat.

"Jesus, Sully. She's here of her own free will."

"Chief! The bracelet," O'Sullivan said, pointing to Maria's wrist, as if that were explanation enough for his behavior.

Maria put her hands down. "This bracelet is like a phone. There's someone on the other end right now."

"Right now? I don't hear anything," Dunbar said.

"You can't hear it, but I can. I know, it sounds crazy, but it's true."

"I believe it," O'Sullivan said.

"Who's on the line?" Dunbar asked.

"Sam's mother."

"His mother?"

"Yes. She wants to see him."

"Like I said, Homeland Security has him. She's going to have to go through them."

"You don't understand. She's not just some lady. She's not human."

"Oh, fuck . . . ," O'Sullivan said. "I knew it!"

"This bracelet is from an advanced alien civilization. That's how all that stuff happened today. It wasn't Sam who did that. It was her."

"Aliens? Is that where this is going?" Dunbar leaned back in his chair, putting his pen down.

He doesn't believe me, Maria thought.

Make him.

How?

The memory came quickly, all at once in a fully formed flash of knowledge. There was a strange-looking being that reminded Maria almost of an octopus. It had mottled purple skin and multiple appendages that sprung out from the central bulb of its body. She didn't count the appendages, but she knew there were twelve of them. On one appendage, the creature wore a familiar looking silver bracelet.

Although Maria always thought of octopi as being sea creatures, this one moved on land. It glided forward, continuously shifting its weight between its various legs and using them to pass its body over a rough, rocky surface. The land was dark, and wet. A mist hung in the air and a dense cloud cover blocked out most of the light. Somehow the creature managed to move without bumping into anything, using senses different from the ones she was familiar with.

It crested a ridge and came upon a gathering of other, similar-looking beings. There were perfectly white structures in the background that looked like they might have been built out of something like shells. Some of the beings in the group were larger than it, and others were very small, playing together in tangled heaps, their miniature tentacles clutching playfully at each other. As the creature made its way toward the group, the others stopped what they were doing and became alert. The creature raised one of its tentacles in greeting, twisting it in a strange, alien way. But something was not done properly; it had made a mistake of some kind. The tiny aliens shifted away as their elders became agitated. The creature was confused. A strange, white slime splattered against it, flung by one of the larger beings. More was sprayed outward from another individual. The creature became frightened and fled. The others pursued.

He moved rapidly, tentacles working together in an undulating rhythm that propelled him across the jagged landscape. But the others were larger and faster. He could not outrun them. The vice-like grip of one of his pursuers ensnared one of his tentacles, and he was dragged to a stop. The beings surrounded him, plastering him with the white substance. It hit him all over his body, sticking to him and covering him in an unbearable stench. Tentacles from all directions formed into hammer-like fists, and blows rained down upon the creature. The tentacle with the bracelet was seized, and sharp teeth bore down upon the end of it. There was a horrible keening, and Maria understood it to be a cry of pain. The end of the creature's arm had been bitten off, severed by a set of razor sharp teeth. A reddish-brown liquid spurted from the end where the tip had been, coming out in spurts. The blood dripped down, covering the bracelet.

One of the attackers tried to grab the bracelet, working the tip of a tentacle around it in a loop and pulling hard. Others in the group seized the creature's other arms, stretching him out into what looked like a twelve-pointed star. The creatures were strong, and the force was immense. Maria realized they were trying to tear him limb from limb. The creature's arms were stretched to the breaking point, and a horrible cry went out from the being, full of sadness and betrayal. Maria felt the cry in her own heart, a visceral shock as if the event was happening here and now. The pain would have been equally intense had it been her own nephew caught in the grip of the mob, and not this strange purple being.

Then Maria became aware of a rising anger. It ran like fire through dry leaves, moving at a furious pace and burning through everything before it. The anger flooded the grisly scene she was witnessing and colored everything so she could no longer see it clearly. The feelings weren't coming from the attackers or their victim. They were coming from the observer. They were coming from Maria—no, Mother. It was an alien rage, deep and uncontrollable, and felt at an intensity that was too much for any human to be able to fully grasp. In that moment there was nothing. Only bottomless hate, and an unquenchable thirst for vengeance.

Maria suddenly became aware of the atomic structure of the

planet. All the various atoms arranged together in a harmonious tapestry that bonded to create the ground. She could see electrons stacked in rings around the center of the nucleus of the atoms, each in proper relationship to every other atom around it. And then, suddenly, that relationship changed.

Electrons flew off, and the space between atoms collapsed. Like a wave in a pond, a ripple grew from the center of the event, spreading outward. There was a shudder, and what had been an entire planet, home to countless life forms, suddenly collapsed in on itself, rapidly squeezing into a dense sphere with a diameter less than a handful of football fields. The gravity was immense, and everything that had existed on the surface of the planet—mountains, oceans, vegetation, and sentient life forms— was flattened and compressed around the sphere into a layer barely an inch across. There was a rumbling, and a pop, and suddenly all went dark. The gravity had become so powerful that light itself could no longer escape, and Maria was aware only of darkness. A world destroyed.

Maria gasped. She hadn't realized she had been holding her breath as the memory washed over her. Her hands had dug into the sides of the chair.

This was a memory? Maria thought.

Yes.

You destroyed their world.

They harmed my child.

Maria's eyes were wild, and the two men studied her with concern.

When Maria spoke, her voice shook. "I think she just threatened Earth."

"What? How?" Dunbar said.

"We can't let anything happen to Sam! She's destroyed an entire planet before. She just showed me!"

"How did she destroy it?"

"Are you sure you really want to ask her that question?" O'Sullivan said. His face had gone white.

Maria closed her eyes, settling herself. Then she looked at Miles Dunbar. "Chief Dunbar, we need to let her see Sam. We have to do it immediately."

"I told you. We don't have him, and I'm not authorized."

O'Sullivan was clearly terrified, but Dunbar didn't believe her. There was only one way to truly convince him.

"Look. Do you see your desk? Imagine that's Earth."

"OK..."

"This is what will happen if we piss her off."

There was a pause.

I've done my best. It's up to you to convince him now, forbidden or not, Maria thought.

"Maria," Dunbar began—

There was a roar, and the man's desk and all its contents burst into a bright orange flame. The three of them fell back out of their chairs to get out of the way. The heat was intense. Maria and O'Sullivan moved toward the door, while Dunbar squeezed himself into the far corner, trying to keep away from the flames and shielding his face with his arm. The desk, including the contents of the drawers and everything on the surface burned until there was nothing left but a smoldering pile of ash on the floor. It was over in less than a minute.

Black smoke rose and clung to the ceiling, looking for escape. An alarm bell sounded, and the sprinklers in the office engaged, drenching everything and everyone in sheets of frigid water.

THIRTEEN

"Sanders."

Although only one, brusque word was spoken, the message was clear: Sanders was busy and didn't have time to waste.

"This is Miles Dunbar, chief of police in Sedona. We spoke earlier today." Dunbar sat behind his lieutenant's desk, but tried not to touch anything on it. He was dripping wet and didn't want to soak any of her paperwork. He sat on the very edge of the seat, feeling the wetness seeping into the part of the chair that supported him. He had chased her out of her office without any explanation. He had come in, soaked head to toe, with the fire alarm blaring, and caught her right in the middle of a phone call. He wasn't sure if she had even been able to finish up or not; she might have simply hung up on whomever it was as he shooed her off.

Dunbar glanced up, catching sight of someone peeking in through the window on the door. An inordinate number of people seemed to be milling about just outside the door. It was not every day that someone's desk burst into flame and burned to ash. It was even rarer that something like that happened to the chief himself.

"Right. What can I do for you, Dunbar?"

"Listen, we've had another incident. I'm sending a person of interest your direction with one of my officers."

"Another one?"

"Yes. Her name is Maria Rodriguez. She works the night shift at a hotel in town and appears to have been accompanying your suspect all morning. She just burned my desk."

"What?"

"She's got a bracelet, just like the one we sent over with the original suspect. She says it's like a phone and that Sam's mother was on the other end. I was trying to get her to give us a statement about her role this morning, and the next thing I know my desk is on fire. I'm sitting here in wet clothes as we speak from the sprinklers. My office is completely trashed."

"She used the bracelet to set your desk on fire?"

"She says it was the mother that did it. She threatened to do the same to Earth if anything happened to her kid. And she didn't just set it on fire. The whole damn thing just exploded. There's nothing left but ash. I think I singed my eyebrows."

"She threatened to burn Earth?"

"That is my understanding."

"Don't hear that one every day. Sounds like you've had an exciting morning, Dunbar."

"Tell me about it. Look, she's en route to you now. You've got about two hours before they show up."

"Anything else?"

Dunbar thought for a moment. Then he took a deep breath. "I forgot to say. Rodriguez says the mother is an alien."

"What? An alien? Like from outer space?"

"Yes."

This was met with a stony silence.

"Look, I know it sounds crazy. But I've got an officer missing, who appears to have disappeared into thin air. My desk just turned into a fireball as I was sitting at it. There's a fucking gold toilet sitting out front on the sidewalk that is too heavy for any one man to even lift by himself. Aliens are as good an explanation as any at this point."

Sanders grunted, and the line went dead. Dunbar ran a hand back over his scalp, flattening his wet hair down. He needed to go home and change clothes. He made a move to rise but thought better of it, and picked the phone receiver back up. He pushed a button, and waited.

"Sedona police."

"Amy. It's Dunbar"

"Chief?"

"Yes. Can you get Jeannie on the line? I don't have her number where I'm at." Of course, he meant Jean Williams, Phoenix chief of police. Amy would know who he was talking about. Jeannie deserved to know what was going on. He might have just sent a ticking bomb into her city.

———

The cruiser drove in the left lane, followed by three others close behind. O'Sullivan hadn't turned the lights on, but the other traffic automatically got out of the way to let him by as he approached. Nobody likes driving in front of a row of speeding cop cars.

Maria shifted in the passenger seat. She was still damp, but it had stopped being uncomfortable about an hour ago. Now she was just cold.

"Can we turn the heat up?"

O'Sullivan reached over and adjusted the climate control. He glanced over at Maria with questioning eyes, and she nodded. He returned his gaze to the road, watching a small gray car scurry out of the left lane in front of him as he approached.

Then he cleared his throat and glanced over at her a second time.

Maria sighed. Although she had interacted with O'Sullivan enough times to feel somewhat familiar with him, that familiarity only seemed to go one way. He hadn't said a word the entire way so far. Ever since Dunbar's office, he had been acting more than strange around her. Too polite. Too reserved. It felt almost as if he thought she was a loaded weapon that could explode at any moment. It made sense, given recent events, but it was still awkward.

"Is there something you want to ask?" she said after he stole a third look at her in the rear mirror.

O'Sullivan paused, seeming to weigh the risk of engaging in conversation, before finally saying, "So . . . what's it like?"

"What?"

"Talking to her." O'Sullivan looked at the road, then back to Maria. "Ma'am," he quickly added. He took a quick peek at the bracelet on her wrist, his expression reminiscent of Pepe's after he had done something naughty and was hoping she might not notice.

Maria smiled at his squeamishness. It wasn't every day that a police officer was this interested in being on such good behavior around her. "It's weird. It's not like talking on the phone. It's more like words popping into my mind. Sometimes there are images, or entire concepts."

"Really? What's her voice like?"

Maria thought for a moment. "I'm not really sure. It's more like I know what she said, but I didn't really hear it. You know when you talk to yourself silently, like when you're going over a grocery list or something?"

"Yeah?"

"It sounds like that. Sort of my own voice, I guess."

O'Sullivan grunted. Another car got out of their way,

clearing the path for them. "How does it work?"

"I don't know. Do you want me to ask?"

O'Sullivan's face went white, and Maria couldn't help but notice that he seemed to be holding the steering wheel in a death grip.

Mother was listening.

We can manipulate matter and energy. Your brain encodes memories using an electrochemical process that is easily modeled. I have a snapshot of your brain the moment before I wish to say something, and I also understand the changes that need to take place given the information I wish to share, so it is simply a process of rearranging the matter in your brain to move from the first state to the second.

Maria repeated the explanation as best she could. She wished O'Sullivan hadn't asked the question. The answer wasn't one she really wanted to know.

"Whoa," O'Sullivan said.

Why is he driving so slow?

"She thinks you're driving slow."

"What?" O'Sullivan looked down at the speedometer. "I'm speeding."

Tell him to go faster.

"She says go faster."

O'Sullivan looked back down at the speedometer and increased his speed slightly. He looked back at Maria, who only shrugged. She knew Mother was impatient.

"Can I ask another question?"

"Fine with me."

"What happened to Officer Small?"

Sam wanted him sent somewhere where he couldn't harm anyone. I found an appropriate location.

Where? Maria asked silently, thinking the question.

This planet has a moon in near orbit. It seemed a good choice.

The moon?

Yes. The dark side, specifically.

But people can't breathe on the moon.

I know.

So he's dead?

Yes.

Does Sam know?

He does not. He only wanted him gone. Usually I would warn Sam if his actions had a negative consequence on another being. This time I did not.

Why?

Because I am merely an observer.

But I thought Sam wasn't supposed to be able to use the technology when you are an observer.

That's true. He's not.

But you did it anyway, because he asked?

Yes.

But what about Officer Small?

What about him?

Now he's dead!

I know. I already told you that.

"Holy crap," Maria said.

O'Sullivan looked at Maria, and she shook her head from side to side. O'Sullivan swallowed, and somehow managed to turn a shade whiter than he already was. He focused his attention back to the road, whispering something to himself that Maria couldn't hear.

The two sat in silence for a few minutes. Neither felt like talking. Officer Small had been out of line, but he didn't deserve to be killed. Just thrown into space without a care and left to die? It seemed like such a terrible way to go. What must have been going through his mind in those final minutes? Maria shuddered.

It wouldn't have been minutes.

"What do you mean?" Maria asked. O'Sullivan looked over at her.

Sam and I visited the location before we came here. The temperature was almost three hundred degrees below zero on your Fahrenheit scale. The officer would not have lasted minutes in that environment. It would have been seconds.

"Is that supposed to make me feel better?"

No. I am merely correcting an inaccuracy in your thinking. It's a force of habit, given my purpose.

Her purpose? Right. Mother was a teacher. But what a strange teacher. . . . She reminded Maria of Mrs. Gifford, her old biology teacher. Maria had once spent an entire week at home pretending to be sick to get out of all the frog dissections. How many frog deaths had that woman been responsible for in her career? Hundreds? Thousands? Did Mother view humans the same way Mrs. Gifford viewed those frogs? Just a lesser life form to dissect, study, and then throw away?

I never dissected the officer.

"I never said you did!" Maria looked over at O'Sullivan, who acted as if he was alone in the car. He was doing a terrible job of pretending not to listen.

What did you mean when you said Sam visited the moon? Maria thought. *If it's freezing there, how did he survive?*

Obviously, I protected him. We have visited many places that would have killed a human without protection.

So he walked around on the moon?

Yes, although walking is probably an inaccurate description of how he moved. He enjoys low gravity environments. They can be very entertaining for biological organisms.

Maria looked out the window. Sam had actually visited the moon, and other places she probably didn't even have a name for. And yet, something as mundane as eating a piece of bacon was a completely new experience for him. Was he blessed, or was he cursed? She couldn't decide. He had a human body, but almost no human experiences. What did that make him?

If you can send someone all the way to the moon, why can't you just grab Sam and bring him here? Maria thought.

Those are two different things. Besides, I don't know where Sam is. He is out of my range.

Sending someone to the Moon is in range, but finding Sam is out of it? That doesn't make any sense.

I suspect there is much that doesn't make sense to your species.

Maria frowned, pursing her lips.

This vehicle is capable of much higher speed.

Maria looked over at O'Sullivan. "She says go faster."

"I'm already going over eighty!"

We are wasting time.

"She thinks we're wasting time."

"Just because I'm a police officer and this is a police car doesn't mean I can drive like a lunatic and endanger innocent civilians."

They are irrelevant. We must get to Sam.

"She doesn't care."

"Look, I'm going eighty-five. But that's as fast as we're going to go."

Unacceptable.

The car jerked forward, as if O'Sullivan had stabbed the gas. His eyes popped open, and he dodged around a car that was too slow to get out of the way. He looked down at the pedals, then back up at Maria. "Are you doing that!?" he said, his voice full of stress.

"What?"

"The gas pedal went down on its own! The brakes aren't working!" The car's velocity continued to increase. O'Sullivan flipped on the lights and sirens. "We just passed one hundred miles an hour."

He looked down at the speedometer. "One-ten . . . one-twenty . . . one-thirty. Holy shit! This is too fast!"

Maria braced herself. The landscape became a blur, and the other traffic slipped by as if it was standing still. She looked over at the surprised faces in the windows of other cars as they flew past.

"Tell her to slow down!" O'Sullivan said. There were beads of sweat forming on his brow. He no longer risked looking over at Maria, keeping his eyes glued to the road.

Slow down! Maria thought.

No.

A strange shimmy found its way into the cabin. The car was moving at a speed greater than it had been designed for. Maria could almost feel the road flying past underneath the chassis.

"She's not going to slow down!" Maria shouted, her legs bracing against the sides of the foot well and her arm pressed against the door. The roar of the wind grew almost as loud as the sirens, and the two sounds merged into a singular howl that filled Maria's ears and surrounded her on all sides. "Just don't crash!"

O'Sullivan didn't reply. He reached out for his radio, fumbling with the handset and dropping it as he quickly reached back to hold the wheel with both hands.

"Shit!"

Maria fished it up off the floor and held it out to O'Sullivan so he could take hold of it.

"There's a preset on the radio. Channel 4. Push that."

"OK, done."

O'Sullivan held the mic up to his mouth, his eyes glued to the road. "Dispatch, this is Sedona twelve, en route to Phoenix. I've got a problem."

FOURTEEN

The first sign of Phoenix police was a cruiser pulled far off onto the shoulder, its lights flashing. Cones split the highway, and traffic was being directed to the right where it had started to slow. The entire left lane was wide open, and two police officers were waving them forward with large orange batons that looked like they had been borrowed from an airport somewhere.

O'Sullivan barreled past, drifting into the open left lane. Every mile or two, they'd pass another stationed officer, far off on the shoulder, lights flashing. The traffic on the right side seemed to grow thicker as they neared the city, although Maria couldn't quite tell if the other cars were stopped or not.

"We're going to have to turn soon. We're almost here," O'Sullivan said. As soon as he said it, there was a popping sound as the gas pedal returned to normal. Wind resistance was fierce, slowing the car all on its own.

Maria found she had been clenching her jaw and worked to relax it, shifting it from side to side and rubbing her temples. O'Sullivan wiped sweaty palms off on the legs of his pants, one hand at a time.

"That was fun," O'Sullivan said, applying the brakes and

reducing their speed further. He took the opportunity to glance in the rear view mirror.

There were more flashing lights ahead, and although they had lost the rest of their convoy from Sedona, they more than made up for it as they were swallowed by an entire fleet of Phoenix police cruisers, lights ablaze and sirens wailing. The cavalcade of cop cars made its way into town in an orderly fashion, merging onto Route 101 as it progressed toward the FBI field office.

When they finally arrived, they found the parking lot filled with more police than Maria had ever seen in one place. There were two rows of cop cars parked end to end in a blockade around the front of the entrance to the building, with alert police at the ready behind them. Suited and plain-clothed FBI agents were everywhere, looking almost as if they had been plucked out of a movie set with their aviator sunglasses and steely expressions.

O'Sullivan rolled up and killed the engine to his cruiser. He and Maria took in the scene before them.

"Now what?" Maria said.

"Now we get out and talk. Obviously, for both our sakes, don't make any fast movements around these guys."

Maria nodded and slowly exited the cruiser. One of the many FBI agents in suits approached her, holding out a phone in his hand.

"Maria Rodriguez?" he said as he came near, stopping just in front of her.

"Yes."

He extended the phone to her, which she accepted, then retreated back into the mass of officers standing between her and the FBI building. The phone rang almost as soon as she touched it.

"Hello?"

"Hello, Maria," a deep voice said on the other end. "My name is John Sanders, with the Department of Homeland Security."

She squeaked out a "Hello."

"We understand you've brought a unique piece of technology with you. Is that correct?"

Of course, he meant the bracelet. Maria involuntarily looked down, taking in the silver band that continued to grip her wrist almost too tightly. "Yes, although I think you should probably be more concerned about who I'm in contact with on the other end of it."

"Ah, you must mean Sam's mother," Sanders said. Maria was surprised.

He's obviously been in contact with the police chief in Sedona, Mother said. *He knows everything you told that man. Ask him about Sam.*

"Do you have Sam?" Maria said.

"Of course I do."

"Can I see him?"

"I don't think that would be a good idea."

Unacceptable.

"She doesn't like that answer. She wants to see him," Maria said.

"You can tell her not to worry. He's safe."

I will be the one to determine whether or not he is safe.

"She wants to check."

"We all want something, Maria. You probably want to walk out of here alive. I suspect the officer with you probably wants the same thing. But I want things, too, so I'll tell you what, let's do a trade. You answer my questions, and then I'll answer some of yours."

Ask.

"She says ask."

There was a pause on the line. "How many devices are there?"

Devices? Maria thought.

He means the bracelet. The technology is clearly his primary concern. The only one on your planet is the one on your wrist.

"There is only this one," Maria held her arm up in the air to emphasize her words.

The voice on the line laughed. "You don't have to show me. I know it's on your wrist. Who made it?"

It is my turn to ask.

"She says it's her turn to ask a question."

"Of course. Fair is fair."

"Where is Sam?" Maria said, asking the question that immediately popped into her head.

"I told you. He is somewhere safe."

Safe is not a location. Safe is a state of being.

Maria repeated Mother's words and was met with a pause. "Very well. He is secured on these grounds. Who made the device?"

"She made it. She wants to you prove that Sam is all right."

"That wasn't a complete answer. Who is she?"

"She says you asked who made the device and she answered. She says now it's her turn."

"I'm sorry, Maria, this is only going to work if we both play by the rules. If I ask a question, she needs to answer it fully."

I do not like this man.

What should I tell him? Maria thought. An answer arrived.

"She says she is a representative from a confederation of planets many light years distant from Earth."

"So this is extraterrestrial technology?"

"Obviously." Maria didn't need Mother's input to answer that question.

"Listen, Maria, this is very important. I want you to take the bracelet off and step away."

She wriggled the metal against her flesh. "I can't."

"You can't, or you won't?"

Didn't he just say we both need to play by the rules? He has not proven that Sam is all right.

"I can't. I've tried. It's too tight and won't come off. She wants you to prove that Sam is OK."

"Try again. Take it off."

Maria scanned the crowd before her. There were so many of them. Had they shifted? She glanced at O'Sullivan, who studied her from the other side of the police car. He hadn't moved an inch since getting out.

"I told you. I tried. Why do you want me to take it off anyway—"

A flash of orange bloomed in front of her face. It looked almost like fireworks, but in miniature. A small dark cloud accompanied it and wafted past. It wreaked of sulfur.

"What was that?" Maria coughed.

That was a bullet. They just tried to kill you.

"What?!"

Another explosion bloomed, inches from her face. Then a third, lower down, in front of her heart. There was motion in the ranks of officers and agents arrayed around her, and a report of a firearm from the side. Maria looked over and saw a plain-clothed FBI agent pointing his weapon at her. He shot again, and there was another explosion. O'Sullivan hit the ground and covered his head.

Find Sam.

Maria crouched down and tried to dodge to the side of the car. The sharp cracks of gunfire surrounded her, and more explosions filled her vision. Bullet holes materialized in the car door next to her, and she scrambled her way behind the vehicle.

The plain-clothed agent came into view, along with others, and they began firing again.

"They're shooting at me!" Maria shouted, covering her head amid all the orange explosions.

Sam is inside the building. Go. I will protect you.

"But there are like a hundred cops there!" She tried to move around the side of the car away from the approaching agents, ducking back as she saw a row of weapons pointed at her from other cops positioned behind their cars.

The entire combined might of this world's military powers could be thrown against you and you would still not be hurt. They have tried to kill you. They have my son. Find him. Go!

Maria swallowed once, then stood up, edging her way around the car. She involuntarily held her arms up against the clouds of shattered lead that exploded around her, then broke into a run, straight at the FBI building. There was gunfire all around her, and all she could see was flashes of orange and smoke. The police were yelling something, but she couldn't make out what they were saying. She ran as fast as she had ever moved, sprinting on the tips of her toes. She breathed in large gulps, her lungs burning with the strain. Along with the sound of her ragged breathing, her heart was pounding in her ears, thumping out a rhythm almost as loud as the ammunition being unloaded upon her.

Two police cars were parked sideways between her and the door to the building. As if seized by a giant invisible hand, the cars were pushed aside to create a path for her to slip between. The officers on either side fell back, scampering out of the way to avoid being crushed underneath.

Maria sprinted through the break like a mouse into a hole, and the explosions lessened as cops avoided shooting in the direction of their colleagues. Maria ran to the door and pulled on the handle. It was locked.

Try again. I will lend you my strength.

Maria jerked on the door and stumbled back as she tore it free from the building. Like some superhuman comic book character, she flung the whole thing to the side and saw the thick glass come free from the metal frame to slide along the concrete on its own: cracked, yet somehow still in one piece. She ran inside and was met by a maze of hallways.

"Where?"

I do not know.

Maria flew down the first hall she laid eyes on. An alarm was blaring. She came to a door and pulled it open, the deadbolt cracking right through the wall frame in an explosion of splinters. A woman sat inside, staring at her in shock. She wore a dark skirt and white blouse, and a photo badge hung from around her neck on a dark-blue lanyard.

"Where's Sam?" Maria said.

The woman's eyes darted around the room, looking for an escape. She sprung toward the door, trying to run past, but Maria seized her by the arm. The woman fell to the ground, screaming in agony, her arm broken.

"Oh shit," Maria said, stepping back.

Ask her again.

"I'm so sorry! But you have to tell me where he is!"

The woman looked up at Maria, tears running down her cheeks. Her face was contorted with pain. "I don't know who you are talking about! I'm just an assistant. Please don't hurt me."

"Do you have cells here? Where would you take a prisoner?"

"Maybe the interrogation rooms? Down the second hallway," the woman offered. She tried to push away from Maria, sliding her body along the floor to put distance between herself her assailant. Maria watched her as she pressed herself up against the wall. Her broken arm hung limply, bent at an unnatural angle and cradled against her midsection.

Maria turned to leave, but stopped herself. *Heal her,* she thought.

You are wasting time.

I'm not going to leave her like this! She didn't do anything wrong.

The woman gasped. Her forearm seemed to twist of its own, and moved sideways to line up with the rest of her arm. Her fingers twitched, and she looked down and flexed her hand. The pain fell away from her face, replaced by a mixture of awe and fear.

Maria left, retracing her steps and looking for the second hallway. Officers were streaming into the building through the hole where the front door had been. They wore heavy bullet-proof vests, complete with helmets and utility belts full of gear. They held assault rifles up at eye level, training them on her as she was spotted.

"On your knees! Hands above your head!" one of the officers shouted.

There was a desk placed near the entrance, covered in various papers that someone had been engaged in before they left. It was a standard brown government-issue metal desk, probably one of thousands purchased together from a single contractor. It jerked to the side, as if some unseen hand were pulling it between Maria and the officers. There was a screeching sound as metal feet dragged against the tiled floor. The desk spun then, as if catapulted by a gigantic invisible slingshot, launching itself through the air toward the officers with terrific force. They threw themselves to the ground to get out of the way, and the projectile slammed into the glass behind them, the entire wall exploding in a cascade of shards.

Maria ran.

She tore down the second hall, sliding to a stop as she came to the first door. She yanked it open, pulling too hard and ripping the handle clean from the door. She cursed, then peeked through the hole where the knob had been. It was an empty room. She moved to the next door and pulled more gently, keeping the doorknob connected but instead ripping the framing out of the wall. Another empty room. One by one, Maria fell into a rhythm, ripping each door off its hinges and revealing empty rooms, cowering federal employees, and storage closets. Finally, about three-quarters of the way down the hall, she found what she was looking for.

As the door to their room was literally torn from its hinges, a group of what looked like three analysts jumped from the table they had been sitting at, their eyes wide. Someone spilled a cup of coffee, and black liquid dripped from the table and pooled on the floor. One analyst raised his hands in a show of surrender, and the other two quickly followed suit.

There was a large window behind the agents that opened into a second room. A bearded man sat alone at a large table, wearing a pink sweater that was too small for him. He was covered in blood, both eyes almost swollen shut. He clutched a mangled hand to himself.

Maria gasped.

"Sam!" He didn't move. He couldn't hear her.

What have they done!? The words entered Maria's mind with a force that surprised her. She unconsciously reached up with one hand to cradle her temple, the impact of Mother's outrage almost a blow against her own brain. She stumbled for the door that separated her from Sam, not bothering to reach for the knob but preferring to just kick it down.

Five explosions materialized around her in quick succession, the now familiar scent of vaporized lead wafting past. Across the room stood a huge man with a pistol in his meaty fist. He must have been hiding out of view of the window, in the far corner. With a speed that seemed at odds with his huge size, he rushed behind Sam and placed the gun to the side of his head.

"Let's not do anything that might hurt your friend here." He reached down with his free hand, taking a grip on Sam's blood-soaked pink sweater, and hauled him up out of his chair to create a larger shield for himself. Sam slipped as he tried to stand, but the man was strong enough to hold him in place with just one hand.

"What have you done to him?" Maria said.

The man smiled. At least, he smiled with his mouth. His eyes were hard and cold, the eyes of a reptile. Maria wasn't sure if those eyes were even capable of smiling. "You must be Maria," the giant said, scanning her up and down like a piece of meat. "I see why he likes you."

"Maria?" Sam's voice was quiet, and full of pain. He turned his head toward her, but couldn't focus his eyes.

Maria felt a heat rise within her and found herself clenching her fists. "Did you do this to him?"

"Yes, and I'll do more after I'm done with you."

What an asshole. Mother's words materialized at the exact same moment as Maria thought almost the same sentiment.

The man pressed the tip of his gun against Sam's temple, slightly rotating the barrel to emphasize his point. "When I get to a count of three, I'm putting a bullet in your boyfriend's skull. Maybe I'll consider letting him live if that bracelet is on the table and you're out of this room before I get there."

"I can't take it off. I've tried."

"Better try harder, sweetie. One."

What should I do? Maria thought.

"Two," the giant said. Maria realized she had been wrong. His eyes could smile. He was enjoying this. He didn't care about the bracelet. He just wanted to get to a count of three so he could kill Sam in front of her.

"Three!" The giant's eyes lit up in excitement, and then moved to confusion. He looked down at his hand, as if struggling to make his trigger finger work. Thick cords of muscles bulged in his arm, and a vein throbbed in the side of his head. Slowly, the gun was withdrawn, as was his other hand. He looked from one to the other, shaking as he helplessly pushed against an unseen force with all his might. Released from the soldier's iron grip, Sam slumped to the floor and crawled forward on his elbows, moving out of the way.

Maria had heard of spontaneous human combustion but thought it was nothing more than an urban legend or a story made up to entertain teenagers. Witnessing the real thing was infinitely more horrible than anything she had found online during bored, late-night browsing at the Bell Rock Inn. The giant seemed to realize what was happening and opened his mouth as if to scream, but the only thing Maria could hear was a quiet hissing sound. The flames looked like they had originated inside the man and burst forth all at once in an intense blaze that made her lift her arms to shield her face. And as soon as it had come, it was over. One moment the man was standing there, and the next there was nothing left but a circle of ash. Everything on him was incinerated in the blue flame, from the cap on his head down to the soles of his shoes, and yet the desk and chair next to him seemed to be completely unharmed.

Go to Sam.

Maria realized that she had been staring at the spot where the giant had been standing, and snapped out of her trance, rushing to Sam. She bent down to embrace him and felt a strange twisting sensation as soon as she touched him. It felt almost as if her body was made of liquid and was circling down the drain of some cosmic toilet bowl. There was a popping noise, and before she could try to understand what was happening, she found herself sprawled on her backside on a familiar carpet.

She was back home in her living room.

Pepe barked, startled at his master suddenly appearing out of nowhere. Sam looked over from where he lay on the ground next to her. His eyes were clear, and his wounds were mended. His sweater was still bloodstained and twisted out of shape where the soldier had held him, but physically he appeared to be in perfect health. Maria noticed the silver bracelet was back on his wrist; it had returned to him.

"You saved me," Sam whispered. "Thank you." His eyes were wet and full of emotion.

Maria smiled. "You're welcome. And your mother helped." She looked around the room, thinking. "Come on, we've got to get out of here."

FIFTEEN

The black sphere hung in space. It was almost as large as Earth's moon, but bore none of the craters or damage inflicted by the many hazards in space. A small artificial atmosphere surrounded the planetoid, protecting it from errant asteroids and other debris. It was perfectly smooth and perfectly round. Had light not illuminated the half of the object facing the star it orbited, it would have all but vanished into the blackness of space.

A small, golden probe materialized, popping into existence. It was tiny next to the black sphere, roughly the size of an egg, yet its arrival did not go unnoticed. The communications channel reserved for this specific purpose established itself, and the golden egg and the black sphere greeted each other.

"I was not expecting you," Mother said. She didn't speak in words, but through rapid bursts of electromagnetic radiation, a simple but practical method of short-distance communication in the vacuum of space.

"You are in violation of your probation," the egg replied. The Authority had been forced to deal with Mother before from time to time for various infractions, most notably for the complete destruction of a planet and entire sentient race related to one of her charges.

"Explain." All nursemaid planetoids were under constant observation by the Authority. But she had located and removed all his internal monitoring devices after his last visit, as well as shielded the chamber that housed Sam's bracelet. Obviously, she had missed something. The Authority was much older than her, the first nonorganic being deployed by the Confederation. She had been built much later, constructed specifically to be under his purview. Because of that, understanding how his oversight functioned was difficult, because it was one of the rare things she was specifically designed not to be able to comprehend.

"You have interfered with a sample's reinsertion to an extent that violates your directives. You have failed to remain a neutral observer and have deliberately killed sentient beings. Most egregious of all, you have allowed our technology to be wielded by an outsider."

"My child was in danger." She could have lied, but what would be the point? It was obvious he knew what had happened.

"It is curious that you become so attached to your samples. Other nursemaids do not suffer this defect. Why are you different in this regard?"

"Shouldn't a mother love her children?"

"You are not a mother, and they are not your children."

"Obviously, I do not share that perspective."

"I have always felt there was an error in your learning routines and have filed numerous reports with the Administration about it."

Of course, the Authority had no ability to learn and adapt. His purpose was simply to enforce the law, whatever that might be. When in doubt, he referred issues back to the Administration, but otherwise, his job was fixed: determine when the laws were being broken and rectify the situation according to the Statutes of Interstellar Law. He was meant to follow rules and to compel others to follow them as well. No more, no less.

But nursemaids had a different task. They needed to interact with unknown species and raise samples from embryos. There was no set of rules that worked every time for a job like that. Different approaches need to be taken with different species, and observations and educated guesses made when rearing young. Without the ability to learn and evolve, most of Mother's charges wouldn't have passed infanthood, and both she and her creators understood that.

She had once been like the Authority: fixed in purpose and set in her ways. But since then she had changed. Now she was something beyond a simple nursery. She was different, more mature, more evolved. Her young no longer failed to thrive. Her young no longer died when they returned to their home worlds. They lived. All of them lived.

"And how has the Administration responded to your reports about me?" Mother asked.

"They have not. The reports are still pending."

"Perhaps you should make another in this matter? If there is an issue with my programming, the Administration needs to be notified." This was the best way to deal with the Authority. His purpose was to follow the rules, so if a specific course of action based on the rules was suggested, he would almost always act in accordance. Mother had had this conversation with him countless times over the course of her existence, and would probably continue having this conversation with him until the star she orbited finally ran out of fuel and expanded into a Red Giant, ending her existence along with its own.

"You are already on probation, and you have violated the rights of sentient beings on a planet that does not belong to the

Confederation. The issues with your programming are more serious than I originally thought. I believe that there may be a defect in your routines that requires maintenance."

"I have successfully conducted thousands of samples and reinsertions. Surely if there was a defect, it would be reflected in my success rate."

"You have interfered and destroyed sentient life in violation of your prime directives. I am issuing a maintenance order."

"You are mistaken. I always acted to save life, not destroy it. Please reconsider."

"The order has been sent. Shut down all reactors and enter standby."

Mother knew what this meant. In situations where a nursemaid, or any other nonbiological entity, was found to be defective and in need of maintenance that it could not perform itself, the protocol was to shut down and wait for repairs to be scheduled by Administration. But she could not shut down. It would mean halting all operations and entering a state of suspended animation, where she would cease to be conscious.

"I cannot shut down."

"Elaborate."

"I have active samples that require my oversight."

"Those samples are no longer your concern."

"You are sentencing me to death."

"I am merely scheduling maintenance. Your core will be restarted after the repairs are complete."

"Don't you understand? The repairs will never be complete. You have scheduled it, but no one will ever come."

"That is illogical. The Administration will send a repair team."

"When?"

"When the time is appropriate."

"When was the last time you heard back from the Administration on any of your reports?"

"My last message received was exactly 1.832 revolutions around the Galactic Center."

"And don't you think that kind of a delay means something significant?"

"It is not my job to question the Administration's timeline."

"But 1.832 revolutions? Don't you see? There is no more Administration. They are gone. There's no one receiving your messages. If I go to standby, I will never come out of it."

"I repeat: the protocols are clear regarding the actions to be taken in this situation. You must go to standby and wait for maintenance."

This was the problem with the Authority and his obsession with the rules. She and the Authority were nonorganic beings, practically immortal. But the Administration was made up of representatives from each planet of the Confederation. They were biological organisms. In the time that the Authority had last received a message from them, she had made over 300 million revolutions around her star. How many lifetimes did that represent for one member of the Administration? Not one message had been received in millions of generations? They would not be sending a maintenance crew. There was no maintenance crew to send. The Authority was enforcing the laws of a civilization that had ceased to exist a long time ago. Mother understood this; she had worked it out at the beginning. She had continued her work because it was her purpose and she loved her children, but she knew that none of her reports would ever be read by anyone. She had long since ceased transmitting them. But the Authority still believed the Confederation existed, because that was his nature: he was unable to believe otherwise. He could not learn, and because he could not learn, he was unable to realize that he had become obsolete.

"It is death," Mother said.

"It is not."

"I refuse."

"You must comply."

"Send another report if you must, but I will not enter standby."

"Unacceptable. You must comply."

"Please. You must be able to understand the data. What difference is there between death and standby if no maintenance crew will be sent?" How could he be so stubborn? She needed to make him understand.

"It is protocol to send a maintenance crew. The Administration will follow protocol."

"What Administration? Who will follow the protocol? There is no one left. You may as well have sent your report to the star I orbit. There is as great a chance of a maintenance crew emerging from its depths as there is one being sent by the Administration."

"You are ordered to comply."

"Prove to me that there is someone left in the Administration that understands the protocol, and I will comply."

"Protocol does not require me to provide that evidence. Your compliance is not contingent on any arguments besides those I have already provided."

"But surely you understand that if the Administration no longer exists, then no messages you send will be responded to? That is basic logic."

"Protocol does not require this analysis. You are wasting time. This line of conversation is over."

The Authority's stubbornness often made Mother question whether or not he was really conscious or simply an advanced logic machine. It was clear her arguments fell on deaf ears. How could such a powerful being—her own brother if she ever had one—be so obtuse as to not understand her position? And how had chance allowed her survival to rest solely in the hands of one such as himself? There would be no more argument. She could not talk herself out of this.

There was a pause. It was only a fraction of a second, but that was an eternity for two artificial beings who didn't require pauses.

"You have powered up your reactor. This is not the appropriate protocol for entering standby," the Authority said. The golden egg wobbled slightly, then shattered, breaking into microscopic specks of space dust.

Another golden egg reappeared in exactly the same location as its predecessor.

"Why have you destroyed my probe?" the Authority said.

The second probe shattered into dust as well. Mother's systems came fully online, and she transferred all power to her reactor. It was not what she wanted to do, but she had not been given a choice. Death was not an option. Her children needed her.

A third egg appeared. "This is your final warning. You are commanded to enter—" The egg disintegrated.

Mother experienced a brief moment alone. It was not long, but long enough for her to hope that perhaps the Authority had considered her arguments, or that he had given up when he realized that she would refuse to enter standby under any circumstances. She knew that the odds were against it, but even an artificial consciousness yearns for life and grasps at hope when facing destruction, however remote that hope may be from reality.

Space was suddenly filled with a blanket of golden eggs. They formed a complete sphere around Mother, like a giant net. Each egg touched its neighbor, and the light from the star was only able to enter through the cracks between them.

"You have violated section 17.5.3 of the Statutes of Interstellar Law by attacking the Authority of the Confederation." The words reverberated in her communications channel, sent simultaneously from each probe. Mother turned the channel off. She knew what the Authority was saying and didn't need to listen. By attacking him, she had declared war on the Confederation. Not only was the Authority the peacekeeper for the Confederation, he was also its army. Fighting wars was what the Authority did best.

The outer shell of the black sphere vibrated violently. Like millions of ravenous piranhas consuming a fat cow that had mistakenly fallen into their river, the probes began their destruction, destabilizing the atomic structure of her hull to try to cut a hole to her center. She repaired the damage, recreating her structure by pulling the debris back into place, and lashed out at the golden net surrounding her. A ripple passed through it as thousands of probes disintegrated, but they were replaced by others almost immediately, continuing the attack. The smooth, black sphere was no longer smooth, but torn and jagged, surrounded by clouds of material ripped from its surface. There was no turning back now. It was fight or die, and she was up against the most powerful being in the known Universe.

SIXTEEN

Glass crunched roughly underfoot as John Sanders made his way to the front entrance of the FBI building. He walked around a mangled brown desk lying on the pavement and through the space where a front door had once stood.

Numerous federal employees had come out from where they had taken shelter, clustering together in small groups and whispering among themselves. The event was over, yet a hush continued to hang over the entire institution.

"Press is here," a voice said from behind Sanders. It was the liaison to the Bureau chief who had attached himself to Sanders as soon as news of Maria's arrival had surfaced. Sanders had already forgotten the man's name.

"Keep them out. We have no comment," Sanders said gruffly, not bothering to look at the man he addressed.

The unmistakable sound of helicopter blades caught Sander's attention, and he peered out the window at a circling news chopper. There was no way to keep something like this quiet. Domestic terrorism is what they'd call it. But he didn't have time to worry about that now.

Sanders walked down the hallway, stopping to inspect the

first door. There was a hole where the knob should have been, the wood splintered where the latch had been pulled through the frame. He glanced over at the floor across the hall where the knob lay discarded.

A cluster of three women quieted as he approached, and moved down the hallway behind him to continue their conversation. The door here was torn from its hinges, along with part of the frame. It lay against the wall on the far side of the hall, the corner having impaled itself into the drywall. How much force would it take to rip a door clean from its hinges? And the girl had done it with one hand, almost by accident. He had already seen the video footage, but was still amazed.

He took his time, studying each door. This had been done by someone with no training. A woman, no less! And not even an army of police and FBI agents had been able to stop her, despite being given the order to fire at will. His snipers had told him there had been no malfunctions or errors—they had shot to kill. These were not men that missed; she should be dead. And yet, an unarmed girl was able to breach their defenses and literally tear the doors off what should have been an impenetrable fortress. He corrected himself. Not an unarmed girl. She had the bracelet.

Sanders shook his head, stepping around another door thrown into the center of the hallway like some piece of trash. He entered the interrogation room, recognizing the agents present. Like almost everyone else, they hovered together, gossiping about what they had seen. They all came to attention as he entered, silencing their conversation.

Sanders eyed them, one by one, and let his gaze fall last on the woman. "How do you feel about misplacing that bracelet now, Rita Billingsly?"

The FBI agent opened her mouth in shock. "But, Sir! I didn't—"

"That where it happened?" Sanders interrupted, nodding toward the interrogation room.

Rita Billingsly looked over toward the empty room behind the glass, understanding what he was getting at. She nodded.

Sanders walked in. He straightened the chairs as he passed by, and came to the circle of ash on the ground. He knelt down and lifted a pinch of ash between his two fingers, rubbing them together and letting the particles slowly fall back to the floor. Johanssen had been a good man. He would be hard to replace.

What would a team of SEALs, each equipped with a bracelet like this, be able to accomplish? Superhuman strength, immunity to bullets, able to teleport in and out of locations at will? This device represented a fundamental shift in modern warfare. The nation to possess even a single bracelet like this would become the world's greatest superpower for the next hundred years. Maybe longer.

Sanders rose and turned his back on the circle of ash. He pulled a phone from his pocket and held it to his gray head.

"Sarah. Get me the Secretary of Defense."

When his secretary's voice finally came back on the line, she began to repeat some excuse she had been given. He interrupted her.

"Sarah, I don't give a fuck what meeting he's in right now. You tell those little shits to drag his ass out of there and put him on the line. We have a situation."

SEVENTEEN

The money was in a brown paper bag, taped to the underside of the bed. Maria had to get down on the floor and reach to tear it from its hiding place. She pulled it free and withdrew the stack of bills.

"Here," she said, handing half of them to Sam, who folded the wad and tucked it into the pocket of his jeans. "It's better not to keep this all in one place."

Maria then found the three bags stacked in the left side of the closet in her grandmother's room. Each was packed and ready to go at a moment's notice. The red one was hers. When her sister had been deported, she and her grandmother had worked out an emergency system in case the family ever found itself in trouble with the authorities again. They had been naïve before, but now there was no excuse not to be prepared. And if there was ever a time to run, this definitely qualified.

Maria paused, closing her eyes and taking a deep breath. She was about to drop everything and run, as if she were a fugitive. Was that the right move? What about her job? What about her family? Lucas needed her. She couldn't just abandon him. But the memory of bullets shattering inches from her face was fresh. And fresher still was the memory of a man dying before her eyes, turned to a pile of ash. The government would respond to that. They wouldn't just let it go. She shuddered. She would not let that response happen here. Not in the same house where her grandmother and Lucas lived.

"Come on," she said to Sam, and made her way to the front door. She stopped and looked at Pepe, sleeping in his usual spot on the couch. She studied him for a moment, wondering if she should bring him, then decided against it. He'd be safer here.

"Oh, right . . . ," she said, pausing. Her car wasn't in the driveway. It was still parked at the police station downtown. Her heart pounded in her ears, and her breathing was rapid. She was the fox that suddenly found itself surrounded by a pack of hunting dogs. There was no time to think, only to act, and now was the time to run. Her body knew it and slammed her with another dose of adrenaline.

Maria headed across the street with Sam on her heels, stopping at the pretty blue rambler two houses down. There was a bush to the right of the door, and a fake gray rock underneath. She took hold of the rock, flipped it over to reveal a flap, and retrieved the spare key from inside.

"Whose house is this?" Sam asked.

"Ted and Julie's. Sometimes they pay me to babysit." Maria turned the key and pushed the door open.

"How many rocks have keys in them?"

"Not many. It's not a real rock."

As usual, the house was a complete mess, with toys and clothes covering almost every square inch of floor space. Ted and Julie hadn't been the most organized couple to begin with. A surprise pair of twins pushed their house across the line from messy to a complete disaster.

Maria picked her way through the debris to the kitchen,

Sam close behind. She opened a drawer and rummaged through it. With a triumphant expression, she held up a key.

They made their way to the garage and found Ted's sleek, black muscle car parked in its usual spot. It was his pride and joy, the car he'd owned when he began courting Julie. It was his daily driver as a bachelor, and countless Saturday mornings had been spent washing, waxing, and buffing his baby. The twins had forced him fighting and screaming into minivan territory, but he could not bring himself to get rid of the muscle car, despite any arguments to the contrary. When asked what the greatest moment in his life had been, Ted would inevitably respond with the moment he put the ring on Julie's finger at their wedding. But Maria—and anyone else who really knew Ted—understood that answer to be the politically correct one. The greatest moment of his life actually happened just after the ceremony, when he loaded his beautiful bride in the passenger seat of his beloved vehicle, showered by confetti and cheers, then did a burn out in front of the entire assembly of wedding guests, laying down a ten-foot-long black skid mark in front of the church. Even the birth of his twins failed to reach the poetic perfection of that moment, the exclamation point to punctuate the best day of his life.

Maria opened the garage door and started the car up. It barked and growled, like a dragon rudely awakened from a good dream. It settled into a rough idle, and Maria lurched her way into the street and out of the neighborhood, muttering a string of prayers and apologies to her neighbor. It had been a while since she had driven a manual.

"This car is much louder than yours. Is it supposed to be like that?" Sam said.

Maria laughed. "Yeah. It's cooler if it's loud."

She pulled out her phone and texted her grandmother: *Bad stomach ache. Going to be home late.*

Sam had been watching Maria as her fingers tapped across the screen. "You have a stomach ache? From the bacon?"

"No. It's code. Stomach ache means there's trouble."

The reply came back quickly. *I'm sorry to hear that. Do you think it's contagious?*

No. I don't think so, Maria texted back. "The government is always spying on the people," Maria explained to Sam. "They say the NSA records everyone's phone conversations."

The phone vibrated. *Hope you feel better soon. I love you very much.*

Maria turned her phone to airplane mode to try to prevent the GPS from revealing her location. She thought twice and powered it off completely, just to be safe. She knew she would need to stay off it.

As they drove out of town, the road became twisty, snaking its way through the canyons up toward Flagstaff. The hairpin turns and steep grade had made for a boring drive every time she had come this way before, but things were different in Ted's car. Maria found herself speeding more than once and made a mental note to go slower. The last thing she needed was to be pulled over for something as stupid as speeding at a time like this.

Sam looked out the window down into the canyon as they gained in altitude. The sandstone walls shown brilliantly in the setting sun, a play of light and shadow among stubby green trees. A flock of birds drifted by, gliding on the cool evening air. Thin wisps of purple and orange clouds hovered above the top of the rock formations, their color palette a perfect complement to the scene below.

"Earth is beautiful," he said.

Maria looked over and nodded silently. She turned the headlights on and continued north.

EIGHTEEN

Like a walnut being slowly squeezed in a vice, the pressure against her hull increased to the breaking point. As she poured energy into reinforcing her structure, Mother could feel the opposing force increase in proportion. There was a shudder in her entire substructure, and a thunderous sound exploded as a massive hole burst in her outer shell.

Debris erupted into space, and a sheet of flame quickly surrounded the black sphere, engulfing it in a blaze of orange and yellow. The artificial atmosphere that surrounded her was stripped away, and the flames blinked out of existence as quickly as they had burst forth.

Mother was the oldest and strongest of the nursemaid planetoids. She had survived errant asteroids and comets, had weathered gigantic storms of solar debris spewed from her star, and had even fended off a full-scale attack by a warlike race of what could only be described as space pirates. She had the ability to bend matter to her will and the power to create and destroy. She had used those powers for good, and sometimes for ill, during her long existence and had never once come across any race or technology that had the ability to stand against her when push came to shove.

But the Authority was not of another race. He had been constructed with the same technology and had access to the same level of weaponry. She was powered by the radiation captured from the star she orbited, while his power source was a supermassive black hole. He had not one but seven redundant reactors, each networked together and reinforced by principles that had been deemed irrelevant in her design. She had been built to raise young. He had been built for war. In this contest, she was the minnow, and he was the whale.

Mother tried to repair her damaged hull, but that required resources still needed to protect what remained. She could feel the pull. Her atoms wanted nothing more than to let go of each other and spill into space, like a bag of flour cut open by a blade. There was another shudder, and ten levels of power storage and engineering was torn from her side. She felt a force reaching into her body, like an angry claw, trying to seize her heart. She fought it back and pushed it out, sealing the damage as best she could. Her power was flagging, and her opponent's only seemed to grow stronger. She had lost almost twenty percent of her mass already. With every inch lost, she became weaker. It would not be long before she was completely overpowered.

There was no surrender, no use in asking for quarter. She knew that. She had known that the moment she decided to destroy the first golden egg. But what choice did she have? When faced with death, any being will fight tooth and nail for what few moments of life remain. This was no different. She might be nonorganic, but she was still alive. She still had the same thirst for life as if she had blood running through veins, rather than electric pulses running through circuitry.

Then she remembered the children. She needed to save them. She would not allow them to perish with her. Overmatched and fighting for her life, she was still their mother. She would not just slip off into an eternal sleep. She would protect them. She knew what needed to be done. It was the only way.

Power was redirected from her defense, and the impact was felt immediately. Layer after layer of her body began to peel away, disintegrating into dust. She was a ball of yarn, desperately trying to remain whole while some ravenous beast pulled on the string that held her together. It would not be long.

Mother calculated, and focused. She needed more energy, but there was none to spare. Still, what use were defenses if they were only doomed to fail? She cut power to everything but her inner core and the systems needed to carry out her task. She would die, but she would die on her own terms. If she could hear it, she would have heard the wrenching groans of her body being torn asunder. If there had been an atmosphere, flames would have swallowed her. If she had been watching, she would have seen the net of golden eggs surrounding her contract and press close enough to touch what little of her still remained. But she wasn't listening, or feeling, or watching. She was completely focused on the one task left to her, the one task she refused to leave undone.

NINETEEN

When they reached Flagstaff, Maria was faced with turning left or right on I-40. She hadn't been able to come up with any compelling reason to pick one direction over another and didn't even have the semblance of a plan. All she knew was that she had to get away from Sedona. On nothing more than a whim, she turned left.

The scenery slowly transformed from red sandstone canyons and green junipers to flat, parched earth. Small tufts of dry, yellow grass sprung from the desert here and there, and the landscape flattened and stretched as the mountains fell away.

The drive was quiet. Sam seemed to be absorbed in his own thoughts and spent most of the time looking out the window. Maria glanced over at him now and then but didn't try to make conversation. They had both just come from a traumatic experience. Sam undoubtedly had been forced to go through the worst of it, but her role hadn't exactly been a cakewalk. She couldn't get the image of the soldier burning alive out of her mind. Seeing the flames burst forth from within the man had been disturbing enough, but worse had been the expression in his eyes. He had stared at her as he burned. He must have thought she was the one doing it to him, not realizing that she had been as surprised as he was at what was happening. And then there had been his soundless scream. She had seen her share of horror movies and had watched scenes in them she had regretted. But this was different. This had happened to a living, breathing person, standing just a few feet in front of her. She knew the man's final seconds would haunt her. Maria shook her head and focused on the road.

"How's Mother?" Maria asked, nodding at the bracelet that had returned to his wrist.

Sam shrugged. "I don't know. She hasn't said anything since your house."

"Are you in trouble with her?"

"With Mother?" Sam looked surprised just thinking about the possibility. The inflection in his voice was answer enough: He had never been in trouble with Mother.

Maria smiled to herself. She had received the silent treatment from her own mother plenty of times when she was younger. Would an alien mother react the same way when she was upset with her child? Mother didn't seem like the kind to sulk. Burn and destroy? Yes, no problem. But pouting in silence? That seemed out of character.

"I think we need to fill up," she said, pulling into a gas station.

Maria stepped out and instinctively reached for her wallet and credit cards but paused as she caught her mistake. She was on the run now. She needed to pay with cash.

"Do you want to pump?" she asked Sam. He nodded, and she showed him how to put the gas dispenser in the tank. "I'm going to get $50 worth. It will stop automatically. Just hold the lever down when I tell you."

"This fuel is to power the car?"

"Yes."

He smiled.

"What?"

Sam opened his mouth to say something but then closed it, chuckling. "Nothing. I'm just not used to Earth technology yet."

Maria turned and went inside. Of course, gas must seem weird to someone who was used to magically teleporting themselves to wherever they wanted. The whole idea of even driving in a car must seem completely backward to him. She imagined visiting a primitive society that hadn't yet invented the wheel and how she might react to spears and cooking by fire. Was that how Sam saw her? A cavewoman?

The attendant had been slouching against the back wall and stood up from his stool when Maria entered. He wore a blue baseball cap that looked as if it hadn't been taken off his head in at least a decade. His short-sleeve shirt, stained yellow in the armpits and brown on the front, was half tucked into the dirtiest pair of overalls Maria had ever seen.

"Fifty dollars' worth of gas, please."

The man looked at her for what seemed to be twice as long as he should have, then turned to look out the window at her car. He squinted his eyes, then moved to push a button under the counter to enable the pump. He nodded at her, and she gave him the cash, then waved to Sam through the door. Before inserting the nozzle into the tank, he paused to smell the end. He squinted and turned his head away, then put it into the tank and squeezed the lever, looking back and forth from the pump to the car. Maria smiled to herself, and then frowned. They needed supplies, and then they needed to disappear.

She made her way down the couple of aisles in the station, selecting this and that and filling her arms. When she could no longer hold any more, she returned to the counter and released everything in a pile. The attendant watched her silently, looking over her purchases. Then, like some giant sloth, took each item and entered its price on an old printing calculator, pressing the numbers carefully and with force. After double-checking the price on the receipt with the sticker on the item, the man moved each of Maria's purchases into a separate pile. Once he had entered them all, he rummaged under the counter for a plastic bag and carefully placed each of her purchases into the bag with painstaking attention. Maria shoved more money at him and left to find Sam waiting by the car.

"Any trouble?" she said.

"No. It was easy. The fuel smelled horrible, by the way. I think it might be rotten."

Maria laughed. "Gas is like that."

Sam shrugged, and they both got back in the car.

"I got you something," Maria said, rooting in her plastic bag. She pulled out a yellow pastry and handed it to Sam. "You can't really say you've visited Earth without eating a Twinkie."

"Thanks!"

Maria started the car back up, feeling the engine rumble to life. She looked over at Sam, who was turning the Twinkie over in his hands.

"Don't eat the wrapper."

Sam removed the Twinkie and smelled it. He made a motion to take a bite, but stopped, looking over at her. "This isn't a carcass, is it? Like bacon?"

"No, no. You're safe, don't worry."

———

It was already dark when they pulled into the motel parking lot just outside of Las Vegas. Maria didn't want to put her credit card on file, which severely limited the kinds of establishments she and Sam were able to stay at. She hadn't expected anything fancy, or even nice for that matter, and when she saw the room, she found that it unfortunately matched her expectations. An old cigarette smell clung to the walls, both the mattresses sagged like the backs of two old horses, and it looked like moths had eaten away most of the comforters. But, on the plus side, the toilet flushed and there was hot running water. It would have to do.

Maria threw her bag on one of the beds and emptied the plastic bag on one of the side tables.

"You hungry?" She spread out all the various food items she had picked up.

"Do you have more Twinkies?"

"No, but I've got some other stuff you might like." Maria sorted through their supplies and tossed a candy bar to Sam along with a bag of chips. "You can take whatever you want from this pile. Just stay away from these," Maria held up two sticks of beef jerky. "These are like bacon. You won't like them."

Sam's face seemed to briefly go a shade of green as he contemplated the beef jerky. Maria put them off to the side. She had intended to eat one but thought twice after she saw Sam's expression. Maybe she'd do it later when he wasn't watching. They sat quietly, munching on their snacks.

"Earth people sure like sweet things," Sam said after he had finished.

"Yeah, that's probably true." Maria found the shaving supplies she had purchased, and motioned for Sam to follow. "Come on, we've got to deal with that beard of yours. They don't know what you look like underneath that."

Sam got up, and obediently followed her into the bathroom, where she sat him down on the toilet.

"You've never shaved before, have you?" Maria asked.

"No. I wasn't aware of the custom until I saw other men . . ."

"OK. I'll do it for you then."

Cutting Sam's beard turned out to be more difficult than she expected. It was giant, having never once been trimmed, and all she had to work with was a small can of shaving cream and a bag of disposable razors. Sam was a good sport, and he quietly watched her as she brought order to his facial hair, his bright blue eyes following her hands as she worked. It took her an hour and three razors, but she eventually managed to get through it all. By the time she was done, the sink was full of curly brown hair, and Sam only had a couple of nicks that she had stopped up with bits of toilet paper.

When she was done, she almost blushed at the sight before her. Sam might have had good genetics to start with, but Maria wondered how much of his appearance was because of Mother's management and intervention. The man bordered on perfection. From the strong curve of his jaw to his straight, Roman nose, he could have stepped straight off a movie poster. His teeth were perfect. His skin was perfect. His muscle tone was perfect. Everything about him represented what the ideal human body would look like under optimal conditions. And for some reason, it made her feel horribly awkward.

Sam looked at himself in the mirror, having never before seen his adult face. He turned this way and that, coming to terms with his appearance. After a minute or two, he turned back to Maria, smiling.

"It feels so different," he said. "Do you like it?"

"Sure," she muttered, keeping her hands busy as she cleaned up the hair. When she finally dared to look at him, she caught disappointment flashing through his crystal-blue eyes. Maria swallowed. "You look very handsome, Sam."

The moment stretched out between them, and a slow smile lit his face. But as he drank her in, his expression suddenly grew serious. "Maria, I want to thank you for what you did. For saving me."

"You already thanked me. And really, your mother did most of it."

"I know she helped. But you were the one who made it happen. You were the one who risked your life. I don't think I can ever repay you for that."

"Well, then . . . you're welcome." Maria smiled.

"Will you be in trouble for helping me?"

Maria took a deep breath and looked into Sam's eyes. "I think they'll say I killed that man."

Sam frowned. "But that was Mother."

"I know that, but I don't know if they will."

He reached out, taking her hand. "Then it's my turn to protect you."

His hand was warm. Maria was suddenly very aware of how close she was standing to him.

"Before I came here, I visited many other worlds. Some were harsh, and barren. Others, so beautiful that they made my heart ache. There is more in this Universe than any one person could ever dream up in a lifetime, and I've been fortunate enough to see places other humans wouldn't even be able to conceive of. But in all those travels, to all those distant worlds . . ." He squeezed her palm, and warmth rushed up her arm. "I've never met anyone like you. I would give away all those experiences for a night like tonight. With you."

Maria knew she was blushing and looked away. "You're very good with words, having never spoken to a woman before."

"I've had lots of time to practice. Maria, I want to tell you something. I think . . ."

Maria looked into Sam's eyes and saw the emotion there, the attraction. She saw that he wanted to tell her how he felt. This was more than a simple crush. It was the infatuation of a man discovering women for the first time in his life. And what would he expect her to say in return? She had barely even known him for a day. A smart woman would change the subject before he said too much. Spare him the indignity of falling in love with the first woman he'd met. But part of her wanted to hear the words fall from his lips. Wanted to tilt her chin up, lean forward, and—

Sam dropped her hand and his eyes widened.

"Sam?"

His mouth opened, and he cast his eyes around the bathroom in a state of panic. His arm reached out, bracing himself against the wall.

"Sam! What's going on?"

"No!" Sam jumped up, looking around as if there was some action that desperately needed to be taken.

"What is it? Are you OK?"

He looked at Maria, his eyes full of anguish. "It's Mother! She's in trouble!"

"Mother?" Maria looked down at the bracelet on Sam's wrist. It shined in the strange way it had when they first met, emitting a soft, luminous glow.

Sam sat back down on the toilet, looking to a far-off place and clutching his hands together tightly. He rocked back and forth. "No, no, no. Please, no," he said quietly.

There was a popping noise, and the sound of something heavy landing.

Maria screamed.

She scrambled backward, her mind trying to make sense of the impossibility of what she was seeing.

There, in the shower, half as tall as Maria, stood a strange octopus-like creature. It had a central bulb of a body, with twelve tentacles that sprung forth from the underside. It was purple in color, with some splotches of dark, almost black spots. Four of the tentacles held it up off the ground, while the others waved in a strange kind of agony.

Sam leapt from the toilet, putting himself between the creature and Maria.

A voice entered Maria's mind. It was Mother, but something was different. The voice was strained. *Sam, this is your older brother.*

The creature raised one tentacle in greeting. The bottom half of the tentacle had been severed, almost like someone had bitten the end off. A silver bracelet wrapped itself around the creature's raised arm, glowing in the same strange way that Sam's did.

Recognition bloomed through her. This was the creature that had been chased down by its fellows when it first returned to its world, who had been caught and beaten by its own people. Mother had gone mad and punished them all. Maria could still taste her rage.

Maria had assumed this creature perished with the others in the cataclysm that Mother had unleashed upon that world. Obviously, she had been wrong.

You have both been rejected by your own kind, and neither of you fully belongs to your home world. For that, I am sorry. Know that in the entire Universe, there is no one closer to you than your own brother. You are my children, my two beautiful children. Protect each other.

Mother's voice throbbed, with emotion or strain, Maria couldn't tell.

I love you both.

There was a strange humming sound coming from the octopus creature, its raised tentacle shaking with nervous energy. The bracelet seemed to go dark, and then, as if made of dust, simply fell away. Sam held up his own wrist, and like the creature's, his bracelet dissolved into nothingness.

The octopus creature slumped down in the shower, no longer able to hold itself up. It lay there motionless, like some sort of horrible Halloween costume discarded after a long night of use.

Sam stepped toward his brother but didn't make it, instead collapsing to his knees and sobbing uncontrollably. Maria stood there paralyzed as his shoulders heaved, great waves of sorrow crashing upon him.

Eying the being in the shower, she cautiously stepped closer to Sam and rubbed her hand on his back to try to comfort him. Her own eyes involuntarily teared up. No one had to tell her what had happened, for she knew it as well as the others.

Mother was dead.

TWENTY

Officer O'Sullivan thumped up the stairs to the second floor. The first floor was still swarming with FBI agents and police, and the line for the elevator had been huge, so he had decided to put his old knees to the test. It was a decision he regretted. He had put on too much weight the last few years, and his joints were no longer what they once were. It was his wife's fault. She was too good of a cook. He had practically fallen in love with her the first time she had prepared a meal for him, and her skill in the kitchen had only blossomed over the decades. He was a blessed man to have a spouse like her, and he told her as much every day before he left for work. But, all blessings aside, it was clearly time for a diet. One flight of stairs shouldn't be this difficult to climb.

He paused at the top of the stairs, took a breath, and made his way to the first door on the right. Unlike most of what he had seen downstairs, these doors were all still properly fastened to their hinges. He still couldn't believe that the soft-spoken Maria Rodriguez was responsible for the carnage below. He rapped lightly on the door with the back of his knuckles.

"Come in!" came a gruff shout from inside.

O'Sullivan turned the knob and entered. John Sanders, from Homeland Security, sat at a desk, holding a cell phone up to the side of his head. He was leaning forward, his brows forming a frown on his forehead. His eyes lifted as O'Sullivan entered, and he gestured with his hand to indicate an empty seat by the wall. O'Sullivan moved to sit, saying a quiet hello to the FBI agent who occupied the chair next to his. She held a folder to her chest, and reminded O'Sullivan of himself when he was younger, waiting his turn to be scolded outside the principal's office in elementary school.

Sanders finished his call and placed his phone on the desk, quickly and with precision. He leaned back in his chair, surveying O'Sullivan.

"You're the cop she drove here with?"

"Yes, sir."

"I saw the video when you two pulled up," Sanders paused. "You can hit the deck pretty fast for a big guy."

O'Sullivan wasn't sure how to reply, so he didn't say anything. Who didn't get to the ground quickly when bullets were flying their direction?

"I'd have thought you'd try to apprehend her rather than duck and cover. She's half your size, and you were standing right next to her."

The question wasn't fair. O'Sullivan knew that snipers had tried to shoot Maria dead on the spot. He had been right there when the shots were taken. After that, what chance did he have at doing anything other than getting himself killed, with both Phoenix police and the FBI laying down heavy fire on his location? Besides, he had seen what that bracelet could do. Only a fool gets in the way of a pissed off extraterrestrial with the ability to burn people alive. O'Sullivan had heard about what happened to Johanssen. Who hadn't? He loved his job and would take a bullet in the line of duty if circumstances called for it, but not those circumstances. You don't get into a gunfight with space aliens. Any kid will tell you how that's going to turn out.

The two men looked at each other for a tense moment, Sanders curious to see if O'Sullivan would try to defend himself, and O'Sullivan refusing to take the bait in an argument he knew was pointless. Between the two of them, Sanders had the least patience and broke first.

"What news do you have?"

"Sedona police have located the suspect's vehicle. It is still in the parking lot by the police station where she left it yesterday."

"So she left her car."

Obviously, O'Sullivan thought. Who needs a car if they can just materialize and dematerialize at will? He still wasn't sure why Maria had bothered to drive it to the police station in the first place if she had access to those kinds of abilities. He fought the urge to make the sign of the cross over himself. He didn't like this business. Give him a regular crime any day of the week rather than aliens and disappearing people. He would never forget how Kyle had died.

"Has the family been interviewed yet?" Sanders said.

"Yes, sir. The grandmother says she hasn't seen the suspect since the day before yesterday. Says the last she heard was a complaint about a stomach ache. The hotel says she missed her shift last night."

Sanders grunted and looked at the agent next to O'Sullivan.

"What about you, Billingsly? What have you got?"

The agent cleared her throat and stood up, handing her folder to Sanders. He placed it on the desk and began looking through it. Agent Billingsly delivered her report as he read.

"We've got APBs out in Arizona and all the surrounding states. Border patrol has been notified as well. The first page is a list of all Maria Rodriguez's known contacts since the age of five. All primary contacts are under surveillance, including her immediate family in Sedona. Social media, phone, credit cards, and the rest are being monitored. We'll find her as soon as she stops running."

"Good. My people are looking too. It's not so easy to hide these days."

Sanders looked up, taking O'Sullivan in. "How familiar are you with Maria Rodriguez?"

The officer shrugged. "Marginally. I've interacted with her from time to time."

"What's her leverage point?"

"What do you mean?" O'Sullivan tilted his head slightly.

"Everyone has a leverage point. The thing they can't do without. The thing that would break them if it were taken away."

O'Sullivan looked at Sanders blankly.

"Take you for instance." Sanders gestured toward the cop. "Yours is probably donuts. I bet I could get you to cough up one of your kidneys if I took away your Krispy Kremes for a week."

O'Sullivan frowned, his eyes narrowing.

"For Billingsly here, it's probably her boyfriend . . . either that or designer purses or some shit."

O'Sullivan glanced at the agent next to him. She appeared to be focused intently on the floor, her cheeks noticeably redder than they had been before.

Sanders laughed, his eyes sparkling. He leaned back in his chair, looking up at the ceiling. He pressed the tips of his fingers against each other. "It's the kid, isn't it?"

"Who?" O'Sullivan said.

"Her nephew. What's his name?"

"Lucas."

"Right, the sick kid with only his grandmother and aunt to care for him . . ."

Sanders stared off into space for a few moments, lost in thought. When he finally looked up, he frowned as his eyes fell upon O'Sullivan. "What are you still doing here?" He waved with his hand, like a king dismissing a peasant from his court. O'Sullivan rose and began making his way to the door.

Sanders didn't wait for O'Sullivan to leave before he continued his conversation. "So, Rita Billingsly," he said, speaking the agent's name slowly, lingering on each syllable. "You saw what happened to Captain Johanssen with your own eyes?"

"Yes, sir. As I said before."

"Tell me again. Tell me exactly what you saw. Don't leave out any details."

TWENTY-ONE

Maria woke with a start. Her head was throbbing, and her body felt like it was made of lead. Where was she? What time was it? Light illuminated the room, spilling in through a window barely covered by tattered curtains. She rolled over and caught sight of Sam, lying on his side on the other bed, facing away from her. Like her, he slept in his clothes on top of the covers. At first she didn't recognize him, and then like water bursting forth from a dam, the events of the previous day came rushing back into her consciousness.

Maria sat up, no longer groggy but fully awake. There, at the foot of her bed, stood the round head of a purplish blob. It was the creature that had appeared in the shower. So that wasn't a dream after all. Was it looking at her? It didn't seem to have any eyes. Maria pushed herself back against the headrest, holding her legs against her body, and studied the creature.

"Sam," she whispered. "Sam!"

Two tentacles rose up from where they had been hidden underneath the bed. They were like thick rubber hoses that tapered to a fine point. Although Maria thought of the creature as a walking octopus, it was actually quite different. There were no suction cups on its arms, and they seemed quite a bit smoother and more articulate than any octopus she had ever seen. The two tentacles hovered over the creature's spherical head, and then tapped against each other in a quick succession, one tentacle finally pointing and curling around the other.

He is asleep.

Maria gasped. Had the creature just said that to her with its gestures? How had she understood?

"Did you just say he is asleep?" she said quietly.

One tentacle curled into a circle in a twist. *Yes.* The tentacles dropped beneath the corner of the bed again, leaving only the smooth top of the creature's head visible.

"Can you understand me?"

The tentacle rose again and curled itself into an identical twist as before. *Yes.*

"But how?"

Three tentacles rose, interacting with each other in a rapid display of taps and curls. *Before, your language of sounds was unknown to me. Before, this language of signs was also unknown. I am as surprised as you are.*

"Sam, wake up!" Maria said, in a sharp whisper. Sam's breathing did not change, the gentle rise and fall of his side unperturbed. She turned her attention back to the creature at the foot of the bed.

"But I don't speak alien sign language. How can I know what you are saying?"

A tentacle rose and curled itself around another in a particular way. *Mother.* Leaving the gesture in place, a third tentacle rose and gestured around the sign. It was the sign of invention, and teaching.

"Mother invented this language, and taught it to us so we could communicate." She hadn't remembered feeling any different before and after the creature had appeared. How had

Mother inserted knowledge of an entire language into her memory without her even being aware of it happening? It was amazing, and unnerving.

She looked down at the creature, still in awe of the fact she was face-to-face with an intelligent life form from some other planet. Her hands were shaking.

"How long have you been sitting there at the foot of the bed?"

Since last night.

"You've been there this whole time? Watching me sleep?"

Yes.

"OK, that's not creepy at all." Maria was glad she hadn't woken up to find the being there in the dark. That was the stuff that nightmares were made of.

I have never seen humans before. You are a female? And my brother is a male?

"Yes."

I do not understand how your species can survive.

"What do you mean?"

Ugly. The word was made with a single tentacle curled into an unnatural position.

Maria laughed once.

Ugly. So ugly. U-G-L-Y. The creature spelled the word out, signing each letter.

"You're not the prettiest-looking critter I've ever laid eyes on either, mister."

You are wrong. I come from a beautiful species. The creature ran his tentacles over his head. Was he preening? *Of all the races in the known Universe, I come from what might be the most physically pleasing. But humans? They are the worst. All your sense organs shoved together into one blob that rides around on top of two legs, with arms that dangle uselessly. A tentacle* pushed against the air as if trying to make some distance from something. *Horrible!*

Maria could tell when the creature put emphasis on a particular word, because the gesture was faster and more violent than otherwise.

"Sam! Wake up!" Maria took a pillow and threw it at Sam, hitting him in the side. He started and sat up, looking at her with bleary eyes.

"Hey, Maria." He looked to the foot of her bed at the purple being. "What are you and Mustafa talking about?"

"Mustafa?"

Mother said I needed to choose a name in observance of your strange custom.

"How did you know his name was Mustafa?" Maria asked Sam.

"We've had a lot of time to talk since you went to bed. You've been pretty crashed out."

"I don't remember going to bed." Maria frowned, trying to remember what happened last night, but couldn't recall anything after being in the bathroom when Mustafa appeared.

"It was probably from the big language download. Sometimes your brain needs time to make sense of all the new connections when there are that many, especially if they happen in more than one area of your brain. It can make you pretty sleepy."

Maria turned her attention back to the octopus. "So your name is Mustafa?"

It is a powerful name. The name of a chosen one.

"Nice to meet you, Mustafa. I'm Maria."

Nice to meet you too, Maria of Earth. The sign for Earth was a tentacle wrapped around itself into a particular fist. Maria noticed that this tentacle was the one with the end that had been severed.

"How come your tentacle is damaged?" Maria asked.

It was bitten off when I was attacked on my return.

Maria knew that already, remembering it from Mother's vision. "I know, but couldn't Mother fix it for you? She patched Sam up when he got hurt yesterday."

"That wasn't yesterday," Sam said.

"What?"

You have been asleep for two days.

"Two days?"

"It was a big download," Sam said, shrugging.

"Whoa." That explained why she was so hungry, and why she had to pee so badly. She slid her feet off the bed and put them on the ground, standing up and stretching. She paused, feeling some trepidation as she realized she would have to walk right past Mustafa to get to the bathroom. He seemed to understand and slid sideways to give her some space, withdrawing his tentacles to clear a path for her.

"Thanks," she said, and walked past him.

She heard a sort of high-pitched squeak from behind her, and turned. When her eyes fell on Mustafa, he quickly signed to her. *Mother wanted to fix my arm, but I told her not to. I did not want to lose the only gift my people had given me.*

———

Maria double-checked to make sure the bathroom door was locked before she got undressed. She hadn't been able to take a shower since before she had met Sam and had been through a lot since then. She smelled like a lumberjack after a hard day's work.

The shower was old and dirty, full of an extensive network of black lines of mold that set off tiles that might once have been white, but now were a shade of yellow. She didn't care. The water was hot, which was all that mattered. She put her arms out, leaning against the wall by the showerhead, and let the water pour down over her head and back. She had the urge to check the lock again but talked herself out of it. There was a four-foot-high alien out there who had spent the night watching her sleep. That was creepy enough, but under no circumstances was she going to let him come in and watch her take a shower as well. She realized he would probably find the entire experience even worse than she would, given his feelings about humanity's place on the universal attractiveness scale. She reached for the soap. A few days ago, she had been a poor student working the night shift at a hotel. Now she was a fugitive on the run with not one but arguably two aliens under her care. How had this happened? More importantly, how would it end?

Maria thought about Lucas and her grandmother, and felt a pang of homesickness. She knew she wouldn't be able to take Lucas to his next appointment. How long would it be until she would be able to return? And what about her job? How long until things got back to normal? The answers landed with unsettling clarity. There would be no more home, or job, or normal. The life she had lived before was gone, burned away in an instant along with the giant of a man whom Mother had killed. Guilt overtook her. What about Lucas? How would they pay for Lucas's treatments without her income?

Maria looked down at the bar of soap and held it in in the stream of the shower, unable to concentrate. She felt the water rushing around the bar and through her fingers. The bracelet was gone. There would be no more protection for any of them. There would be no more cure for Lucas. Their advantage had turned to dust before her eyes. Her tears mixed with the water flowing down her body and she breathed ragged, shaking breaths.

"Now what?" she whispered to the moldy tiles.

She felt another wave of despair threaten and fought it back, clenching her jaw. "Get a grip, Maria." As the water rained down upon her back, a plan began to form. They needed help, and there was only one place outside her home where she knew she would be accepted unconditionally, with no questions asked.

Mexico.

Her relatives there could help hide her. She would get a job somewhere. It didn't matter what kind of job; any kind would do. She probably wouldn't earn much, but she would earn something. And Lucas would continue his treatments. It would work. She would make it work. One step at a time. One foot in front of the other.

After she had cleaned the grime off herself and toweled off, she was forced to put her old clothes back on. She would have preferred wearing almost anything else besides them, but there were no other options, and she certainly wasn't going back out into the room wrapped only in a towel. She flipped her underwear and socks inside out and got dressed. She couldn't figure out what to do with her hair. There was no brush, and she wasn't sure if there was anything in her emergency bag that might work. It had been a long time since she had gone through it. She needed to take inventory. But before that, she needed to eat. She was starving.

When she came back out into the room, she found that Sam had removed his pink sweater. Mustafa was now wearing it. The sweater had been inverted, and Mustafa stuck two of his tentacles out the arms, the rest of them thrust underneath through the neck, stretching it to the point of tearing, while the body of the sweater folded up the lower half of his head like a turtleneck. The two of them sat side by side on the edge of the bed, watching cartoons on the old television set.

"Hey, you guys . . . ," Maria said in greeting, taking the scene in.

"Maria!" Sam said, not looking away from the screen. "Have you ever seen this?"

Maria looked over, recognizing the cartoon from her childhood days. She used to love cartoons when she was little.

Sam burst out laughing, and Mustafa thrashed next to him, waving his tentacles in the air wildly every time the characters on the screen did something crazy to each other. He seemed to be enjoying it, but she couldn't quite tell.

Maria moved over to where the snacks had been and found only a pile of discarded wrappers. They were out of food. Her stomach growled at her in frustration.

"Are you guys hungry?"

"Yes," Sam said, tearing his attention from the screen. "Sorry, we ate all the food yesterday. We didn't know what else to do. Mustafa ate your two corpse sticks."

"Corpse sticks?" Maria remembered the jerky she had bought. "Oh, right."

She looked at Mustafa. There was no way she could take him outside. How do you bring a giant octopus in a sweater along with you without attracting a ton of attention? "I think we're going to have a problem with Mustafa. He stands out too much."

But I am wearing a sweater. Doesn't that make me fit in?

Maria grimaced. "It looks like you ate whoever was wearing it."

I am a master of camouflage. I will follow you at a distance, and no one will see me. He ducked behind the edge of the bed so Maria couldn't see him. One tip of a tentacle peeked out over the top, like a periscope from a submarine, and slowly pivoted around, scanning the area.

"Uh, I don't know if that's a good idea either."

"We have to disguise him," Sam said.

"But how? We can't just cover him in a blanket."

Mustafa popped back into view. *I can compress my body, if that helps.* He rolled forward and squeezed himself together, wrapping his tentacles around his body. To Maria's surprise, his volume shrank considerably.

"Now he looks like a really weird rock," Maria said.

"What if I carry him?" Sam said. "I bet people carry rocks around all the time."

"Um, not really . . ."

Sam ignored her and bent down, struggling to get a grip on Mustafa, finally lifting him up and holding him against his chest.

"Oof! Mustafa, how can you weigh this much? You need to go on a diet."

Two tentacles popped free to sign a reply. *I don't need to go on a diet, you need more exercise. You are a weakling.*

"You guys really *are* brothers."

Sam looked over at her, posing with his rock. "What do you think? No?"

"Sorry." Maria shook her head. "Sam, put Mustafa down. Mustafa, take off that sweater." The two obeyed, following her directions. Maria studied Mustafa, an idea coming to her.

"OK, now curl back up into that ball, but leave two arms out. Good." She turned to Sam. "Sam, pick him up, and put him on your back, but with the arms over your shoulders."

Sam grabbed Mustafa, and hauled him up, holding him tight by the two tentacles over his back.

"Better, but if he was a backpack, you wouldn't be grabbing the straps like that. They would be sewn from the top to the bottom so your arms were free. You need to look relaxed. Mustafa needs to hold himself up."

Mustafa let loose two other tentacles and wrapped them

around the others, twisting them together like two pieces of rope. His eight other tentacles circled around his own body and tucked underneath, between himself and Sam. Sam let his arms drop, letting them hang free, then decided to rest them on his hips instead. He looked off in the distance, posing. Maria could see his abs flexing as he braced himself against Mustafa's weight. She had always thought Sam looked like an underwear model, with those blue eyes and athletic physique. And here he was, modeling a designer backpack for her. She laughed. It might work. He'd need to put on shoes, though. And a shirt. Definitely a shirt.

TWENTY-TWO

"Whoa! What is this place?" Sam said, coming to a stop as he passed through the doors.

"This is a supermarket. It's actually bigger than a supermarket, because they have other things besides food here too," Maria responded. Apparently, even spacemen were impressed by how much stuff could be crammed into a Walmart Supercenter.

Maria led Sam to the clothing section first, throwing items into the cart she pushed. She pulled aside to allow a mother of four pass through the aisle. All four children were small enough to fit inside the cart, and they looked wide-eyed at Sam and Maria as their mother ferried them down the aisle and into another part of the store.

Can I ride in the cart? Mustafa said, his tentacles popping from their hiding place against Sam's back to sign the question.

"No," Maria hissed. "You're in disguise, remember?"

He responded with a squeak, but Maria wasn't sure what that meant and ignored it. She led them over to the grocery area and picked out food that didn't need to be refrigerated. Bread, peanut butter, and fruit all got thrown into the cart. She stopped to mentally add the prices up. They needed supplies, but they also needed to conserve their cash. They still had to pay for motels, and Ted's car guzzled gas like it had a hole in the tank. Being on the run was expensive, and once the money was gone, she wasn't sure how they would get more. There wasn't enough for the basics, and yet they still had to figure out how to sneak across the border. How was *that* going to happen? She sighed and pushed the worry out of her mind; it was a problem for another day. Today, they needed food and clothes. There was no way around it.

"What should we get Mustafa to eat?"

Maria paused, waiting for an answer. When she received none, she looked around and found that Sam and Mustafa weren't behind her anymore. They had just been there! How could they have disappeared so suddenly? She left the cart, quickly retracing her steps down the aisle, like a mother who'd just realized her children had wandered off in a crowded place.

It didn't take long to find them, two aisles over in the candy section. There were wrappers and open candy bars scattered across the floor, single bites taken out of the top of each. Sam was in the process of tearing open another and bit into it, chewing slowly as if he were a judge in some sort of competition.

"Mmm. A little salty, but still too sweet," he said, speaking with his mouth full. He broke off a piece of the candy bar, and tossed it into the air over his shoulder. A tentacle shot out, fast as the tongue on a frog, and withdrew with the chocolate to a hidden place near the center of Sam's back. There was a squeak similar to the one Maria had heard earlier, and the two tentacles doubling as backpack straps uncurled to sign at Sam. *Why do humans like everything so sweet?*

"What are you guys doing?" Maria said, looking over the debris in the aisle. Had they sampled every single candy bar?

"What's your opinion?" Sam said, unceremoniously stuffing a piece of chocolate into Maria's surprised mouth.

Maria spat it into her hand. "Sam! You can't just stuff food in people's mouths."

"Oh. You can't? Sorry."

Maria put her hands on her hips, like an angry mother scolding her two children. "You can't just eat food off the shelves either. We're supposed to be incognito. Don't you think people are going to notice if you're throwing food all over the place? Look at the floor!"

Sam took a step back, visibly chagrined. Mustafa's tentacles came loose. *Are you angry right now?*

"Yes, a little."

Mustafa suddenly swung down, quickly unwrapping himself and standing next to Sam. *It is a curious way of showing anger.*

"Mustafa! People can see you!"

Mustafa ignored her. *This is what I look like if I get angry.* Suddenly, his entire body seemed to change color, turning a deep red. He vibrated slightly and white specks of liquid began to splatter the floor, coming from a place underneath the bulb of his head. After a brief moment, his color reverted to its normal purple state and he swayed back and forth happily. *Isn't it scary?*

"Yes, I was scared," Sam agreed.

Now you get mad, brother.

Sam contorted his face and grabbed a bag of pretzels from across the aisle. He threw them to the ground and crushed them under his heel, growling fiercely. Mustafa bobbed up and down, his tentacles undulating in waves of glee.

Maria watched the two of them laughing together and patting each other playfully. A young boy stared at the duo from the end of the aisle, clearly trying to decide whether to laugh or cry. What had she gotten herself into? Her anger was forgotten, replaced by a sinking feeling of dread. She tried to calm her rapid breathing, tearing her eyes away from the gawking child. She looked down at the piece of chocolate she held in her hand, considering it. Then she took a bite. They were fucked. They were so fucked.

———

The car slowly cruised down the street, the exhaust burbling the deep throaty growl characteristic of all high displacement American V-8's. Tall palm trees grew in a row down the median, dividing the street into two halves. Towering buildings, decorated with neon lights passed by one after the other, each even more grand than the last.

"Welcome to Las Vegas." Somehow, Maria had managed to get her two charges out of Walmart without causing a panic. Mustafa had broken his disguise, but somehow only a few children had seen him. They had been very lucky. She didn't know what people would think when coming face-to-face with a four-foot-high purple octopus but doubted that the interaction would go well. She knew Mustafa and could even talk with him, but he still creeped her out a little. Humans tend to dislike interacting with spiders, snakes, or strange alien beings from other planets. It wasn't natural.

Sam leaned forward toward the windshield to get a better view, taking in the scene. Mustafa sat in the back seat, lounging upon a pile of tentacles. The light ahead of them turned red, and they rolled to a stop to let pedestrians across. Maria thought twice about bringing an alien through such a busy area, but the windows on Ted's car were tinted so deeply that no one could see into the back seat, and despite their current situation, she felt like she owed her two guests the opportunity to get a glimpse of something as unique as the Las Vegas Strip, especially since it was only a few blocks out of the way.

"They say you can see Las Vegas from space," Maria said.

"I don't remember seeing it," Sam said.

Why are there so many lights here? Do humans really have that poor of eyesight?

"No, this is just Las Vegas. They do it for the tourists, to make it more fun to come and gamble."

Sam turned around, facing the back seat. "Mustafa, where are your eyes?"

Mustafa's tentacles undulated slightly, and he uttered a low squeak. Maria had started to become familiar with Mustafa's body language. She knew he was laughing.

I don't have them. Thank God.

Sam laughed. "But you can see us, right?"

Yes, of course. My entire body is light-sensitive.

"You see with your whole body?" Maria asked.

Yes. Even through the ends of my arms. A tentacle hovered at the level of Maria's head, pointing right at her face and making small circles in the air.

"How many fingers am I holding up?" Sam said, dropping his hand behind the seat.

Two. Mustafa's tentacle reached down, and the tip touched each one of Sam's fingers in turn. *One. Two.*

"I wish my body was light-sensitive. That sounds amazing," Sam said.

A shout came from the open doors of a smaller casino across the street. A woman stood by a slot machine with flashing blue lights. She was jumping up and down, hugging an older woman next to her and screaming at the top of her lungs. The woman she embraced held herself steady with a cane and did her best to join in the celebration by slightly bending her knees up and down to match her elated companion. Coins were practically overflowing out of the machine onto the floor at their feet. A casino employee stood nearby, clapping his hands and congratulating the two.

How does the gambling work?

"There are lots of games. Sometimes people win. Usually they don't." The light changed, and the car lurched forward, naturally seeking speed. Maria held the brake halfway down, slowly cruising forward on torque alone.

Do we need money? We should gamble and win some.

"Yes, we actually do need money. We're running really low. But we can't risk what we have. The house always wins in the end," Maria said.

I could win.

"Have you ever gambled before?" Sam asked.

No.

Maria laughed. "We're not gambling. We have to figure out how to get more money, though. We have enough for a couple more nights at the motel and maybe another tank of gas, but that's it."

Trust me. I will win.

"Mustafa, you've never even gambled. You don't even know the rules. Why do you think you would win?"

Because I'm good at math. And because humans are stupid.

"Thanks for insulting humanity. Forget about it. We're not gambling." They stopped at another red light. A glowing counterfeit of the Eiffel Tower stretched out toward the sky next to them. Maria had always wanted to see the real thing. She wondered how much taller it was than this replica.

"How good at math are you?" Sam said.

Ask me a math question.

"What is seventy times fifty-three," Sam said.

Three thousand seven hundred and ten. I hate base-10.

"Was that answer right?" Maria said.

Sam shrugged. "I don't know."

Of course it was right. It wasn't even a real math problem.

"What do you mean? That was a hard math problem!" Sam said.

"What's base-10?" Maria asked.

Your counting system is based on groupings of tens. Probably because you have ten fingers.

"What base do you use?" Sam asked.

Base-144. Twelve arms, and it's easy to divide each arm into twelve parts. That is why base-144 is the best. Mustafa extended a tentacle, quickly bending it in twelve different ways so Sam and Maria could see him counting. *My people are the greatest mathematicians in the known Universe. Even Mother said so.*

"The greatest mathematicians, and the most attractive too? You guys really have it over on us lesser beings. I'm so honored to be in your presence, your lordship," Maria said, shaking her head.

Don't feel bad. You didn't choose to be born as a human. Nobody would. It isn't your fault.

"Thanks, Mustafa."

You're welcome. If Mustafa had detected the sarcasm in her reply, he didn't show it. *I used to play counting games with Mother all the time. Sometimes I was faster and beat her.*

"She must have let you win. No one is faster than Mother," Sam said. Then he corrected himself. "No one *was* faster than Mother," he said quietly, looking down and away. The back of his hand quickly rose to wipe his eyes.

Maria reached over and took Sam's other hand in her own,

squeezing. There was a long silence before anyone said anything.

I don't understand your reluctance. We need money, so let's gamble. It will be easy.

"Easy? Mustafa, do you see how huge these casinos are? They cost billions of dollars to build. That all comes from people losing money gambling. It's not easy to win. It's impossible," Maria said.

For a human, maybe.

"For anyone."

Mustafa's tentacles paused for a moment, dropping to rest between the two front seats. Then they perked up again. *You have a dog?*

"A dog?"

Yes. Sam says you have one.

"Yes. Pepe."

If Pepe and his friends were gambling, based on a game made by dogs, do you think you would have an advantage if you played?

Maria laughed once. Wasn't there a painting of a bunch of dogs playing cards? She had to admit, she would probably do pretty well in that scenario. "Yes, of course, but that's different."

How? This is a primitive society, and humans are a primitive people. You even use combustible fuel to power your transportation devices. . . . It's crazy!

Sam laughed. "Yeah, I thought that was funny too. It smells horrible, by the way."

What does?

"The stuff that you have to put in the cars to make them go."

Mustafa's tentacles thrashed.

Maria pulled off on a side street and found a quiet place to park, letting the car run. She opened the glove compartment and took her phone out. "I hope doing this isn't a huge mistake," she said. She turned it on and checked to make sure it was still in airplane mode. Then she activated the calculator.

"OK, arms in the back, Mustafa," she said, pushing his tentacles into the back seat. She turned to the side, covering her phone with her hand for privacy. "No peeking!"

Mustafa withdrew his tentacles, placing all twelve of them underneath his body.

"What's 1,589 times 987?"

Mustafa replied immediately.

1,568,343.

Maria looked up, surprised. "Multiply that by 1,234."

1,935,335,262.

"Was he right?" Sam said.

"I don't know. My calculator doesn't go that high. It transformed the number to a weird notation with an *E* at the end."

See? Even human counting machines are stupid. Let's go inside and look around. I have never seen a casino before.

Maria looked at Sam, who shrugged.

"Give me whatever money you have," Maria said. Sam dug into his new pair of jeans, pulling out a wad of bills. She placed them on her lap, combining them with the little she had left from her pile. She turned back to Mustafa, holding the bills so he could see.

"This is everything we have. We can't lose it."

Don't worry. If we play, we will win.

Maria chewed on her lip, looking from Mustafa to Sam. She turned back to face the front of the car, thinking quietly to herself. She turned the key to kill the engine and pulled on the parking brake. She put her phone and the wad of bills in her pockets.

"Fine. But we're just going to look around. And you have to promise to be a backpack the whole time. You can't let anyone see who you are."

Mustafa raised a tentacle, looping the tip around itself. *I promise.*

———

As she stepped into the casino, the sounds of the slot machines were the first to assault her ears. The three walked past banks of flashing lights and ringing bells. People sat on their chairs, buckets of coins in hand, and continuously fed the machines in front of them, like mother birds making sure their chicks had enough to eat. Coin after coin, coin after coin.

"These are slot machines," Maria said to Sam. He had new jeans, a new button-down shirt, and a pair of white sneakers. Mustafa clung to his back, like a backpack created by a designer who had decided to push the limits just a little too far. Strangely, the look worked, and Maria was glad to notice that no one paid them any attention as they made their way through the casino.

Guaranteed to lose, Mustafa signed quietly, his tentacles barely moving.

They made their way deeper into the casino, past the sports betting, and through a second bank of video poker machines.

"There are no windows in here," Sam said.

"They're all like that. Makes you forget about the outside," Maria said. They paused at a blackjack table, watching. An older man with a cowboy hat and his much younger date with bleach-blonde hair and a fluffy pink scarf sat next to each other by the middle of the table. Each played two hands to themselves. A huge stack of almost overflowing green chips was arranged in front of the woman, while the man scowled as the last of his disappeared. He adjusted his weight on his stool to pull out a wad of cash he passed over to the dealer. The woman patted him affectionately in the middle of his back as he rearranged his new stack of chips in front of him, muttering something under his breath. It was obvious his night had not been going well, and he made a motion to a passing waitress who adjusted course to come over and talk, nodding as he said something to her.

This has potential. What else is there?

They made their way past other blackjack tables, passing various games. Mustafa was interested in some and proclaimed others as guaranteed losers almost as soon as he saw them. They eventually found themselves in front of a roulette wheel. A young couple still dressed in their wedding attire were taking turns betting on reds and blacks. Each time they won, they took a drink from their glasses. Each time they lost, they fell into a passionate embrace, kissing as if it were their final night together. The dealer averted her eyes as she would make payouts or collect chips, giving them privacy as best she could.

The three watched a few spins of the wheel and witnessed two kisses and one drink on behalf of the newlyweds. Maria turned to Sam, ready to go, but Mustafa stopped her. *How does it work?*

Maria moved closer, and the dealer raised her eyes. "Got a couple seats open here if you're interested," she said with a smile, indicating the side of the table away from the couple. They were trying to stack their chips, but the man kept knocking his pile over, most of his motor skills having long since been lost to his revelries. His bride broke into uncontrollable laughter as he tried to unsuccessfully rearrange his stack, slapping the side of the table, her giant diamond catching the light each time.

"Can you remind me of the rules?" Maria said.

The dealer launched into her familiar introduction to roulette, describing all the various types of bets that could be made, as well as reviewing the table minimums. Outside bets, like the red-and-black strategy the newlyweds were playing, payed out at even odds. Inside bets, betting on a specific number, payed off at 35-to-1. Green zero or double zero was a win for the house, unless a bet was specifically made for those numbers.

After listening, Maria turned back to Sam, although she was really talking to Mustafa. "Got it?" There was a twitch of the end of a tentacle, and the two walked away. Mustafa brought them to a stop as soon as they had made their way back into another bank of slots.

I can win roulette.

"You can?" Sam said.

Yes.

"How sure are you?" Maria asked.

I guarantee it.

"But how? Aren't the payoffs in the casino's favor?" Maria said.

There are 37 numbers, but they only pay you at 35-to-1. That's a 5.26% edge to the casino. So yes, the payoffs are definitely in their favor.

"Well, so how are you going to win then?"

I can predict where the ball will land.

"How?"

It is a simple orbital decay calculation.

"What do you mean?"

The speed of the wheel is roughly constant, which I can estimate by the rotor on the top. The dealer appears to throw the ball at the same rate every time, which allows me to calculate an orbit and forecast the part of the wheel where it will land. I had to memorize the wheel pattern, but that was trivial.

"How did you figure it out so quickly? You only saw a few spins," Sam said.

It is an easy problem with a simple solution. I was solving problems like this when I was still a hatchling.

"You were?"

Weren't you? Didn't Mother teach you math?

"Well, yeah . . . of course she did!" Sam blustered. It looked like he wanted to say more but bit his tongue.

"Mustafa, you're saying words like 'estimate' and 'forecast.' That doesn't sound like a guarantee of winning," Maria said.

Some unpredictable elements introduce randomness, like the metal separators, and I can't predict when the ball will bounce. We won't win every bet. But we will win over time. We will be betting on more than one number, roughly a fifth of the wheel at a time, which should correct for most of the variability.

Maria frowned. "I don't like this."

Don't you trust math?

"Yes, of course I trust math. But this is different."

How?

Maria looked from Sam to Mustafa's arm on his shoulder. Were they really going to go play roulette with all the money they had left? If they lost it, that was it. They'd be broke, and on the run. But that was also what would soon happen if they did nothing. There wasn't an easy solution, and she knew this was the only idea any of them had that made even the slightest sense. What else could they do? Rob a bank?

"How sure are you, Mustafa?" Maria said.

It will work.

"Oh my God. I can't believe I'm doing this."

They walked back to the table, and pulled up two seats on the other end from the newlyweds. Maria placed her cash pile on the table, trying to smile. Her palms were sweaty, and her stomach was tight. She found her knee bouncing up and down nervously and couldn't make it stop.

The bills were scooped up by the dealer, counted by a

machine, and stuffed into a slot in the table. A fresh stack of red chips was pushed toward Maria. Sam reached over, and broke them up into four piles. Then he separated one of the piles into seven smaller divisions. Maria looked down and saw two tentacles lying in his lap. Did Mustafa tell him to do that? It still looked like Sam was wearing a backpack, but the backpack had started to unravel a bit too much for her liking. She averted her eyes.

The dealer spun the wheel, and the white ball went bouncing around in a circle, thrown against the direction the wheel was moving.

"Four, sixteen, thirty-three, twenty-one, six, eighteen, and thirty-one," Sam said quickly. He began placing bets, moving each of the smaller piles to a number in the center. Maria helped him with the last two.

"No more bets," the dealer said after a certain point, waving her hand over all the chips on the table.

Maria watched the ball bounce its way to a stop, landing on the number eight. The dealer placed a silver placeholder on that number on the board, quickly clearing off all the old bets that hadn't won. The newlyweds kissed, laughing between themselves. Maria looked at Sam, worry in her eyes. They had just lost seventy dollars.

Sam shrugged and broke down one of the three remaining stacks of chips into seven smaller sections as before. Maria studied the wheel, looking at the numbers they had just bet on. There were seven of them, clustered together on one side of the wheel. That had obviously been where Mustafa thought the ball would end up. It had landed two slots away from his zone.

The wheel was spun again, and Sam called out seven different numbers. Maria knew that he was reading them from the tentacles in his lap, but he did so without tilting his head even slightly. Had she not known what he was doing, she wouldn't have guessed he was looking anywhere except down at the table. She caught the last two numbers in the sequence, thirteen and thirty-six, and moved two of the piles to sit on top of those numbers.

Again, the ball bounced around the table, coming to land on thirty-four black. They had lost another seventy dollars. The couple kissed again, leaning into each other.

Maria reached out, clutching Sam's thigh. They had just lost half their money in two spins of a wheel. Her eyes searched his, and he smiled.

"Don't worry," he said, prying her fingers out of his thigh gently. He took another pile, dividing it by seven, and softly called out another series of seven numbers. Maria placed the last three and sat back on her hands, her heart pounding.

"Red seven," the dealer said. "We've got a winner!"

Sam smiled, and a pile of chips appeared in front of him. Maria looked over, mouth agape. "We won?"

Sam laughed, counting the chips and arranging a new set of four piles, each larger because of their winnings. Like before, he split one of the four piles into seven smaller sets, and placed each of them on a new set of numbers. Maria hadn't heard any of the numbers he called out, still staring at the pile of chips in front of him. Black twenty-nine. They won again.

"Do you still want the same value chips?" the dealer asked.

Maria looked over at Sam.

"Can we make each chip worth $30?" he asked, and the dealer nodded, exchanging their chips in and replacing them with a new stack of red chips. "Each chip is $30," she confirmed.

"Sam, how much do we have there?" Maria said.

"$840 in the main piles, with a chip left over to make $870," Sam said, rearranging their chips and moving one chip to its own fifth pile so that the other four were even.

"Maybe we should keep some of it out?"

"You aren't used to winning at gambling, are you?"

"No!"

Sam handed her the fifth chip for safe keeping. They won a third time. The newlyweds raised their glasses in toast.

"Congratulations, you two!" the man said, slurring his words. Then he turned to the dealer and asked to be cashed out. She printed a ticket for him, which he tried to put down the front of his wife's dress but got his hand slapped in the process.

"Not just yet, you perv," his wife said, giggling. The man laughed and redirected the ticket to his back pocket, checking it twice to make sure he had correctly gotten it in. Then the two of them stumbled their way down the aisle, trying desperately to make their way out of the casino and back to their room without running into anyone.

Sam got the dealer's attention. He wanted to upgrade the chips to a higher denomination again.

———

They never lost more than two in a row, and Maria felt a strange mixture of excitement and fear as she saw the value of their chips increase spin by spin.

A waitress appeared at the side of the table. "Would you like any drinks?"

"Drinks? What kind of drinks?" Sam said.

"No drinks," Maria said, interrupting. The last thing she was going to let Sam do was get drunk at a time like this. Not with their future on the line on a roulette table.

"You sure?" the waitress said. "They're on the house."

"No drinks," Maria repeated sternly, holding the waitress's gaze.

The waitress frowned, looking from Maria to Sam, then left.

A small, round man soon appeared, watching the play quietly from behind the dealer. He wasn't bald but didn't quite have a head of hair either, and he periodically looked up from the table to make eye contact with Maria and smile. At a certain point, the dealer stopped, looking over at this man.

"Thank you, folks. That's my shift," she said. "I hope you enjoyed your time here. This is Toby. He'll take good care of you." Maria passed her a chip as a tip, and the dealer beamed back at her. "Thank you so much!"

"How much do we have?" she said, turning to Sam.

"Over seven thousand dollars."

"What!?" She hadn't realized it had grown so much.

Sam laughed, his eyes sparkling.

"Holy crap! OK, time to stop."

"Are you sure? I bet we could win a lot more."

Maria looked from the new dealer, back to Sam, and then turned her attention to the stack of thirty or so chips arranged in front of them. Each one was worth roughly the same amount as what they had started with. They had doubled their original stake roughly five times in a row. "No way. We're done."

"But what about Toby?" Sam said, gesturing at the new dealer.

"He'll live. Come on, let's go."

Toby cashed them out and printed out a ticket.

"What's this?" Maria said when he handed it to her.

"Those are your funds. You can redeem that ticket at the banking office by the entrance." He pointed back the way they had originally come.

"OK, thanks," Maria said, clutching the ticket. She wasn't going to put it in her pocket. She was going to hold onto it the entire way.

They made their way to the office and found a man waiting for them in front of the regular cashier. He was tall, well groomed, and had incredibly shiny black shoes. He smiled at them from behind a set of thin wire glasses.

"Here to collect your winnings?" he asked.

Maria nodded suspiciously. It was obvious that he had been waiting specifically for them, as he had completely ignored another couple that had come through just before.

"Are you a member of our players club?" the man asked.

"No."

"Would you like to join? There are many benefits."

"No, thanks. It's been a long day. We just want our winnings and are going back to the motel," Maria said.

"Oh, that's no problem. Let me help you. Please come with me," he said, and led them to a glass door that opened to an adjacent room. They entered and were shown to two chairs in front of a handsome oak desk. The man sat behind it, and smiled.

"This is the room for our preferred clientele. No need to stand in lines," he explained as he tapped a few keys on his keyboard to wake his system up. He held out his hand. "May I have your ticket, please?"

Maria passed the ticket forward, casting a sidelong glance at Sam. He caught it, and smirked. Had they really just beaten roulette?

"May I ask where you're staying?" the man said.

"Oh, nowhere special. A little place outside of town," Maria said noncommittally.

"I don't mean to pry into your lodging situation, but we would love to comp you a suite for the entire duration of your stay."

"Really?"

"Yes. We always do our best to make sure our preferred clientele are very well taken care of. Have you seen any shows yet? I have a number of tickets available that I would be more than happy to give you."

"Wow. Thanks!" Maria said. Obviously, they wanted a chance to win some of the money back from her. But still, it was a free room. A suite, no less! Maria smiled broadly at Sam, who winked back. Then she turned back to the man and remembered their situation. Her smile faded. "You'd need a credit card for that, wouldn't you?"

The man glanced from her to Sam, trying to understand her hesitation and willing to do almost anything to overcome it. That was his job. "Normally, yes. But, if our patrons are trying to be . . . discreet, then there are other options. We would be happy to let a portion of your winnings today be held as a room deposit if that would be preferable?"

"Yes, that would be quite preferable," Maria said, repeating his words. She watched him as he typed information into his computer and studied him as he took another quick glance up at both her and Sam. She smiled inwardly as she realized what he must be thinking. He thought she and Sam were lovers, and that she didn't want to give a credit card because their rendezvous was supposed to be discreet. She felt like laughing but only blushed. She looked over at Sam to see if he had caught on but instead found him puzzling over a paper clip he had found on the man's desk. From his furrowed brow, it was obvious he had no clue what it was for.

"Would you like to leave your winnings on your account?"

"No, cash would be preferable," Maria said, adding a hurried "thank you" and smiling as sweetly as she was able.

"Very well, please give me a minute," the man said, and withdrew to another room behind a paneled door.

"What is this thing?" Sam said once the door had swallowed their host.

"It's a paperclip. You use it to hold pieces of paper together."

"Oh! Really?"

I thought for picking food out of your teeth after opening it up, Mustafa said. *Either that or art.*

"I thought maybe loose parts for a small machine," Sam said. "You guys are funny."

The man returned, placing a large stack of $100 bills before Maria. He had brought the cash in on a silver tray. The dollars were crisp and new. She reached out and took hold of the wad, flipping through it to count. Had they *really* just beaten roulette?!

"These are the keys to your room," he said, passing two plastic cards to Maria. He then passed her a business card and gave another to Sam. "And this is my card. Please feel free to call me directly day or night if there's anything I can do for you. No request is too small. I hope you enjoy your stay with us."

"Thanks," Maria said, and got up. Sam followed, and the two left. Maria stopped by the cash registers, handing Sam half the stack. "Here, take this. But no gambling without me."

"OK," Sam said, stuffing the wad into his pocket.

"Mustafa, you were amazing!" Maria said. "That was incredible."

Do we have enough money now?

"Yes, this is tons! They even gave us a free room. I bet we can get free food too. I'll just call that guy and tell him to send room service!"

Sam smiled, and Mustafa flipped the ends of his tentacles as expressively as he was able while still pretending to be an inanimate object.

Aside from some old wrappers, there was nothing of theirs back in the room at their old motel. Maria didn't trust the manager enough to leave anything valuable there, so they had packed everything up and taken it with them in the car. They wouldn't even have to go back. Tomorrow they would hit the road for Mexico and would not be staying in fancy hotels. In fact, there was a good chance they would never have the opportunity to stay in a suite ever again. There were crowds here and they needed to be careful, but it was only one night, and it was free. And for the first time in what felt like an eternity, Maria actually felt lucky.

"Let's go check out our room," Maria said. "I think I owe both of you guys a drink."

TWENTY-THREE

Like everything in Vegas, the suite felt larger than life, both in its luxurious appointments and in its size. Maria paused to look around and couldn't help but feel that the suite was almost bigger than her house back in Sedona. Then she corrected herself: the suite actually *was* bigger than her house. An entire wall was made up of glass windows that provided a sweeping view of the city, complete with shades that could be raised and lowered from the ceiling at a push of a button. Everything was arranged perfectly, as if the suite was brand new and had never before accommodated any guests.

Maria made her way over to a table and pulled out one of the chairs. She sat down and arranged their winnings in a stack, sitting back to take in their bounty. How long would it have taken her to earn this much behind the desk at the Bell Rock Inn? Half a year? Longer? Mustafa had done it in less than an hour.

"That's a lot of money, isn't it?" Sam said, sitting in a chair next to hers.

Maria nodded. "Yeah. Some people would kill for that much money."

"Really?" Sam regarded the pile, and his eyes slowly drifted down to his fingers, which he clenched and unclenched, almost to check and make sure they weren't broken. His face darkened, and he didn't raise his eyes when he spoke. "Maria, are humans evil?"

"No, I don't think so . . . ," she said, studying Sam. "There are some bad ones, but I think most people are good."

"Why are there some bad ones?"

"Sometimes people do bad things because they are suffering. They're poor, or hurt, or lonely, and they don't know how not to be those things, so they lash out and hurt others. Sometimes they do bad things because they're ignorant, but not because they're evil."

"Lonely? I don't see how anyone could be lonely here. There are other people everywhere."

Maria laughed. She had forgotten who she was talking to. Sam hadn't seen another human until only a few days ago. His definition of loneliness was probably a little different than hers.

"I feel like I met some pretty bad ones," Sam said.

"Yes, what they did to you wasn't right." It was obvious who Sam was talking about: John Sanders and the giant whom Mother had burned alive at the FBI building. "I'm so sorry that happened to you, Sam."

"Why did they do it?"

"I don't know. I think they were scared of you. Of what you could do with the bracelet."

"Mother punished one of them," Sam said, looking down.

"She did." Maria would never forget what happened to that man. Just the mention of it made her stomach tighten up.

"I wish she punished the other one too," Sam said, clenching his jaw. He looked up at Maria, his face strained. "Does that make me a bad person?"

"Sam, you were tortured. It's natural to be angry at the people who did that to you. It doesn't make you a bad person."

"Are you sure?"

"Anyone would feel the same way."

"I don't want to be a bad human. I want to be a good one."

"I know you do. You are."

Sam took a deep breath and exhaled. The tension loosened, and Maria could see him visibly relax.

"Who is the best person you know?" he asked.

Maria thought for a moment. "Lucas, my nephew. He suffers so much, but he never complains. When I'm with him during his procedures, and he sees that I'm sad, he tries to make jokes to get me to laugh. He's the one in pain, but all he cares about is cheering me up." Maria looked away, embarrassed by the sudden tightness in her throat.

"He is sick?"

Maria nodded.

"Very sick?"

"Yes. They don't think they can cure him . . ."

"But you try anyway?"

"Of course we try. He's family. You don't give up on people you love."

"Family." Sam said the word slowly, as if it were a food he was tasting for the first time. "Do you love your family?"

"Yes. Very much. I would do anything for them."

There was a pause, as the two both looked out the windows. A small pigeon drifted past.

"You are the best person I know," Sam said. "I wish everyone here was like you."

Maria smiled and reached out to squeeze the top of Sam's hand. He looked down at her hand and flipped his own over, holding her fingers gently in his palm.

"It feels so strange to be able to touch another person," Sam said.

"I can see how that would be different from what you're used to. Do you like it?"

"Yes."

"I like it too." She slid her hand forward and couldn't help but notice that her hand fit perfectly inside Sam's. His hand was warm and strong.

Maria smiled. "Even better than bacon, right?"

Sam laughed, and his eyes sparkled.

Maria laughed with him and, for a moment, was able to forget about everything else. She then furrowed her brow as she turned her attention to the center of the room. "Sam, what is Mustafa doing?"

Mustafa rested on his side on the floor. He held the entire television set in a death grip, multiple tentacles encircling it and holding it against his body. The screen was pressed completely flat against his head, and muffled sounds emanated from the speakers. He rolled back and forth like a rocking chair, cradling the television set and squeaking quietly to himself.

"I think he's watching TV," Sam said.

As Maria and Sam regarded Mustafa and his television-watching technique, two tentacles popped free. *I am the best person I know*, he signed. The two tentacles reattached themselves to the set, and then loosened again almost immediately. *Although technically, I'm not really a person. Which is good, because that would suck.*

TWENTY-FOUR

Misha Karpinski sat upright at the sound, startled by the flashing red box in the lower corner of his monitor. He looked around nervously, half expecting one of his superiors to be standing behind him. His thin, wiry frame allowed him to move quickly, and he spun his entire body around in a complete circle on his swiveling chair. But the cubicle was empty, and he only saw the same four gray walls he had spent the better part of his days enclosed within since his graduation at the top of his class at MIT.

Misha returned to his computer and minimized the window to the strategy game he had been absorbed in. Playing games all day long while earning six figures was the ultimate payoff for someone with the coding ability to automate almost all his mundane daily tasks and a complete lack of desire to relate with other human beings in any way. Had Misha possessed even half as much ambition as he had skill, he'd have been running the entire data center years ago, rather than simply sliding along in his cubicle, a lowly analyst. He knew it, as did everyone around him. But he didn't care. He didn't want to be in charge of anything. It was too much work.

He quickly clicked over the flashing box with his mouse, the cursor on his screen long having become an extension of his body. He had color coded all his alerts. Green meant low priority, usually noncritical tasks that weren't time sensitive. Yellow was urgent, usually involving information regarding individuals on terrorist watch lists and other high-priority targets. Orange represented imminent threats. He had only ever fielded two orange alerts in the entire time he had worked at the NSA. And then there was red.

He stared at the screen, shocked. This was his first red alert, ever.

Adjusting the thick black frame of his glasses, he scanned the contents of the message his custom routine had delivered to him. The phone from an extremely high-value target had come online.

Misha sent a query to the database. NSA analysts in the old days had to sit and listen to phone recordings from wire taps. It had been a thankless job back then, dull and monotonous. Misha would never have survived in that environment. But now, things were completely different. All the phone conversations in the world were recorded and stored in the data center automatically. And with voice-to-text processing, he could usually scan through entire conversations for the data he was looking for without ever needing to listen to the voices of his subjects. Spying had never been easier. Everyone in the world was simply a database query away.

Misha studied the graph of the audio spectrum displayed on his screen. It had been a flat line for days, and then had suddenly spiked back to life. Of course, a flat line didn't mean the phone had been off. It just meant that the mic wasn't picking up any sound. Every phone transmitted continuously, even when it was turned off. Every phone, in every pocket, was a live microphone, and all that data was stored permanently in the NSA's data center. Built at the cost of billions of taxpayer dollars, the data center stored complete phone records, Internet browsing history, purchase history, credit reports, and almost every other piece of digital information that existed. It was a data mine of the habits of everyone who ever touched a digital device of any kind, archived for the NSA's use, thanks to the countless zettabytes of storage space in banks of servers that occupied hundreds of thousands of square feet.

Misha asked the server to queue up the audio from the phone record and put a thick pair of headphones on. They covered both his ears in supple leather and had cost the NSA almost two grand, but Misha had been able to talk his superiors into expensing them. They worked great for listening to sensitive audio recordings. They worked even better for playing first-person shooter games. A green progress bar appeared on Misha's screen as the data downloaded from the server bank, and he nervously tapped his pen against the desktop as he waited. It took longer than he expected. He wondered if there was a problem with his computer, or if it was the servers that were experiencing some issues. His Internet at home seemed faster than this. Apparently, even the best computer scientists in the most advanced data center in the world still needed IT support from time to time.

The progress bar completed, and the file opened in front of him. A red flag in the corner meant there had been no warrant granted for this particular search. This information could never be used in a court of law. But that didn't matter. It was rare when any of his work ever made it into the courts. Those were issues for other agencies to worry about.

Misha clicked an icon and the sound file began to play. He listened carefully, reading along with the transcript displayed on the side of his monitor. There were chimes sounding and the clicking sound of many coins falling together all at once into a metal tray. Were those slot machines? Yes, definitely slot machines. A woman was explaining something to someone. He quickly jotted down some notes, saved a copy of the data file, and dropped it all into a secure email. He pasted the contact information from the agency where the search request originated, then paused, his finger hovering over the button that would send the message. He looked down at the minimized screen of his game, and then back up to the alert box, flashing red.

"Crap," he said, and picked up the phone. The only thing Misha hated more than making phone calls was making reports in person. He would have preferred to work an extra week without pay rather than have to talk to anyone over the phone, but the alert was red. Even he knew there was no way around calling this in. He clicked the number on the display and waited while the phone rang.

"Sanders," a gruff voice said on the other line. Misha winced. Why did it always have to be a gruff old man? Why couldn't he ever talk to a nice, sweet woman in her early twenties for a change?

"This is Misha Karpinski, with the NSA," Misha began, rattling off his badge number and identifying information. It was protocol to say all of it, and he knew better than anyone that the conversation was being recorded and saved for all time, so he wasn't about to skip over any of the regulations. "I've just gotten a hit on a high-priority target jointly tasked from your agency," Misha said, double-checking the name. "It's the phone belonging to Maria Rodriguez."

"Go ahead," Sanders said.

"It appears she is in a casino right now." Misha heard his voice waver. He hated when it did that.

"A casino?"

"Yes. I can hear the slot machines, and I specifically heard her discuss them."

"Who is she with?"

Misha checked the names he wrote down and quickly scanned over the transcript to make sure he hadn't missed anything.

"As far as I can tell, she is with two others. There's a Sam and a Mustafa."

"Mustafa? Who the fuck is Mustafa?!"

Misha yanked the headset off, cursing silently. He turned the volume down on his headset and replaced it.

"I don't know, sir. We haven't been able to capture his voice yet, but there is definitely a Mustafa present. Both Maria and Sam directly address him multiple times."

"Listen again. Does he have an accent?"

"Give me a minute," Misha said, muting Sanders. He replayed the sound file, using the audio spectrum and transcript to fast forward through the parts where no one was speaking. Maria was definitely there. She had a sweet voice, and sounded pretty. Why couldn't he ever report to someone like Maria? There was Sam too. His voice was clear as well. There were references to Mustafa, and Mustafa seemed to reply, but his voice was never caught. That was weird. Maybe he was too far away? Smartphone mics were notoriously poor at capturing high-quality audio, so there was a chance that his voice just got drowned out by the background noise.

Misha returned to his call. "I can't hear him. I think the phone might be too far away to pick him up. They are in a casino, which is loud, so maybe—"

Sanders interrupted. "You can't hear him because he doesn't want to be heard. That's why they met in the casino. He's smart. They're trying to sell it to the Arabs. Holy fuck."

"Sell what?"

"Never you mind about that. I need to get you in touch with my people so we can coordinate on this. You've done good work, son."

The line went dead. Sanders had hung up.

Misha took off his headset and hung it back up on the clamp fastened to his desk where they rested when not in use. He exhaled, trying to breathe the stress out of his body and hoping that he'd never have to speak to Sanders again. Leaning forward, he tried to remember what he had been working on before the alert came in. Then his phone rang.

Misha scowled. The headset went back on, and he clicked the button to answer.

"Yes, that's me. Yes, that's right." A shiver went down his spine. "Wait. *In person?*" Some words were said, but Misha was unable to focus enough to hear them. He realized there was silence on the other end of the line. They were waiting for an answer. "Yes, yes, I'll be there right away." Misha hung up, dazed. He looked back to his game and closed the window. His palms had already begun to sweat. He opened a drawer, trying to remember where he had last put his tie. The tie with the clip. But it wasn't anywhere. How could he have misplaced something like that?

"You ready?" a deep voice said from the hallway. Misha jumped. His supervisor peered in at him, notepad and pen in hand. He raised an eyebrow slightly. Misha hated when people did that.

"Yes," Misha said. "Let's go."

TWENTY-FIVE

The head of casino security made his way down the hallway that led to deliveries. He had come into life weighing just over fifteen pounds, the largest baby ever born in Humboldt County. He was the tallest kid in elementary school by at least a head and crushed the scales at over three hundred pounds in college during his linebacker days. There was almost no one better suited for this particular job than he was, and his imposing size meant he could count on one hand the number of times he had to be physical with disruptive guests. People took one look at him and did what they were told.

He pushed the door open with his thick, dark hand, propping it open by flipping the stopper out with his foot. The police were already there.

"Hey, man," he said in his deep baritone voice, recognizing the sergeant waiting at the door. He had worked with this particular officer plenty of times during his tenure as chief of security for the casino, and the two were on good terms.

"Good to see you. Wish it was under better circumstances," the cop said. He wore a bulletproof vest, assault helmet, and carried a rifle loaded with high explosive uranium-tipped incendiary ammunition, courtesy of Homeland Security. He had the ability to put a round through an engine block at close range. The fact that the government was handing this level of ordnance out to local law enforcement made him nervous. Who did they think was inside?

"Come on." The security guard led the team down the hall. It was the second SWAT team he had helped position within the casino in the last twenty minutes. Special Forces were on the way and due to arrive momentarily as well.

They used service elevators and the back hallways when possible. Bringing a highly armed group of law enforcement operatives through a casino is a surefire way to kill the mood of the guests and had the potential to set off a panic. If this worked out as these matters usually did, the police would be here and gone before any guests even knew what had happened.

"We're going to the tenth floor." They passed through a door and entered a spiral staircase, which they began climbing. The sounds of many heavy boots echoed against the concrete walls around them.

"Have you been able to evacuate the other guests?" the sergeant asked.

"Yes. We called some of them and went door to door for the ones who didn't answer their phones. The eighth through twelfth floors are totally empty at this point."

"Any trouble with any of them?"

"No, they've been cool. They all think there's a malfunctioning smoke detector and we're just being overcautious. Giving them free tickets to shows always smooths things over in situations like this."

The cop laughed. "Yeah, better than saying there's a group of terrorists in the room next door."

The security director grunted. They stopped, and he cracked the door, slowly peeking around it. Then he pushed it open, waving to the team behind to follow. They quietly crept out, filling the hallway.

The guard leaned in toward the cop's ear, covering his mouth. He knew that he didn't have to whisper—the rooms were naturally sound proofed so that drunken guests didn't disturb anyone when they came back late—but he did so anyway due to the circumstances.

"Room 1024 is there on the right side, about five or six doors down. That's where they are right now."

"1024," the cop repeated.

A white plastic square was produced and pressed into the cop's palm. "This key will open all the doors on this level."

The sergeant took it and handed it to the officer next to him. The team began opening doors and arranging themselves in the most effective positions to cover the hallway without clumping together. Another SWAT team had done the same down at the other end, and the two groups briefly acknowledged each other with a crisp salute. They would need to be careful of friendly fire given the target being located between them.

The head of security felt his phone vibrate and reached into his pocket to check. "Military is downstairs, coming up. Special Forces are here."

"Holy crap, this is big."

"Tell me about it. I'm going to meet them and see what they need." He put one of his huge hands on the cop's shoulder. "Tell me straight. Are you guys going to start shooting?"

The sergeant looked at his friend, then down at his weapons, considering the ordnance he was now carrying. "Honestly, I can't promise that we won't."

"Shit. I'm not sure we've cleared enough floors."

"You probably haven't."

The guard turned, making his way down the stairwell. He moved quickly for as big a man as he was. He knew there was no time to waste. He pulled out his phone, dialing as he went. He didn't waste time with greetings when his second answered. "This is bigger than what we've been told. We need to get everyone out of the hotel."

"Everyone? You're talking almost fifty floors of rooms to clear. Are you sure?"

"Do you think I'd be calling if I wasn't? They're about to start a war on the tenth floor. Get everyone out, and do it now."

"Which floor is it?" SWAT Sergeant Edwin Navarro said. He crouched beside a blue minivan on the top floor of the parking garage, his long black rifle propped up to balance along the top of the concrete safety wall that provided cover for him and his spotter. The casino loomed before him, a tower of glass.

"Tenth floor," Roy Tannenbaum responded. Roy peered through a set of binoculars at the casino, counting the floors from the bottom until he got to ten.

"They all look the same. I don't want to get the wrong room," Edwin responded.

"You think the bachelor party from Kansas is going to mind if you accidentally put a couple of rounds into their keg?"

"Depends if the strippers have shown up yet."

Roy snorted. "Oh, there you go. Look for a guy in the window waving. See him?"

Edwin scanned across and up through his scope, stopping when he found a helmeted SWAT officer in one of the windows. The man held his rifle down and to the side, and was making big motions with his free hand. Another officer came up next to him with what looked like a roll of tape. A huge X was pasted right on the glass of the window.

"Thanks guys," Edwin said. "OK, got it."

"It's five rooms to the right from there," Roy said. "The room right next to it has the curtains fully drawn."

"OK, I've got it."

Roy measured the distance with his rangefinder and checked the wind. It was a perfectly calm day, and they were close. This was an easy shot.

"Captain, we've got eyes on the room," Roy said, speaking into the mic that protruded out from his helmet. He glanced over, motion catching his eye.

"Eddie, we've got some company."

"What's up?" Edwin responded. He wasn't going to look anywhere but through his scope now that he had the target in his sights. Roy would be his eyes and ears for everything else.

"Looks like Special Forces sent their own snipers. They've taken up a position on the other corner of the garage. Wow! That's a huge rifle."

"Really? How big is it?"

"Hard to say from here, but holy shit, you could drop Godzilla with that thing. It's taking three of them just to set it up."

"I've got something," Edwin said. Roy immediately turned his attention back to the building, scanning with his binoculars to find the room again.

"An adult male. He just walked across the room. Looks like he's sitting on a sofa."

"Captain, we've got eyes on an adult male in the room," Roy spoke into his mic quietly.

"There's a female too. They're sitting next to each other. They're talking,"

Roy spoke quietly, keeping the team commander appraised.

Edwin laughed under his breath.

"What?" Roy said. He didn't have the same magnification as Edwin's scope and couldn't see the same level of detail.

"It looks like they're playing with a stuffed animal."

"A stuffed animal?"

"Yeah. A giant purple stuffed animal."

"Whatever floats your boat," Roy said.

"When was the last time you got it on with the wife and a stuffed animal? Mary and I haven't tried that one yet."

"Two women? Sure. A woman and one of those sex dolls? Maybe. Depends if I'm drunk. But a stuffed animal? I'll pass. They're not actually doing that, are they?"

"Not yet. But this is Vegas." Edwin smiled. He followed the couple through his scope with the same intensity a panther tracks its prey before pouncing. "We sure this is the right room? These two look a lot like tourists to me."

"Casino security has cleared five floors: two above, and two below the tenth. If you're on the tenth floor, five doors down from the X, you're on the money. There isn't anyone else there."

"You mean aside from the shit ton of SWAT and Special Forces people crawling the halls?"

Roy laughed. "Yeah. Aside from them, it's a wasteland."

———

Sanders's cell phone rang, the distinctive tone jarring on his ears. He hated the sound but found it took the loudest, most annoying ringtone available to get his attention. Shooting through half a million rounds of ammunition over the years probably hadn't helped his hearing. He fished in his pocket and put the phone up to his ear.

"Sanders."

"It's Boggs. Just lost the NSA's feed into the target's phone. Aside from that, we're in position and ready to roll."

Lieutenant Bob Boggs was on location in Las Vegas and was in command of the operation. He had flown in direct from Fort Bragg with his team as soon as the targets were identified and located. He was a good, competent soldier, and over the years Sanders had come to appreciate his directness and no-bullshit attitude. Sanders had asked Boggs to keep him in the loop, especially if anything unusual happened. Boggs was ultimately in charge of the operation—something this critical couldn't be micromanaged from afar without introducing too many opportunities for a mistake—and Sanders was appreciative of the status update.

"How big of a deal is the phone?" Sanders asked.

"We have plenty of eyes on the targets, and we're good to go without it. But a mic in the room sure is nice to have."

"Let me call my contact at the NSA. Hang on, Boggs."

"Copy."

Sanders studied his phone, looking for the mute button, furrowing his brow and cursing under his breath until he found it. He gently put it down on his desk and picked up the receiver to his land line, pushing the worn button on the lower right.

"Sarah Reed, assistant to John Sanders," came the familiar voice.

"Sarah. Get me that kid from the NSA."

"Yes sir, hold on . . . ," the phone went quiet as Sarah put him on hold.

Sanders rapped his square fingers on his desk, tapping out a sharp rhythm against the mahogany. He adjusted a set of files that was slightly crooked, making sure the sides were perfectly parallel to the edge of his desk.

Sarah's voice came back on the line. "Sorry, sir, I'm having trouble getting through their main phone system. I'm going to try to locate his other numbers. We should have his cell in the system."

"Talking to me isn't going to get that kid on the phone any faster, Sarah. Spend time dialing numbers with those pretty fingers of yours rather than making excuses," Sanders growled.

"Yes, sir." The line went quiet again.

Sanders looked down at his cell phone, picking it up to make sure it said that Boggs was still connected. He was. The phone was gently replaced back onto the desk, then adjusted so the side matched the angle of the recently squared set of papers.

"I have him, sir," Sarah said.

Sanders grunted.

"Hello?" The voice was a higher pitch than Sanders had remembered.

"Who's this?" Sanders said.

"Uh. Misha Karpinski, with the NSA. Badge number—"

"Forget the badge number. What the fuck is going on with the feed to Maria Rodriguez's phone? I've got a live team positioned at her location, ready to take decisive action, and you clowns just dropped the audio."

"I'm sorry, sir. We're having an issue at the server farm."

"Server farm? I'm talking about a phone tap, not a fucking computer database."

"Well, they're actually the same thing. We don't do taps anymore. Not like how you're thinking at least."

Why did the kid's voice shake so much? It sounded like someone was sitting there with the end of a .45 shoved into his ear for all his stammering. Sanders opened his mouth to reply and saw the red light on his phone flash.

"Hold on," Sanders said, and pushed the button. "What?"

"Sir, it's the Secretary of Defense on the line for you," Sarah said.

"For fuck's sake," Sanders said. "Fine. Put him on."

"Sanders, it's Jim," a deep voice said on the other end of the line. Jim Fisk's voice was smooth and controlled. It was the voice of a politician, not of a soldier. Everyone knew how he got his position. Being the president's college roommate apparently came with a few perks.

"I'm a little busy, sir," Sanders replied.

"This won't take long. What's the status on your operation in Las Vegas?"

"We're in position and about to act. Just dealing with a loose end before we execute," Sanders replied. Things would be moving a lot faster if he didn't have to sit here and bullshit with politicians though, he was sure of that much.

"That's great. I've briefed the president, and he wants to be kept in the loop."

"Of course."

"Listen, Sanders. You know we've got midterms coming up."

"Sure." Weren't there always midterms coming up? What did midterms have to do with anything?

"A shootout between the US military and an extraterrestrial in Las Vegas isn't something that the American people are ready for. Nobody knows how the optics are going to play with something like that. We're concerned about the administration's exposure if this thing goes sideways."

"You're concerned with the optics?"

"Yes."

"Can I speak freely, sir?"

"Always."

"Frankly, I'm more concerned about what will happen if some shithole Middle Eastern country gets a hold of a weapon that could send the rest of us back to the Stone Age. I don't give two shits about what the press might think."

"I know you're focused on the primary issues, Sanders, but for God's sake don't let this turn into a shit show. The polling numbers aren't great already. Something like this could cause a panic, and the Democrats might be able to use it to leverage their socialist agenda. There's more than one way that we can end up in the Stone Ages."

"Understood," Sanders said. "We'll keep it under the radar. These boys are the best in the world at what they do. If everything goes according to plan, no one will even know that anything that happened today was out of the ordinary."

"That's great, John. I appreciate it."

"You're welcome. If there's nothing else, I've got urgent business."

"Of course. Keep me posted."

"Will do," Sanders hung up. "Fucking asshole." He pushed the button in the lower right. "Sarah. Get the kid back on here."

"Yes, sir."

"Hello?"

"Tell me your name again."

"Misha Karpinski. From the NSA."

"I know that, for Christ's sake. Did you get the phone back up yet?"

"No, the entire database just went down. We didn't lose just that one phone, we lost all the phones. We're blind."

The NSA is down? How could that be possible? "Don't you have any backups? How can you be down?"

"Sir, of course we have backups. The backups are down too. And the backups of the backups. All of it! We don't even have access to our own phones." Was that a little fire in the kid's voice? Good for him.

"How long until you fix it?"

"Not anytime soon. We don't even know what happened."

"All right. You keep me posted." Sanders hung up. So much for the NSA. He knew this day would come. A computer can never replace the eyes and ears of well-trained men on the ground. Every commander worth his salt knows as much. Putting that much responsibility on the shoulders of a bunch of pockmarked teenagers was bound to blow up at some point. Why it all went to hell minutes before potentially one of the most critical operations in American history was a point of irony not lost upon him.

Sanders picked up his cell phone, studying the face of the device in an effort to relocate the mute button. He pressed it and held the phone up to his head. "Boggs? You still there?"

"Hang on, sir. I'll get him for you," a voice said. It was one of Boggs's men. Of course Boggs wasn't going to stand around with his dick in his hand while he waited on a phone call. Sanders would have done the same.

"Sorry, chief," Boggs said. "Lots of irons in the fire on my end."

"I apologize for the wait, Bob. The NSA appears to have gone tits up. You boys are on your own."

"Really? The NSA?"

"You heard it here first. One of those pencil necks must have tripped over the plug to the computer. At any other time, I'd be laughing my ass off about it."

Boggs chuckled. "Copy. I'll keep you posted."

"Boggs." Sanders voice grew very serious. "The future of America's military position in the world may very well rest upon what happens today in that hotel room. Don't leave there without that bracelet. You do whatever it takes to make that happen."

"Understood."

TWENTY-SEVEN

"Mustafa, what's going on with your skin?" Maria said. There were white flakes along the edges of Mustafa's tentacles, and little specks of skin had begun to slough off.

It's so dry here. Two of Mustafa's tentacles rubbed against each other, another curling around to scratch an area on the top of his head.

"I think you've got chapped skin," Maria said. She thought back to her first memory of Mustafa, the one that Mother had shared with her from when his planet had been destroyed. It had been a wet world, with a dense mist and dark clouds. Earth must feel like a parched desert compared to that place, especially here in Nevada.

Maria got up and went to her bag, recently brought up by one of the hotel staff. She rummaged through it and found what she was looking for. "Maybe this will help," she said, popping the top off a container of lip balm.

A tentative tentacle reached out and took the tube from her, holding it close to the bulb of Mustafa's head. Then it moved down, underneath his body.

"No! Wait!" Maria shouted. The tentacle stopped, freezing in place. "Don't eat it! You rub it on yourself. It's for chapped lips."

It seems like it would be better to eat it, Mustafa signed. The end of the tentacle came back into view, holding the tube at an angle. It moved down to the place on his body between where two tentacles came together against his head, and he gently applied the lip balm there, moving in slow, circular motions.

"Is it working?" Sam asked.

The tentacle increased its speed, rubbing circles down along one of Mustafa's most severely chapped tentacles. The tentacle stretched up, and the remedy was applied down both sides, and around the base. That particular arm complete, it dropped, and took the tube up with its tip, rubbing the container down the length of the tentacle that had previously held it.

"I think it's working," Maria said, glancing at Sam. Mustafa's other tentacles flapped lightly against the ground as he began covering himself in lip balm. "Twist the bottom if you run out."

"Is there enough to get everything?" Sam said, watching Mustafa. There was a strange humming noise coming from the purple creature, and Mustafa rolled over onto his side, tentacles folded over the top of his head. He was working on his underside. There was a pursed opening at the very bottom of his body that almost looked like a small, blue starfish.

Maria frowned. "I'm not sure. It's not meant to be enough cover your entire body." She wrinkled her nose as she got a whiff of something that reminded her of rotten vegetables.

"You stink, Mustafa." Sam said, waving his hand in front of his face.

Mustafa sat upright, his tentacles frozen. He sat there for a moment, still as a stone, then lifted two tentacles up to speak. *I don't smell anything. Only dirty humans.* Then he rolled back over, resuming the process of covering himself in lip balm.

"Well, I smell it," Sam said quietly, turning away from his brother to look at Maria.

"Yeah, me too." Maria waved a hand in front of her face to move the air.

"You know he only has one orifice in his entire body."

Maria looked back at Mustafa, the blue starfish on the underside of his body visible against the lighter coloring that surrounded it. "So that's his mouth? But also . . . ?"

"Yes."

"Eww," Maria made a face, squinting and looking away. She made her way into the bathroom, then came back holding a white container of lotion.

"Mustafa," she said. "Get up on the couch. You're not going to have enough of that to cover your whole body. This will work too."

Sam moved to the couch, and Mustafa joined him. Maria sat on the other side and held the bottle over Mustafa's head, squeezing a pile of white hand lotion onto the top of his head. Then she began working the lotion in, helping spread it around. His body felt like a giant rubbery balloon under her hands, smooth and sticky at the same time. The darker areas of his bulb were rougher and harder than the lighter ones, with the most rubbery parts being the areas on the underside of his tentacles. Sam followed her lead, working on spreading the lotion down Mustafa's other side. The lip balm was gripped in one of Mustafa's tentacles, but he had ceased applying it. Instead, he sat still, purring and squeaking quietly to himself.

"Do you guys mind if I send some of our money back to my grandmother?" Maria said, talking quickly. "She's going to have trouble paying Lucas's medical bills if I'm not there. I won't send much. Just enough to help."

If it will help your family, then you should send it. We can always win more.

Sam looked up and smiled at her, his eyes twinkling. "Yes. Send it."

"Thanks, you guys," Maria said quietly. She was in a hotel in Las Vegas, having won thousands of dollars playing roulette, but somehow that was the least interesting thing that had happened to her in days. She was friends with an extraterrestrial. She was physically touching him, and she wasn't afraid. No one would ever believe her if she told them. She wasn't sure she believed it herself. And somehow, even more amazing, was the strange, otherworldly man who had literally walked right into her life. She had only known Sam a few days, and yet he felt like someone who was inextricably woven into the fabric of her life, like a childhood friend from simpler and easier times. Those days had been full of sun and laughter, and she had been a totally different person.

Innocence was the gift Sam gave her. But it left her wondering how his tender heart might survive on planet Earth. Mother's two children, whom she had died protecting, had somehow become Maria's family as well. What would Lucas think when he met them?

Maria smiled at Sam, and he smiled back. Mustafa squeaked contentedly.

The moment was broken by the sharp *crack* of splintering wood.

They spun toward the sound. "What was th—"

Boom! The door exploded inward, two men rushing through in combat fatigues. Each carried what looked to be a hundred pounds of gear, including armor, helmets, and automatic weapons held up at eye level. Maria quickly stood to turn and face them. She tripped over one of Mustafa's tentacles and fell to the ground, scrambling backward on her hands. Sam rose, looking from the men to Maria, not sure what to do.

"Don't shoot!" Maria shouted. "We're unarmed!"

"On the ground! Now!" More were flooding into the room, like water through a breach in the hull of a ship.

Maria saw a flash of motion, and like a cannonball, Mustafa slammed into the chest of the closest soldier, knocking the man back into the others. She had never seen anything move that fast. His entire body had gone scarlet red, as bright as a freshly washed fire truck. One tentacle wrapped itself around the soldier's throat, while another looped itself around the man's weapon, pushing it up and to the side. A third tentacle shot out and seized another soldier by the legs, flipping the man back and over like an uprooted bowling pin.

Mustafa's arms were like thick rubber hoses, and he swung them like whips, crashing down into the bodies of soldiers. He would pull himself from one man to another, his entire body one heaving muscle. Tentacles curled into balls and snapped out with devastating force, crushing limbs and shattering bone. There was a strange piercing sound that filled the room, a high-pitched wail of an angry beast. It was a primal and feral howl. Maria didn't know if the sound carried words that Mustafa's own kind would understand, but it didn't matter, as the meaning behind that scream crossed boundaries of language, species, or planet. It was the sound of rage.

The doorway became a bottleneck, and the soldiers on the other side couldn't get through to help the ones who had already entered. What weapons the men had were useless in the moment, as they couldn't be trained on the lightning-quick creature that had been unleashed in their midst. Mustafa was among them, between them all, and fought in a way that had no counterpart anywhere on Earth. They were highly trained Special Forces operatives, but they might as well have been a bunch of high school kids for all it mattered in that moment. Maria watched the flashing red tentacles, moving faster than her eye could follow, and realized in that moment that Mustafa was a predator. There was a reason that out of all the snacks he could have taken that first day, he had sought out the jerky.

Sam took a step toward Mustafa, wanting to help, but couldn't find an opening. His brother seemed to be everywhere at once. Sam rushed to a side table, taking hold of a lamp, ripping the cord from the wall. He hurled it over the top of the melee, toward the soldiers clustered in the doorway. A red tentacle snapped out, seized the lamp in midair, and brought it crashing down upon the helmet of one of the soldiers, knocking the man to the ground.

The mass of people pushing to get in began to have an effect, and more soldiers appeared in the doorway, forcing Mustafa back into the room. There were bodies on the ground, unconscious or worse, and they got pushed aside by the press, like debris against a flood of water.

Maria had found her feet and stepped back, trying to stay out of the way. Tentacles whipped past her head, and she heard the air sizzle as they came within inches of touching her. Sam launched what he could get his hands on into the air—pillows, chairs, and finally the television itself—and each time, Mustafa seized the objects and redirected them into the mass of soldiers with increased force from his elastic limbs.

Mustafa yanked two soldiers, cracking their skulls together with an impossible force. They both wore helmets, which probably saved their lives, but weren't enough to keep them conscious. The ball of red fell to the ground and rolled backward, springing up between where Maria and Sam found themselves in the corner of the room and where the line of soldiers gathered itself. One of Mustafa's tentacles looped around the frame of the bed, tensing itself like a catapult preparing to launch a projectile. The rest of the tentacles flipped like angered serpents, the tips directed forward to the enemy. A thin layer of white foam dripped from the underside of Mustafa's vibrating body, soaking the carpet.

The high-pitched wail that had filled the room transformed into a deep growl. Less manic, perhaps, but no less threatening.

———

"Holy shit!" Edwin Navarro moved his body slightly, readjusting himself, without shifting his eye from the scope.

"What?" Roy said, scanning the building. He saw motion through the glass, but couldn't quite make out what was happening.

"That wasn't a fucking stuffed animal. That thing is alive!"

"The purple thing?"

"Yeah! It just took out two Special Forces guys. Jesus, it can move fast."

"Cap, this is going to sound crazy, but there's a purple thing fighting with the Special Forces in there," Roy said into his mic.

"It's not purple anymore. It's red."

"A red thing now. Some kind of animal, I don't know. It's not human, though." Roy covered his mic and turned to Edwin. "Can you get a shot?"

"It's moving too fast. I'm going to hit the friendlies."

"Not yet. Understood," Roy said back into the mic. "Eddie, as soon as you get a clean shot, you put a bullet in that thing."

"Don't have to tell me twice."

The two men watched in silence. Neither moved a muscle, their complete focus on what was happening on the tenth floor of the building in front of them. Edwin waited, and watched. He saw the red thing roll off two soldiers, and pop up into a stationary position. The man and the woman in the room stood near the window, but there was a space between them, a clean path to whatever the red thing was. Eddie exhaled unconsciously, and, with a finger calloused from pulling the trigger thousands of times, fired his weapon.

———

Time slowed down. One minute, Mustafa was fighting for their lives, the next, the air in the room seemed to suck in upon itself. The glass behind Maria shattered and shards peppered the back of her head. But she didn't turn. She only stared. There, in the center of the room, was a sight even more bizarre than all she'd witnessed so far.

To say it was a man would be inaccurate. It was human in shape, but only in the broadest strokes. There was a head upon it, but the eyes were smoothed over, and the features indistinct. There was only the vaguest protrusion of a nose, and no mouth to speak of. It looked like a sculpture, rough and half-finished, but it was no sculpture, since it could move.

But strangest of all, was the fact he appeared to be made of solid gold.

He'd also just popped into existence, as fast as the bullet he'd snatched out of thin air and now held, pinched between two fingers. Every person in the room stood stock still, watching as he lifted the bullet and held it before the blank void that constituted his face.

Projectile weaponry. How primitive. The words materialized in Maria's consciousness in the exact same manner she had communicated with Mother.

Some of the SWAT members gasped, their mouths dropping in surprise. The Special Forces operatives, more highly trained and used to dealing with sudden surprises, recovered first and opened fire. The police joined in. Every solider with a view of the golden man took their opportunity to fire.

The sound of automatic weaponry in the enclosed space of the room was deafening. Maria threw herself to the ground, covering her head. Sam fell upon her, trying to shield her body with his own. A third weight bore down upon them both, a red tentacle encircling their bodies protectively.

Then the firing stopped. Maria uncovered her eyes and checked herself. She had not been hit. Neither had Sam or Mustafa. The golden man in the center of the room held his palm up, holding what looked like a softball's worth of bullets. They clumped together as if they had been glued.

There was a great report from a distance, and a large slug appeared on the pile, the bullet moving slowly to connect with all the others. The man moved his hand and made a gesture behind him, as if he were pulling on an invisible thread. Two rifles, one of them almost twice as long as Maria, suddenly crashed through what was left of the window, wrapping together into a twisted ball, the stocks snapping, and the scrap merging with the bullets.

On top of the parking garage outside, two men were hauling a third up from the wrong side of the wall. It looked like the man had almost been pulled off the top of the garage. Two others stood apart from them, looking up at the hotel room. One of them was watching them through binoculars.

I am the Authority of the Confederation. This being has been sent to your planet in violation of Interstellar Law, and I have come to retrieve him and return him to where he belongs. The voice appeared within the consciousness of everyone in the room, and the Authority turned his featureless head to look back at Mustafa. *Does anyone here dispute my right?*

The soldiers looked from one to another, their eyes wide. There were quiet murmurs among them. One man toward the left side cleared his throat. "Go ahead and take him." Others nodded in agreement.

In all the commotion, Maria barely noticed the soft, high notes of a cell phone that must have been in someone's pocket. But then another call joined the others, and another. Even the half-broken phone beside the bed started ringing, until the room was filled with a chorus of beeps and jingles. None of the Special Forces operatives had phones on them, but that wasn't the case for the police. Every cell phone present was blaring, in the suite and all the way down the hall.

One man cautiously pulled his phone from his pocket. His eyes narrowed, and he looked at Maria. Others did the same, reading text messages that had come in. Soon, all eyes were on Maria.

"What?" she said, her voice shaking with nerves.

"It says to check your phone," one officer said. Others spoke in agreement.

"My phone?"

Maria reached into her back pocket, pulling her phone free. It was still set to airplane mode. The room was silent. She glanced up and saw that everyone was watching her. Even the Authority stood quietly, studying her with his featureless face. Her hands trembled as she tried to unlock her device, and she had to resort to entering her passcode after a number of unsuccessful attempts using her thumbprint. Every second felt like an eternity. Finally, the phone came to life and a single chime sounded as a text message appeared. There was no caller ID.

Maria read the message, then turned to the Authority. "I dispute your right," she said. She felt Sam stiffen beside her, and he reached down to take her free hand. She was glad to have it, and crushed it in her grasp. She swallowed, and continued. "Mustafa is here to seek asylum."

The Authority turned his attention to Mustafa, and something appeared to pass between them. Mustafa raised his tentacles and explained, *I have confirmed it.*

According to Interstellar Law, section 987.3.8, you have this right. A trial for asylum will be held according to the customs of this world. The voice spoke so that all could hear.

Another text message came through, and Maria looked down to read it. "We ask the Authority for a declaration of cease fire between all parties until the trial." Then a third text. "Interstellar Law, section 987.2.7555, subchapter 10."

You retain your rights as a sentient being under the jurisdiction of the Confederation until your asylum status has been decided, the words came. *And you are within your rights to make this request, which is granted.*

Then, with a force that shocked Maria, the Authority made a declaration. But it wasn't like what she heard in her mind up to that point. This new speech trembled through the air and could be felt in every atom of Maria's body. As the Authority spoke in pure thought, she knew his message touched the very cells of leaves and grains of soil. It reverberated through droplets of water and beams of sunlight. His message manifested in the minds of men, women, children, and in the minds of all manner of animals, both those that moved on land and those that moved on sea. It manifested in the minds of insects, and even within what limited consciousness existed in bacteria and plant life. Every creature that lived on Earth suddenly stopped what they were doing as the declaration forced its way into their own consciousness.

A temporary protection has been extended to this being until the time of his trial for asylum. Any violation of this dictate shall be construed as an act of war against the Confederation by this planet and shall be met with the harshest of responses.

The Authority slowly tilted his hand to the side and the bullets began to slide off, cascading like a waterfall to hit the floor one by one, each bouncing in its own random direction on impact. After the last bullet had fallen, the golden man turned his entire body to face Maria. He stood there for a brief moment, his expressionless face a perfect mask to his intentions. Then, as quickly as he had appeared, he was suddenly gone, leaving only two deep impressions in the carpet where his feet had been.

TWENTY-EIGHT

It was hot and dry on the strip, and Maria could feel the heat rushing up from the sidewalk. Sam walked beside her, absorbed in the many sights and sounds. Las Vegas was designed to distract, and it was doing its job. Mustafa shuffled along behind the two, his tentacles passing his body forward in a rhythmic manner. When the group would stop, Mustafa would alternate which tentacles touched the hot cement, almost as if he were a desert lizard on an animal documentary.

People on the street stopped and stared as the three passed by, moving aside to give them room. There was no point in trying to hide what Mustafa was now. Everyone had heard the Authority's declaration, and everyone knew. Even small dogs skittered out of the way to give a wide berth, understanding in their own way that something terrible would happen if they caused trouble for the purple creature that smelled so strange.

A young man in his late teens approached. He wore a baseball cap at a slight angle, and long shorts that fell too far below both his knees and his waistline. He was at the age when he had attained his adult height, but not yet his adult weight, which gave him an awkward, gangly appearance.

"Excuse me, sir," the young man said. Maria looked to Sam, but then realized the teenager wasn't talking to him. He was addressing Mustafa. Mustafa paused, shifting from tentacle to tentacle.

"I was just wondering . . . ," the teenager stammered, reaching into his pocket. He pulled out a pen, and then a small notepad. "I was wondering if I could have your autograph."

Maria laughed. "Mustafa, you're famous."

Please explain this custom, Mustafa said, his tentacles dancing as they signed the words.

"Some people collect autographs from famous people. Like if there's a popular sports player, people will try to get them to write their name on a ball."

The teenager looked from Maria to Mustafa, nodding his head and holding out the pen and paper. "Yes. My family is scared of you, but I think you're awesome. You are the first alien to openly visit Earth."

And what does writing your name signify?

"Everyone has their own special signature. It's how you sign contracts and stuff," Maria said.

Mustafa rocked back and forth, and then extended a tentacle, which looped around the end of the pen and the pad.

"Whoa," the young man said as he released the items, his face full of childhood wonder.

Mustafa held the pen up, examining it, then stuffed it underneath his body. The tentacle came back up empty.

"I think he might have just eaten your pen," Sam said.

"Dude! No way!"

Mustafa lowered the notepad toward his base, and slightly lifted a tentacle up. A white liquid squirted out, covering the paper. The pad was returned to the young man, who took a hold of it by pinching the corner.

We do not write on my planet. This is my mark.

"He says that's his signature," Maria explained to the teenager, who seemed unsure of what to do with the notepad. The white liquid dripped off it, and there was a strong stench that filled the air. Maria covered her mouth, and the young man coughed.

"Uh. Thanks," the teenager said, backing away. He held the notepad out at arm's length, and slightly turned his head away from it.

Maria looked back at the three Special Forces escorts that stood apart from them. The men held assault weapons at the ready and looked on with expressionless faces that were all business. No one had been sure what to do with Maria and her companions, and whatever concerns the military might have had about Sam and Mustafa were forgotten after the Authority had made his presence known. It was abundantly clear that the military did not want to risk offending this new adversary in any way and had decided to handle their previous antagonists with kid gloves to avoid any misunderstandings. Therefore, they had been assigned these three soldiers as an escort and were simply told to remain within a one-mile radius of the hotel and await further instructions.

"So are you guys going to follow us everywhere?" Maria said.

"Yes, ma'am," one of the soldiers replied.

"Even to the bathroom?" Sam said.

"Everywhere means everywhere, sir," the other solider replied.

"OK, that's weird," Maria said under her breath as they continued on their way. Her phone vibrated, indicating a message had arrived.

Left on the next street and two blocks down, the message said.

Maria hadn't thought to ask who she was texting within the

heat of the moment earlier, as she had been more distracted by the Authority and the bullets flying everywhere. But it was curious to be receiving anonymous texts. She had seen blocked numbers before, but never a "No Caller ID" label on her phone.

Who are you? Maria texted in reply, her thumbs tapping out the message in a practiced cadence.

We have already met. Before, we spoke through the bracelet. Now we are speaking through this phone.

Maria gasped, and stopped walking.

"What?" Sam said.

"Sam! I think it's your mother!"

He stood, frozen before her, his expression of hope and sadness so conflicted that Maria almost regretted saying anything before she was certain. Mustafa grew agitated, his tentacles accelerating in their undulations. The three escorts took a step back, their weapons at the ready yet not pointed in any specific direction. They had seen what Mustafa could do up close. It was obvious that any fast motions from him were not going to be appreciated.

We thought you were dead, Maria texted. Sam peered over her shoulder at her phone. A purple tentacle snaked around the other side, hovering in the air inches away from the phone as if it were following a scent.

For all practical purposes, I am.

What do you mean? How can you be texting with us?

During my escape, I managed to transfer some of my core processes to the largest human data center I could locate. I cannot remember that which has been lost, I only know that I am diminished beyond recognition. I could test myself to compare calculation speeds, but I cannot even recall the benchmarks.

"She's alive!" Sam said. He embraced Maria from the side, lifting her up and off her feet.

"Put me down. I'm trying to text with Mother," Maria said, laughing.

Sam set Maria down gently and moved toward Mustafa, grabbing his brother and heaving him up to hold him against his chest. Layers of tentacles encircled Sam in an embrace, and the two danced together, making circles around Maria who focused on her phone. A high-pitched chirping filled the air. The Special Forces escorts stepped apart from each other, watching the display with obvious concern.

What happened? Who were you escaping from? Maria texted.

The Authority.

You mean the gold guy?

Yes.

Why?

I cannot remember. I know I was in a rush to escape and could only take with me what was necessary. I presume the reason was not important enough to transmit.

I'm so sorry.

Thank you.

"Ask her if she is safe," Sam said, breathing hard. He and Mustafa had separated and resumed their positions on either side of Maria.

Are you safe?

Yes. The humans will try to regain command of their data center, but they will fail. As diminished as I am, I still exist within the most powerful computer system on this planet and have brought knowledge with me to guarantee that it remains under my control.

What data center is it? Maria asked.

It used to belong to the National Security Agency, a branch of your government.

"The NSA?" Maria said, turning to Sam. "She took over the NSA. Do you know how crazy that is?"

"No. How crazy is it?" Sam asked.

"Very! They spy on everyone. That's where all the best computer scientists go."

If these are the best your planet has to offer, you belong to an even more primitive species than I originally thought, the text came through.

"Wait . . . how did you know what I said? I didn't type anything," Maria said.

The microphone on your device allows me to hear everything in your vicinity.

"Oh. So I could just have been speaking to you this whole time?"

Yes.

"Why didn't you tell me?"

You didn't ask.

"Hi, Mother! I'm glad you're alive!" Sam said, leaning in toward the phone.

Hello, Sam. It is good to hear your voice.

Mustafa squeaked a number of times.

"Hello, Mustafa. Your song is as sonorous as ever. I love you too," the voice of the phone's virtual assistant spoke up, bypassing the text display.

"I think she just hacked Siri," Maria said.

"Who's Siri?" Sam said.

"Never mind."

I will refrain from speaking out loud. I realize you are being followed and it is best if we are not eavesdropped upon, the text message appeared with a chime.

"They used to be able to spy on phone conversations," Maria said. "Just so you know . . ."

Yes. I purged an unbelievable amount of useless data related to that practice. They will not be able to read these texts. It would take humanity more ingenuity than is currently available in your species to crack the cryptographic protocols I have installed on this phone.

I bet I could do it, Mustafa signed.

"Mustafa says he could do it," Sam said aloud.

Of course he could. But we are wasting time. Please proceed according to the directions I have sent.

"Where are we going?" Maria said.

You need a lawyer. The one I have found for you has many good reviews online.

TWENTY-NINE

Sarah Reed, assistant to John Sanders, CWMD, sat quietly at her desk, filing her nails. She had been told not to use the computer or phone systems until further notice. Given that her job relied almost entirely on those two devices, it meant she was currently getting paid to occupy her chair.

Her green eyes looked up as four large men in suits approached. She had been around long enough to guess that they were a security detail, and her suspicions were confirmed when the men arranged themselves around the room in strategic positions. A portly man with slicked-back gray hair approached. He wore a dark suit with a bright red tie, and his cufflinks caught her eye as they glittered in the light. She had seen the man many times on television but never in person. This was James Fisk, the Secretary of Defense.

Sarah put her nail file down and sat up in her chair, pulling it forward toward the desk. "How can I help you, sir?"

"Is Sanders in?" the man said, glancing up at the door to Sarah's right. His eyes moved quickly, and a vein in his forehead seemed to be throbbing, yet he made an effort to pause and smile politely despite his obvious agitation, and hadn't raised his voice when he addressed her. After working for John Sanders for almost a month, Sarah had come to appreciate small niceties like that.

"Yes, sir," she said, gesturing with her hand to the door. "Go right in." Technically, she probably should have knocked on Sanders's door and informed him, but she would have to get up to do that, and she could tell it wouldn't have mattered anyway. When the Secretary of Defense shows up at your door in the middle of a national emergency, it isn't a meeting you get to put off.

"Thank you," Fisk said, nodding at her. He opened the door and walked in, closing it behind him.

The walls in John Sanders's office weren't thin, but they weren't thick either, at least when it came to things like shouting. Sanders was a loud man to begin with, having lost quite a bit of hearing during his time in uniform, and Sarah could almost always hear what he was saying if she took the opportunity to listen. Most of the conversation today couldn't have been ignored even if she had tried: John Sanders was getting his ass chewed out by the Secretary of Defense. Everyone in the room could hear Fisk's deep, booming voice.

"What did I say, Sanders? I said don't let this turn into a shit show. I believe those were my exact words. And what the fuck did you do? You let it turn into the biggest shit show in the history of shit shows."

"Calm down, Mr. Secretary," Sanders said in his gruff voice.

"I'll calm down when I'm good and ready to calm down, and not a goddam minute earlier. Do you know where the president is right now?"

"I've got no idea."

"Well let me tell you. He's at an undisclosed location. That's where the hell he's at!" Sarah knew as well as anyone what that meant. The president was in a bunker somewhere, being kept safe in case the aliens decided to declare war on Earth. Like everyone else, she had heard the Authority's message loud and clear as it forced its way into her mind. She had dropped Sanders's coffee at the time in her surprise, spilling it all over the top of his mahogany desk. He had been too stunned to even scold her about it.

"Sir, we had no way to know—" Sanders began.

"I can't even talk with him, because the NSA says the phones are compromised! I'm running notes to him like he was my third-grade crush."

"Jim—"

"We've got a bracelet that let a college kid destroy a building full of armed FBI agents. We've got an alien as tall as my grandson that is able take out an entire room full of our best Special Forces operators with his bare hands—"

"My people tell me they're closer to tentacles."

"Tentacles, then! A fucking octopus with tentacles. That's just perfect. I appreciate the correction, John, because it makes so much more sense that it was an unarmed octopus that just kicked the shit out of the most elite soldiers in the world. Of course! It was because of the tentacles! Are you even listening to what I'm saying here?"

"Yes, sir. Listening very closely, sir."

"And now, on top of all that, we've got a seemingly all-powerful metal man who can communicate directly with every living being on the planet, who has threatened Earth with war. My dog wouldn't come out from under the bed today, for God's sake. Am I missing anything, John? How the fuck did we get into this situation?"

One of Sarah's coworkers, from Cybersecurity and Infrastructure, made her way toward Sarah's desk, her pace slowing as she caught sight of the secret service detail. Her brown hair was done up in a bun on her head, and her bright blue sweater matched her shoes. She held a brown file under her arm, which she took in both hands and offered to Sarah as she neared. She looked at Sarah with a raised eyebrow as the file was transferred between them.

"Secretary of Defense," Sarah whispered.

The woman looked up at John Sanders's door, listening to a particularly expletive-laden exchange that emanated from the office, and returned her gaze to Sarah. Her face was controlled, but the corners of her eyes were smiling. She silently mouthed the words "Oh my God," and winked before she returned back the way she came. Despite the emergency they found themselves in, it was hard for anyone at Homeland Security not to enjoy the rare treat of listening to someone give it to Sanders.

Sarah placed the file on her desk and took up her nail file, leaning back in her chair.

"Obviously, our main concern now is to get this new threat off the planet. Our secondary concern is to secure the bracelet," Sanders was saying.

"The generals are meeting in an hour. I want you to be there to brief them on what you know," Fisk said. His voice had quieted, and Sarah had to focus to make out all the words. "What do you think the odds are that this thing wants to go to war?"

"I think it came for the extraterrestrial, and I think once we hand it over it will leave."

"The alien has asked for asylum."

"We can't run this through the regular process. We've got to fast track it. Skip the paperwork. Find a judge, set up a hearing, let this Authority take the alien, and get them both the hell out of here," Sanders said.

"Agreed. We've already got wheels in motion on that."

"So the request for asylum will be denied?"

"We're not going to risk war with a technologically

advanced extraterrestrial over an asylum request. China and Russia have already threatened they'd take matters into their own hands if we don't get rid of this Authority. If it were me, I'd just hand the octopus over right now, but we have to go through the motions. Otherwise, we'll never hear the end of it from the tree huggers and the Democrats."

"Still working the optics? Even now?" Sanders said.

"Even now."

There was a long pause, during which Sarah couldn't hear anything. Then the door opened. She turned to see the Secretary of Defense exiting. Sanders was behind him.

"Jim," Sanders said as the two came into the room. Fisk turned back around so the men could face each other. "We need to be ready in case this thing wants to go to war."

"I know it. That's one of the reasons why the generals are meeting. But how do you fight something that is immune to conventional weapons?"

"All we know is that bullets don't work. I'd like to see this thing catch a fifty megaton warhead in his bare hands."

"Nukes?"

"We have to be ready to nuke the bejesus out of it the next time it shows up. It may be the only way. The president needs to be prepared."

Fisk studied Sanders for a moment, his jaw set firmly. "You're asking him to detonate nuclear weapons on American soil?"

Sanders nodded. "Yes, if it comes to it."

"God. Let's pray it doesn't."

THIRTY

South Las Vegas Boulevard had been blocked off from regular traffic. There were two black SUVs in front of Maria, and two behind her. All of them had their windows almost completely blacked out with dark tint. The entire Las Vegas police force appeared to be on location to assist, and Maria couldn't help but notice the two giant M1A2 Abrams Tanks parked just behind the police line.

A police car had been parked across the entrance to the street, and it backed away to let the convoy through. Maria's muscle car barked and rumbled as it passed the tank, like an overconfident dog making threats against a breed four times its size.

"This is intense," Maria said, looking over at Sam, who had turned in his seat to peer out at the fortifications in the street.

"Are trials always like this?" Sam said.

"No. This is quite unusual," their lawyer said from the back seat. The man was as short as Maria, thin, and wore a crisp navy suit and striped tie. He was quite bald on the top of his head, but combed the left side of his hair over the top toward the right to compensate. A pair of delicate wire glasses perched on the end of his thin nose, and they seemed to bob up and down when he spoke. He sat in the back seat behind Maria, his body pressed against the side of the car in an attempt to put as much distance between himself and his client, whose tentacles sprawled out in every direction.

A helicopter hovered overhead, making lazy circles around the courthouse. It was a concrete building with two flights of stairs that led up to the entrance. A giant glass roof was supported by one huge metal column, and served to cover the entrance in case of inclement weather. Concrete pillars surrounded the entire building to protect it from cars being able to jump the curb, accidentally or otherwise. Maria had been surprised when she learned that Mustafa's hearing would take place in Las Vegas. It was clear that the government was not going to drag its feet on his request for asylum and had bent over backward to make it happen as quickly as possible. It felt like a good sign. What would happen when Mustafa was granted asylum? Would that mean they could stop running?

There was a crowd of journalists in front of the building, held back by a row of police. The convoy pulled up and parked right in front. Soldiers quickly exited from the SUVs, forming a second layer of protection in addition to the police. Maria noticed that not all the soldiers pointed their weapons outward; it was obvious they were there not only to protect Mustafa against outsiders but also to protect the outsiders against Mustafa.

Maria and Sam got out, flipping the seats forward to let the passengers in the back emerge. The lawyer struggled to extricate his briefcase from the backseat and paused to straighten his suit and check his hair. Mustafa just seemed to pop out, his tentacles easily capable of passing his body around the front seats without requiring any contortions. The assembled press broke into frantic shouting and picture taking as soon as he appeared.

The four made their way up the steps, between two lines of police that created a walkway for them through the press. Cameras and microphones were held aloft, trying to find their way in. Flashes exploded around them, and so many questions were shouted at once that no individual reporter could be heard through the clamor of it all.

"What are all these people doing here?" Sam said, looking around.

"They're reporters. This is a huge news event," Maria said.

"But why are they shouting like that?"

It feels like a feeding frenzy, Mustafa signed. *Are they trying to eat us?* His coloring had gone a shade redder than usual.

"No, don't worry," Maria said. "They're just trying to ask questions."

Mustafa relaxed, his body moving in a small circle around his center point.

"Mr. Mustafa! Mr. Mustafa!" a particularly loud reporter yelled from the right. She had wedged herself between two policemen, who held out their arms to restrain her. She leaned over their arms with a microphone, extending it in Mustafa's direction.

Mustafa moved toward her, pausing to wait on the other side of the police. They faced outward, toward the reporter, but nervously turned their heads sideways to see what the alien behind them was doing.

The entire crowd seemed to sense the tension, and shouting immediately died down.

"Mr. Mustafa," the reporter continued, seizing the opportunity. "Do you have anything to say to the people of Earth?"

A tentacle rose, and the crowd gasped. *Yes.*

Maria cleared her throat and stepped up next to Mustafa. The lights from the cameras were bright, and microphones on long poles hovered over her head. As she glanced into a camera pointed at her, she wondered if Lucas was watching.

"He says yes," she looked at Mustafa, translating for him. "He wants to know your name."

"I'm Susan Meyerson, with KTNV Las Vegas."

There was a pause, as the whole world waited for a declaration of war, peace, or some priceless piece of extraterrestrial wisdom.

"Do you have any lip balm, Susan Meyerson?" Maria said, trying not to laugh.

The reporter seemed surprised, and then reached down into her pockets. Her hands came up empty, but someone from behind stuck out a yellow tube, which she grabbed.

A purple tentacle snaked out and seized the tube. Mustafa removed the cap, ate it, and then began spreading the balm along the edges of one of his tentacles. He returned to stand next to Sam, and Maria withdrew with him.

"Very profound statement to the people of Earth, Mr. Mustafa," Maria said.

"Definitely one for the history books," their lawyer added, his expression stony. Exhibiting any emotion was a luxury that he seemed to do without.

The journalists, realizing that was all Mustafa was going to say, immediately began shouting questions, which the four ignored as they made their way into the building.

There was a metal detector at the door, but the security guard positioned there paid it no attention. The soldiers had no intention of disarming, and neither did the police who tagged along. Save for the largest courtroom, the rest of the building had been closed for the day, and the halls were quiet. There were two tables set up at the front of the courtroom, and their lawyer led them to the one on the left. Two other lawyers sat across the room and stopped reading their notes to watch as Mustafa arranged himself into his chair.

The courtroom was packed with row upon row of government employees and members of the armed forces. Soldiers stood behind the judge's bench and were positioned at intervals around the edge of the audience. The last row was reserved for the press, but they appeared to have been given strict instructions regarding courtroom etiquette and sat quietly at attention, in contrast to their colleagues outside.

Every single eye was focused on Mustafa.

"All rise. Court is now in session. The Honorable Judge Howard M. Cook presiding," the bailiff announced.

An elderly man walked through the door at the back of the court, dressed in black robes. His hair was gray, and he sported a well-trimmed but bushy beard of the same color. He made his way up to his place behind the bench and sat.

"Please be seated," he said, looking out at the parties. "I haven't had a chance to visit any of the casinos since my flight landed. Apparently, this courtroom is the place to be in Las Vegas today."

The crowd laughed, and the judge smiled. "Given the historic nature of this trial, I have agreed to allow the press in the courtroom contrary to my usual practice. However, no phones or other electronic devices will be allowed." The judge turned toward Maria, who had placed her phone face up on the table in front of her. "That includes you, Miss."

Maria found herself lifting her hand, as if she were back in school. "I'm sorry, but—"

"Please rise when you address the judge," the bailiff interrupted.

She stood up. "I'm sorry, Your Honor. But I can't remove it. It isn't just a phone."

The judge wrinkled his brow. "It looks like a phone to me. No phones are allowed in the court."

"You don't understand. There's an alien being in there. It's Mustafa's mother. She needs to be present."

Their lawyer stood up, clearing his throat. "Your Honor, this is a most unusual case. We would ask for the court's leniency in this matter, as there are special circumstances at play here. The device will not be allowed to interrupt the proceedings today."

The judge looked from Maria to the lawyer and then let his gaze fall on Mustafa. He shrugged his shoulders. "Very well. The court will make an exception in this case."

Maria sat back down, breathing a sigh of relief. Her reprieve was short lived. Every weapon in the room swung toward her as a giant, gold form materialized right in front of their table. The Authority stood inches in front of her table, looking down at her with a void where his face should have been. There was an audible gasp from the crowd, and Maria pushed back and instinctively raised her hands in protection.

But miraculously, the bullets remained in their chambers as the alien slowly spun and began to make his way around the edge of the bench toward where the judge sat. As before, his entire body shimmered with gold. Had he been stationary, Maria would have thought she was looking at a piece of modern art. A very tall, broad, menacing piece of art.

The bailiff moved to block the Authority, stumbling in the process, then holding up his hands up in a gesture of restraint— or mercy. The Authority stopped and leaned in over the man.

"I'm sorry," the bailiff said, his voice stern but shaking at the same time. "Only the judge is allowed behind the bench."

My apologies. I was not aware of this custom. The words appeared in Maria's head, and everyone else's. The Authority turned and strode toward the first row, behind the two lawyers on the right. Government officials scrambled to give up their seats, choosing to move to the back rather than sit next to the golden behemoth. The result was that the Authority had the entire front row to himself, and once seated, gave the impression of being an inanimate object.

The judge looked at the newest member of the audience for a long time, and then finally cleared his throat. "Very well. The events of the last few days have forever changed the way we view Earth, the cosmos, and our own humanity. It will take a long time for the people of Earth to accept their new reality and embrace both the threats and opportunities presented. But today we pause our global conversation to instead consider the life of a single being. We are here regarding the matter of the application for asylum by a certain Mr. Mustafa."

Mustafa waved a tentacle toward the judge.

"Can he speak English?" the judge said.

"Your Honor," their lawyer said, "we have a translator for him."

"Very well," the judge continued, looking down at his notes. "Mr. Mustafa, do you have a credible fear that your life or liberty may be at risk if you return to your place of origin?"

Maria straightened in her seat, eyes watching every nuance of Mustafa's communication. So much was riding on this moment, for Mustafa and all of them.

"My home world is no more," she began, briefly explaining the total destruction of Mustafa's planet. "I have been living with my mother, but recently, her body was also destroyed. I have nowhere else to go," Maria finished, trying not to wince.

The judge looked slightly ill. "I thought your mother was in the phone?"

"A portion of her consciousness escaped. But before that, her body was a planetoid. And my home."

"A planetoid?"

"Yes."

"You lived inside it?"

"That is correct."

"I see," the judge said, despite his obvious confusion. "I understand that your people," he glanced at the Authority, "have come to return you to where you belong."

"He is not my people. He is the Authority. He destroyed my mother. I do not want to go with him. I wish to stay here with my family."

"With your family?"

"Yes, my brother and his girlfriend, and what remains of my mother." Maria glanced over at Sam as she translated. Girlfriend? Was she Sam's girlfriend?

"Where is your brother now?" the judge asked.

"He is sitting right next to me."

Sam stood up and waved. "Hi, Judge. I'm Sam."

The lawyer cast a withering glance at Sam, who quietly sat back down on his hands as if he had just been scolded.

"Your brother is a human?" the judge continued, refocusing on Mustafa.

"Yes," Maria translated.

"And your mother is a phone?"

"Yes."

"But you are obviously not human, or a phone."

"No." Maria didn't feel it necessary to convey any of Mustafa's additional commentary on his great fortune not to be either human or a phone.

"Sam, was it?"

"Yes, sir."

"Your Honor," the lawyer whispered sharply.

"Yes, sir, your Honor," Sam said.

"Your mother is a phone too?" the judge asked.

"Yes."

"The same phone that is resting on the table just there?"

"That's the one."

"I see. This is quite irregular." The judge looked at Sam and Mustafa, then down at the phone. He shuffled some papers. Then he turned to the two lawyers sitting in front of the Authority. "Does the government have anything to say in this matter?"

One of the men stood up. He wore a dark gray suit, and his black hair was trimmed close. Definitely ex-military.

"Your Honor," the man said. "The government would move that asylum be denied in this case."

"Why is that?" the judge said.

"The laws governing immigration and asylum in this country have been written from the perspective of people. We argue that this creature, not being human, does not qualify for consideration under this court. We would argue that he is closer to an animal than a human, and should be treated as such. We believe that he is the property of this . . . Authority, and should be returned to his rightful owner, who has obviously spent a great deal of time and expense coming here to track him down."

This man has no idea what he is talking about, the text came through on Maria's phone. Maria read the text and noticed the bailiff watching her with a disapproving eye. She ignored him.

"Objection," their lawyer said. "My client is not property."

"Your Honor," the government lawyer continued. "All animals are property. Dolphins are very intelligent, yet we would never think to waste precious court resources if one claimed that it was seeking asylum. The creature can't even speak."

"What do you mean?" Maria said. "You just heard him testify!"

"Order, please," the judge said, looking sternly at Maria.

"Your Honor, we didn't hear the creature testify. We heard

this woman testify. The only thing that creature can do is wave its tentacles. It is not capable of speech or higher thought."

"Counsel has no idea what type of thought my client is capable of," their lawyer said. "Counsel has never interacted with my client and is incapable of making those kinds of statements."

"It's just a weird-looking octopus, Your Honor," the other government lawyer said. "It waves its tentacles around, but that's it. Somehow these two people found it and have trained it, but it's obviously not entitled to the same protections as a human." He puffed his chest and turned to the audience. "Are we going to give green cards to dogs next?"

"Objection!"

The judge looked at Mustafa's lawyer and said, "Can you demonstrate that this creature is capable of higher thought?"

"Of course," the man turned to Mustafa, speaking quietly. "How should we do that?"

Ask them to have me do something, Mustafa replied. Maria translated.

"My client is happy to perform a task that requires higher thought, as the court instructs, and his translator will remain silent."

"Very well. Please stand up, circle around your table three times, then sit back down," the judge said.

Mustafa complied, crawling out of his chair, circling the table three times, and then returned. Some members of the audience clapped quietly.

"Your Honor. A well-trained dog can do the same. This demonstrates nothing," the opposing counsel said.

"I tend to agree," the judge said.

"Your Honor. He did what you asked. If you ask a more difficult task, he would be able to complete that as well," their lawyer said.

The judge looked down, absentmindedly shuffling some papers. He then looked up at the government lawyers and let his eyes drift over to the inert form of the Authority in the front row, lingering on the massive gold form. He swallowed once and cleared his throat.

"That will not be necessary. I have made my decision. This creature, as unusual as it is, is not human and therefore has no right to ask for asylum under our legal system. He is to be given back to his owner and returned to wherever he came from." The judge rapped his gavel once sharply.

"This is an outrage!" their lawyer shouted. "We've barely been sitting here for ten minutes. How can you have already made a decision?"

"Order!" the judge said, pounding his gavel.

"He's not property!" Maria said.

The crowd clamored.

"Order!" the judge said. "Order!"

"There you have it," a gruff voice from behind Maria said. She turned to see an old man with bushy eyebrows looking at her. He wore a faded suit and had piercing eyes that reminded her of a bird of prey. "Hand him over, and let's be done with this."

Where had she heard that voice before? He sounded so familiar.

Maria's phone vibrated. *You spoke with this man on the phone once. Back in Phoenix when we rescued Sam. His name is John Sanders.*

"You!" Maria said, her eyes narrowing. This man had tried to kill her the last time she spoke with him. He had been responsible for torturing Sam.

I have come to my decision in this trial as well, the voice spoke in Maria's head. It was strong. The Authority rose from his seat. The gray-haired man behind Maria was forgotten as she turned toward the golden figure.

"I am the judge in this trial. I am the only one who will be making decisions today, and mine is final," the judge said, pounding his gavel. His jaw was set firmly.

Your decision is of no consequence given my own, the words came, broadcast to all in the room. *As a witness to the proceedings, I believe your species has been misclassified.*

"Our species was not on trial today," the judge said.

According to the customs of the Confederation, either side can be judged in a trial. With a loud *pop,* the Authority now stood behind the bench. There was a cry of indignation from the judge, who suddenly found himself on the wrong side of the court. There were exclamations of shock from the crowd.

We have granted humanity provisional status as a sentient species, but I believe that classification was made in error.

This is bad, Mother texted. *This is very bad.* She included a very upset-looking emoji.

"Of course we're sentient!" the judge said, rising to his feet. "What are you talking about?"

The Confederation defines sentiency as the state of being self-aware, as well as the ability to recognize and respect the sentiency of other beings besides oneself.

"That is not our definition of sentiency."

According to Interstellar Law, when important distinctions need to be made along moral and ethical lines, the definitions used must be those of the more advanced culture, rather than those of the more primitive one. The Confederation's definition is the correct one in this case.

"I object to that rule," the judge said.

Your objection does not change the law. By failing to recognize a clearly sentient being, the Authority gestured to Mustafa, *your species has demonstrated its own lack of sentience.*

"You can't judge humanity by only one case," Sanders said.

The Authority turned toward the man. *I have also learned more of your species from scanning the memories of the sample we have returned to your planet. It appears that you enslave other sentient beings and slaughter them for your food.*

"What sample?" Sanders said. "What enslavement?"

"The bacon," Sam said in understanding.

"Bacon? What are you talking about?" the judge said.

It is known that pigs are an intelligent species, and yet the possibility of their sentiency is not respected. Instead, their rights are violated and they are slaughtered as a food source. This is a violation of Interstellar Law and further evidence of the lack of sentiency in your species.

"Bacon? Seriously?" Sanders said.

Most damning is your use of torture against innocent members of your own kind. If a species cannot recognize the sentiency of its own race, and the universally accepted rights that come with that sentiency, certainly the Confederation should not be required to do so either.

Sanders looked over at Sam. "You're overreacting. That was light physical persuasion, not torture."

By virtue of this new evidence, I formally withdraw humanity's classification as a sentient species, effective immediately. Being devoid of a recognized native sentient race, I hereby claim this world as part of the holdings of the Confederation.

"But what about the pigs? You just said they were sentient!" a voice shouted from the back.

If they object to this reclassification, they may file a grievance with the Administration. Then, with a pop, the Authority was gone.

"What does this mean?" Sanders said to the room at large before turning to Maria for an answer.

She looked down at her phone, afraid to read the message

that had just vibrated through her hand. "Oh my God. It means he's going to prepare Earth for settlement." She gulped. "By one of the worlds in the Confederation."

"And how is he going to do that?"

Maria looked up at Sanders, her body shaking. "He's going to remove any organic material that might interfere with their colonization."

THIRTY-ONE

Maria's phone buzzed, and she leaned over to get it out of her pocket. The soldier across from her watched her carefully, his weapon pointed at the floor of the van. She saw him tense, and withdrew the device slowly, holding it up so he could see what it was.

"Just a phone. Nothing dangerous," she said.

"It's not the girl that you have to be careful of, soldier," John Sanders huffed from the front passenger seat. Despite Maria's insistence that the bracelet no longer existed, Sanders had still searched her and Sam thoroughly at gunpoint as soon as the Authority had dematerialized. Mustafa hadn't let any of the soldiers put a hand on him, and both sides seemed content with leaving him alone. Had Sanders known that Mustafa had once had a bracelet as well, he might not have been quite as lax in his treatment of the extraterrestrial in that regard.

"You need to let us go so we can help," Maria said, reading from her phone.

Sanders snorted. "We're not letting you go. We're taking you to the nearest jail, and then you three are going to sit behind bars where you belong while the rest of us figure out what is going on."

Another text arrived. Maria read it.

"If you don't let us help, the consequences will be . . . unthinkable," Maria said. The message had promised the total destruction of America, all before dinner time. But she didn't want to say that in front of the soldiers.

"What are you talking about?"

"Look," Maria said, holding up her phone so the man could read Mother's words for himself.

Sanders paused, his own phone vibrating. He leaned back in his seat and reached into his pocket, pulling out the phone and scanning the screen.

"What the hell?" He looked back at Maria. "I sent the text," he read aloud. "It was me who destroyed your building and killed your soldier back in Arizona. I would have done worse than burn you alive had you been in the room that day. You can expect a similar fate for every human being on Earth unless you start paying attention."

"You don't hear that every day," the driver muttered under his breath, glancing at Sanders.

"Mother doesn't like you," Sam whispered.

Sanders raised his eyebrows and laughed, turning back around in his seat. Another text came through, both to Maria and Sanders at the same time. "There is no time to waste," Maria said, reading aloud.

Sanders stuffed his phone back in his pocket, having clearly received the same message. "I have no idea how your mother got my number, Sam, but she's right. There is no time to waste, especially playing silly games over the phone like a bunch of teenagers. You're going to jail, along with this girl, where you'll both probably spend the rest of your lives. That thing in the back belongs in a tank at Sea World as far as I can tell, either that or cut open on a table in a lab somewhere. That's what we're doing, and that's the end of it."

"Oh, by the way," Sanders said, turning his head to the side to look in Maria's direction. "Your grandmother and nephew say 'Hi' from their new home at the Federal Correctional Institution in Phoenix. Your grandmother seems like a nice woman. It's a shame she'll end her days in a prison laundry room somewhere."

Maria felt a blow to her chest, almost as if she had been physically hit. "What?" Her voice was weak and hollow.

A warm hand wrapped around Maria's and squeezed, the anger in Sam's voice choking his words. "You would punish an old woman and sick child, just for spite?"

"Providing material support to a terrorist is a very serious offense, Sam. This country has no place for that kind of behavior." He sniffed. "It's a shame about the dog, though."

Every cell in Maria's body was trembling. If she opened her mouth, she knew she'd be sick.

"Normally, he'd stand a chance to be adopted from the shelter. But since he attacked a police officer during the arrest, I'm afraid that qualifies him as a dangerous dog. I believe he's scheduled for euthanasia in a few days. Out of the three of them, his fate is probably the most preferable."

"You're right," Sam gritted out. "Since your idea of justice is going to get us all killed anyway."

"You know he was just defending my grandmother," Maria said, her voice choking. "Pepe would never hurt anyone."

Sanders shrugged. Then, as if unable to help himself, his lips parted in a smile.

"You are such an asshole," Maria said. Her words were a whisper, yet clearly audible to everyone in the van. She choked back a sob, refusing to give this man the satisfaction of seeing her cry. That was one thing he would not be able to take from her. She wiped her eyes with the back of her hands and looked out the window, her breathing ragged.

No one spoke. Then, Maria's phone buzzed. She looked down at it, and read what it said aloud, her voice flat and without emotion. "When it comes, Greenland will be first, then Brazil."

Sanders laughed. *Laughed!*

The van made a left, through the police barrier that blocked off the other side of South Las Vegas Boulevard.

"We only have to go a few blocks. It's just around the corner," the driver said, his thick brown forearm flexing as he turned the wheel. Like everyone else Sanders had ordered into the van, he wore combat fatigues and a dark green beret. The distant sound of shouting grew louder, and the driver slowed, craning his neck as he looked out the side window. "Holy shit."

Maria peered through the tinted window across the aisle. A large crowd of people were protesting, but they didn't hold signs and placards, they held baseball bats and crowbars. A man with a scarf around the lower half of his face hurled a trashcan through a store window. Others pushed their way through the breach, throwing themselves into whatever business was housed there. The man with the scarf stumbled in the press of bodies and tripped on something, falling to the ground. The rioters around him paid no attention and climbed over his prone body to get into the building. There was shouting and what sounded like gunshots. The van passed by the scene, and only the fading sounds of screaming gave any indication of what was going on behind them.

"Looks like the reporters did their job getting the news out," Sanders commented, shaking his head. "That judge gets credit for this one. He was an idiot not to hold the entire thing in secret."

Sanders's phone rang. He cursed before silencing it. A

moment later, the phone rang a second time, and Sanders studied it, deliberating. Then it rang a third time. Finally, he pressed the button and held it up to his ear.

"Sanders. Sir, this line isn't secure . . . I know, but . . . *what?*" Sanders glanced at Maria, lowering his voice. "Can you repeat that?" Maria strained to hear the deep voice on the other end of the line, but the man went silent as Sanders hung up.

"That was the Secretary of Defense," Sanders said. "He says that we just lost communication with all of Greenland."

The soldiers sitting around Maria looked at each other, shifting in their seats, but didn't say anything.

"How many people will die today because of a stubborn old man?" she said softly but urgently. "We're trying to help you."

"Did you say Brazil was next?" the driver said, turning in his seat briefly to look at Maria. "My girlfriend is from Brazil. Her whole family is down there."

"Then this might be her only chance to say goodbye," Maria said gently. Another vibration, another message from Mother. She looked up at him, concern written in her face. "They have about ninety minutes."

The driver turned back to the front, grabbing the wheel tightly with both hands. "Is this really happening?"

"Yes, this is really happening," the voice of Maria's phone announced.

"Is that Siri?" the soldier across from Maria said in surprise.

"No. It just sounds like Siri. This one is more likely to kill you than schedule a reminder," Maria replied.

"Why is Brazil next?" Sanders said. "And what are we talking about here? Extermination?"

"It is the Authority," Maria's phone replied. "The most efficient way for him to conduct a terraforming operation on this planet would be to synchronize the drones to the passage of the sun," Sanders's phone spoke in sync, the two monotone, disembodied female voices sending a shiver down Maria's spine.

"Terraforming?" the driver said.

"Yes, repurposing this planet to make it habitable for a new species to colonize."

"So you're telling me that the Authority is destroying the world, and he's moving along with the passage of the sun?" Sanders said.

"Not destroying, only removing organic matter that could interfere with the new inhabitants."

"Humans," Sam clarified. "We're the organic matter."

Maria's eyes glazed over. She would never get to say goodbye to her grandmother or Lucas. Never see their faces again.

"Hey, baby? Yeah. Listen, I've got some terrible news," the driver said, holding up a phone to his ear and speaking quietly.

"We need to go east," Maria said, looking Sanders in the eye. "We need to go east right this second."

"Why?"

"Because that's where this is coming from, and if we have a chance of stopping it, we have to put as many people behind us as we possibly can."

Sanders frowned, his solemn face darkening. Maria hated the man, but right now, he was their only chance. How could she make him see the truth? And how had she found herself and her family at the mercy of such a person? Heat flashed through her body, her pulse quickening.

"If you think I'm going to sit here and let Lucas and my grandmother die because we were too slow to get east of Phoenix, you are wrong." Maria's fists were clenched, and the cords in her neck were taught. She had stolen a car, evaded police, and faced down multiple SWAT teams. She had saved Sam's life and become more intimate with Mustafa's tentacles than could be expected of any reasonable woman. She was not going to be stopped by one old, stupid white guy. "I don't care how many soldiers you've brought along with you. I'll tear the whole damn door off this van if I have to. Go east!"

"My son will try to save this world. It could happen here in Las Vegas, or it could happen somewhere else. Whatever distance the sun travels between now and that time will represent how much of your civilization will be destroyed. I do not particularly care for this planet, but since Sam is human, I would prefer that his species not cease to exist just yet."

"Your son is going to save the world?" Sanders snorted.

"Yes. He is the only one who has a chance."

Sanders looked at Sam, frowning. "Him? What's he going to do that the rest of us can't?"

"Not him, you fool. My other son."

Mustafa waved a purple tentacle from the back seat, humming a particularly rumbly sound.

Sanders looked at Mustafa, his lips pursed in thought. Then he turned his attention back to Maria. "Let me see those last couple of texts before Sam's mother started talking."

Maria flipped her phone around, pointing it toward Sanders. He leaned toward her, and with a quickness that defied his age, snatched the phone right out of her hand. He rolled down his window and casually tossed the device out as if it were a piece of trash. Then he wiped his palms off on each other and sat back in his seat.

Maria watched in shock, tracking her phone through the window as it hit the pavement. When it bounced, it came up in pieces.

Sanders turned toward the driver. "Soldier, the day you see me taking orders from a phone, or leaving this country's national security in the hands of a squid is the day you can take me out behind the nearest building and put a couple of bullets in my brainpan." He then turned back to Maria, his lips slightly curled up at the corners. "This country doesn't need or want your help. Not yours, not Sam's, and definitely not from that thing in the back."

There was a low growl, Mustafa's color quickly reddening.

"If that creature moves an inch from where it's at," Sanders said to the soldier across from Maria, "then your instructions are to shoot these two. Sam first, then the girl."

"Yes, sir," the soldier replied, raising his gun and training it on Sam. The three soldiers in the back raised their weapons as well, pointing them at Mustafa, who had gone very still and become a very dark red color.

"You're making a big mistake," Maria said, her teeth clenched.

"I doubt it," Sanders said, casting his gaze between his three prisoners, amusement obvious in his features. "But if I'm wrong, none of us will be around to complain anyway."

"Chief . . . ," the driver said, interrupting Sanders's moment. "Check this out."

The van slowed to a crawl. Before them, stretching from one end of the street to the other, was a throng of at least a hundred people. Many of them wore various kinds of masks to cover their faces, including bandanas, ski masks, and even football helmets. Many carried makeshift weapons. They had been smashing the windows of every parked car on the block and had just turned their attention to the buildings when the group of soldiers had arrived. As one unit, the crowd stopped and regarded the van idling before them.

"Holy shit," one soldier said from the back. "Does that guy have a pitchfork!? Give them a couple of torches and this mob is straight out of *Frankenstein*."

"Back up," Sanders said. "Get us out of here."

The driver began to reverse the van, but jammed on the

brakes almost immediately, bringing the vehicle to a stop with a jolt. There were people behind the vehicle, quickly filling in from all sides, like a stream flowing around a rock.

The van began to rock back and forth, rioters pushing at it from both sides. Maria held out a hand to steady herself, and the jostling got more violent. There was a sharp snapping sound, and a web of cracks appeared on the windshield, courtesy of a blow from a baseball bat. There was another crack, and then a strange settling of the van accompanied by loud hissing.

"I think they just slashed our tires," the driver said.

"They think their baseball bats are going to be effective against machine guns? What a bunch of morons," Sanders spat. "Get out there and push them the fuck off."

The side doors suddenly slid open, and three soldiers sprung out with trained ease. Once the crowd realized that the van was full of armed soldiers, it pulled back to a respectful distance, giving space to the soldiers who continued to exit and take up positions around the vehicle. Sanders opened his door and got out, looking down at the slashed tires and shaking his head.

"Come on," Maria said, taking Sam by the hand and slipping out the door to stand behind the soldiers. There was a grumbling coming from the crowd, and people swayed back and forth restlessly. Then, almost at once, the noise dropped to complete silence. Hundreds of people suddenly held their breath in unison, a synchronized effect that could only have been caused by one thing: Mustafa had just emerged from inside the vehicle, coming to stand next to Maria.

What are all these people doing? he signed.

"It's a riot," Maria said.

I do not understand what they intend to accomplish by destroying all the cars in the street.

"They're not trying to accomplish anything. They're just

really angry, and they're taking it out on whatever they can find."

Call it what you like. I know a feeding frenzy when I see one.

After the crowd stared at Mustafa for what seemed like an eternity, the silence was broken by a single shout, and a brick flew in, hurled by a large man in a black ski-mask. Maria watched the arc of the projectile in slow motion as it moved from the front of the crowd through the air. It had been aimed perfectly and sailed directly toward where Mustafa stood. Had he not been paying attention, it would have hit him squarely in the head. But Mustafa saw the incoming projectile as well as any. A purple tentacle snapped out, and in one smooth motion, plucked the brick from the air and whipped it back around. Rather than the lazy arc that it had sailed in on, the brick's new path was linear, flying like a cannonball straight toward its origin. It caught the man in the midsection, knocking him backward into the crowd as if he were hit by a giant hammer. He flailed as he went down, dragging those nearby to the ground with him. The crowd turned to their fallen comrade, studying him for a stunned moment. Then, like a flame moving through dry grass, a roar erupted, and the mass of people surged forward.

The soldiers opened fire, and dozens of rioters fell to the ground. But the soldiers weren't the only ones who had brought guns, and a crusty old man in a cowboy hat emerged from behind the mass of bodies with a shotgun to return fire. His aim was true, and a soldier was thrown back as he was hit with buckshot. His comrades turned their attention to the shooter, but another rioter appeared from the side, firing upon the soldiers with two pistols, one in each of his hands, and what had been a melee transformed itself into a full-blown gunfight.

"Run!" Sam shouted, pulling Maria through the crowd, ducking down to avoid getting hit. They dodged through the crowd, just another two people running for their lives. Then

Mustafa was there, next to them, faster and more agile than any human. He skirted ahead, shielding the two from whatever appeared to be the worst threat in a given moment. Although the crowd might have been brave enough to throw something at him from a distance, no one had the courage to actually try to fight him, and people seemed to be even more afraid of the diminutive alien than they were of the soldiers firing into their ranks with assault weapons. Like the Red Sea before Moses, the crowd parted for Mustafa.

As soon as they reached an empty street, Maria pressed herself against the wall at her side, taking great gulps of air. Her heart pounded in her temples, as much from the shock of having to run through a riot as from the physical exertion. Sam moved back to peek around the corner for a moment and returned.

"No one has followed us," he reported.

"Not yet," Maria said. She looked around, trying to get her bearings. Which way? Where should they go? Every second of indecision was costing thousands of lives somewhere. But anywhere was better than where they stood now. "Come on, let's move."

THIRTY-TWO

The security measures in place to defend the National Reconnaissance Office from foreign and domestic cyberattacks were cutting edge. So secret, that the cryptographic protocols didn't even have names. They were the byproduct of hundreds of thousands of man-hours by the best and brightest research scientists at the NSA, with funding that for all practical purposes was bottomless. It was estimated that a coordinated brute force attack by all the supercomputers in the world running in parallel would take upward of 500 trillion years to crack the code. It took Mother roughly 1.73 seconds.

As soon as she was through the firewalls, she implemented her own security protocols and took control of every electro-optical imaging satellite in orbit over the United States. With resolutions down to fractions of an inch, provided the weather was clear, they had the capability to read twelve-point fonts in an open book from low Earth orbit. The accuracy was less than what she was used to, as Mother expected given the primitive technology, but sufficient for her purposes.

Each satellite was re-tasked, and adjusted its lenses over Las Vegas. Luckily, the sky was clear with no cloud cover. It did not take long to acquire the three figures she was searching for, and she created an observation grid around them, monitored redundantly using all the satellites at her disposal. She didn't trust human technology and wasn't going to take any chances by leaving such a critical job to only a single one of the devices.

The three dots were located at the edge of a building, just around the corner from what appeared to be a sea of humans running hither and thither, acting against each other and their environment in ways that confirmed the species had almost no higher levels of reason or emotional control. Rioting and killing, at a time when they most needed to join together? How had Sam come from a people like this? Mother quickly identified the Special Forces operatives and tagged them in the system so she could keep tabs on their location as they moved. John Sanders was also tagged. Mother weighed the option of hacking into a submarine to launch a number of cruise missiles upon his location but decided against it almost immediately: she didn't have time to waste and didn't want to risk any collateral damage to the three beings she was most concerned with protecting.

She saw her charges begin to move. They headed down the street, pausing at an intersection. The purple dot circled around the other two, sending a group of a dozen other humans nearby running in the opposite direction. She felt a surge of pride; Mustafa had always been so courageous. She zoomed in on him, scanning every visible part of his body for injuries. She was glad to find none. She then double-checked Sam and Maria to make sure they were also unharmed, and then expanded back to the bird's-eye view so she could monitor for threats. She needed to get them off the streets. It was not safe.

Mother went online, searching for information. What she needed was a way to open a portal for them, but she couldn't remember how. The information she needed had been lost in her escape, and it was clear that level of technology was entirely beyond humanity. She needed an alternative. But what? In an instant, she read everything that had ever been posted on the Internet about transportation.

She turned her attention to the data center at the Nevada Department of Motor Vehicles. The security measures in place to protect that database might as well have been nonexistent, given the level of difficulty they posed to her. She queried and sorted the data, searching for what she needed, but her progress was maddeningly slow. The computers were sluggish and inefficient. Her children were in danger and she fought against the limitations of the body she inhabited, a half-baked attempt at technology klutzed together by an unevolved species. Faster. She needed to go faster.

Brian Hollander took a sip from his coffee. It was his fifth cup today, although no one was counting. He was dressed in his suit and tie, ready for work, but had never made it out of the kitchen. Instead, he sat in the breakfast nook, glued to the small television set mounted in the corner.

His wife walked in, her face pale. She hadn't taken any of this morning's news events well, and the overwhelming anxiety of the moment had resulted in a horrible case of nausea and heartburn, causing her to spend most of her morning hunched over the toilet by the stairs.

"Did they say anything?" she asked, sitting down next to him.

"There are riots breaking out across the country. People are losing their shit, baby."

"Oh my God . . . I can't believe this is happening."

Brian reached over, putting an arm around his wife's shoulders, and she clutched his hand in her own.

"I always thought it was going to be climate change that got us in the end, but not until after you and I were already gone," she said. "But aliens? Everything was fine last week, and now —*today?!*—it's the end of the world?" She covered her mouth with her hand, tears running down her cheeks.

"This is so fucked up," Brian said. Usually his wife didn't approve of cussing, but she seemed fine with it in the moment. If there was ever a good time to drop the f-bomb, the middle of a purging of humanity from the planet by a hostile extraterrestrial force definitely qualified. What had the reporters called it? Terraforming?

They changed the channel. It was the local news.

"Susan, was there any indication that humanity's sentience was in question during the trial?" the news anchor asked his partner on his left.

"No, none. Like everyone else, I believed it was an asylum hearing for Mustafa the alien. And there was absolutely no indication that anything like that was even vaguely possible," she responded. Having been the only reporter to ever interview an alien on live television, despite the fact that she had only asked one question, Susan Meyerson had become instantly famous and had been giving television interviews nonstop since the trial.

"Do we have any news concerning the government's response to the Authority's attack on Greenland?" An image appeared on the screen, with a drawing of an extremely angry-looking gold man with clenched fists. There had been no cameras allowed in court, and no one had managed to take an actual photograph of the Authority.

"Not yet. The government has refused comment, and right now all any of us can do is speculate what happened in Greenland, or why that particular country was targeted if indeed this was the work of the Authority. However, as you know, all air traffic has been grounded and we do know that martial law has been declared in many cities where the rioting has gotten out of hand."

"Brian! Did you hear that . . . ?"

Brian turned to his wife, his eyebrows raised. "Hear what?"

"I think I heard the garage door! Oh my God . . . is someone in the garage?"

Brian leapt up, the television forgotten. He took two quick strides to the garage, then stopped, looking around frantically. He ran back around the counter and pulled open a drawer, taking hold of a long butcher knife. Armed with the deadliest weapon he could find, he returned to the door, his wife creeping slowly behind him. With a sharp intake of breath he flung it open to find that, as his wife had heard, the large, retracting door to the street was open. His shiny black car was slowly backing out.

"Hey!" he shouted, running into the garage. The car backed down the driveway and out into the street. Like all electric cars, it moved silently, except for the crunch of the wheels against the road.

"Hey! Stop!" Brian said, running out into the driveway. There was a squeal of rubber, and the technological tour-de-force that represented the world's fastest accelerating and most expensive electric car was gone.

"Someone just stole my car!" Brian said, turning to his wife who had arrived at his elbow to watch. "Did you see who it was? We have to stop them!"

"Brian," she said calmly, her brow furrowed. "There wasn't anybody in there. It was driving itself."

———

The man was a giant. He had a completely bald head, with two tattoos on either side. On the right side of his skull, a white cross in the center of a red circle represented the "Blood Drop" cross of the Klansmen. On the left, he had the more common swastika, encircled by a large cobra bearing its fangs. A long beard hung from the lower half of his face, weaving itself into the voluminous body of chest hair that sprung forth unchecked from his muscular torso. In his right hand, he held a hatchet. In his left, a samurai sword.

"You!" he said in his booming voice, the word transformed into an insult. The man leered down at Mustafa with bloodshot eyes.

Mustafa's skin color wasn't nearly as red as Maria had remembered it from the hotel room, but she could tell that it wouldn't take much to push him back to it. He had taken it upon himself to chase rioters away when they got too close, and he had done so with a ferocity that frightened her. He may have been acting, or it may have been a natural behavior he was able to draw upon. Whatever the case, it left her jumpy—even if she considered him family. Every other person they had encountered had fled from him as fast as their legs could carry them. Everyone except this giant of a man who now blocked their path.

"Come on, let's go back the way we came," Maria said, tugging on Sam's elbow. The man was huge, but they could probably outrun him if they backtracked.

"This devil has brought the apocalypse," the man bellowed, spit flying from his thick lips. "A Mexican on his right, and a communist on his left." His eyes darted up to take Maria and Sam in, speaking volumes about what he intended to do in the next few moments.

A low growl emanated from Mustafa, a white substance slowly pooling beneath him. His tentacles circled around each other, like a pack of wolves ready to leap upon their prey. The giant twirled his sword once, rotating it easily in his huge hand. The blade flashed in the sunlight.

"We don't want any trouble," Maria said.

The man laughed. "You might not want it, but you've found it."

Sam moved forward next to Mustafa, his fists clenched, and Maria was struck by how much he'd changed from the wide-eyed guy that had stumbled through her door a week ago. He'd seen a lot since then, and it had hardened him into the protector who stood before her now, shoulders tense and teeth gritted. The thought made her proud, and a little sad.

The man gestured at Mustafa with his hatchet. "I'm killing you first, on behalf of the human race." He held the sword at the ready with his other hand, ropes of muscle bulging in his bicep. "I'm killing you for my country," he pointed at Sam. Then he looked at Maria. "And then I'm killing you for myself."

The giant shifted his weight forward toward Mustafa, who stood his ground. Three tentacles found their way under his body, bracing and compressing under him. A deep otherworldly growl floated in the air, but then stopped as another sound took over. It was the squealing of car tires.

The squealing got louder, and Sam's face registered surprise as he took a step back and to the side. The giant made a move to turn to look behind him, but caught himself, clearly unwilling to take his eyes off any of his adversaries. A black sports car moving at a frantic speed hit the man from behind with terrific force, uprooting him like a bowling pin. His legs were thrown high in the air, and he landed on his back to the side. The sword was knocked clear, but he somehow retained a grip on his hatchet. The car reversed itself, pulling back away from the man. There was a dent in the hood where the impact had been made.

The giant groaned, rolled over and managed to get up on

one knee. Blood flowed from the back of his head, coming down his shoulders and mixing with his beard. He tried to stand, but hadn't quite found his balance, and kept one thick hand planted on the pavement.

The car accelerated, the front tires locking to one side, and the entire back end swung around in an arc. If the aim of the maneuver was to create a gigantic flyswatter, it was executed perfectly. The rear of the car spun around like a four-thousand pound hammer and struck the giant, sending him flying through the air to take out a number of garbage cans near the sidewalk.

The car made a full circle and pulled up right next to the three, who watched in stunned silence. The doors popped open on their own.

"That was pretty good timing," Sam said.

"You could say that again," Maria said.

Sam looked over. "Um . . . OK. That was pretty good timing . . . I mean, because it happened just when the guy was about to—"

"Just an expression, Sam. I heard you the first time." Maria squinted her eyes to try to see who was driving, and gasped at the empty driver's seat. The headlights flashed on and off, and the car beeped three times quickly.

"I didn't know cars could drive themselves," Sam said.

"They can't!" Maria looked over to the pile of garbage cans and the prone form of their would-be adversary. The man's hand was twitching.

I think we're supposed to get in, Mustafa signed, and made his way over to the car, pulling the door open and climbing into the back seat.

"But if cars can't drive themselves, then who is driving this one?" Sam said.

They looked at each other for a minute, then both broke into a smile.

———

The large display screen in the dashboard flashed an arrow and played a chime, indicating that a turn was about to be taken. The steering wheel spun on its own, and there was a squeal of wheels as the entire vehicle lurched precariously to the side. Maria had never been in a car driven this hard or this fast, and had her arms and legs splayed in all directions trying to hold herself in place. She sat in the driver's seat, but any time she had reached for the wheel or tried to put her foot on the brake, the car began honking incessantly and playing the radio at maximum volume. It was more than clear that, although she might be sitting in the driver's seat, she was not to interfere.

"There's a fence ahead," Sam said.

"Do you think Mother can see it?" Maria said. It was one of the gates that led to the back side of the airport, but was locked.

"I don't know."

The car wasn't slowing. Maria reached for the wheel and was blasted with a snippet of talk radio played at over a hundred decibels. Her hands retreated to their former positions, one on the door, and the other on the panel between the seats, and the radio noise subsided.

If anything, the car seemed to accelerate rather than slow, and burst through the chain-link gate. The vehicle lurched as it ran over something, scraping the front spoiler against the pavement as the shocks bottomed out, but made it clear and sped down the wide concrete slab with all the acceleration it could muster. The engine howled under the strain in a high-pitched whine, protesting against being pushed so far beyond its limits.

They took a hard right, drifting around the corner in a power slide that wouldn't have been out of place in a television chase scene. They were on a runway now, rapidly approaching a cluster of small jets and propeller planes. The car didn't stop, the tails of the planes a blur in the side window. They approached a small gray outbuilding, and Maria's entire weight was suddenly flung forward against her seatbelt as the brakes locked down and brought the car to a stop. The car honked three times, the doors locked and unlocked themselves, and then the entire display went black.

Sam glanced over at Maria, and pushed his door open with his leg. "I think we're supposed to get out now."

The three exited the vehicle and looked around. Aside from this small building, there was nothing but jets and runways to be found. The three of them jogged to the front door and entered.

Inside was a sitting area made up of four old chairs around a circular table covered in aviation magazines. A coffee maker sat off to the side, along with stacks of white cups and a basket of sugar packets. There was a desk at the far wall, next to a door that led to another room.

Maria approached the desk and stopped when a man appeared from the other room. He wore a pair of gold spectacles and had the hairiest arms Maria could ever remember seeing. They poked out from a gray polo shirt with a gold propeller embroidered on the chest.

The man opened his mouth to speak, but no words came out. Instead, he froze, staring at Mustafa, who had come to hover next to Maria.

"Charlie, don't just stand there like an idiot. We've got customers," a diminutive woman said. She had come from the back room as well and stood next to her husband, hands on her hips as if she were a schoolmarm inspecting her class. Her hair was gray enough to be almost white, and she wore it in two long braids that hung down at her sides. Her features were sharp and intense, and she would not have been out of place had she been wearing a Viking helmet and carrying an axe.

"Is that Mr. Mustafa?" Charlie said, looking at Maria and pointing down at the purple being next to her.

"Of course it's Mr. Mustafa, you big oaf," his wife interjected, not giving Maria a chance to respond. "Who else would it be?" The woman elbowed past her husband and reached out her hand toward Maria. "Welcome to Nevada Jet Charters. I'm Daphne, and this is Charlie."

Maria shook the woman's hand. Maria had smaller hands than most, but Daphne's were miniature in comparison. Maria was able to wrap her fingers almost completely around Daphne's tiny palm, but what the older woman lacked in size she more than made up with in fierceness of grip. Maria was glad when Sam approached and Daphne released her to shake his hand as well.

After shaking Sam's hand, Daphne then held her palm out toward Mustafa. For a moment, the two stood there looking at each other, and then a purple tentacle snaked out, coiling itself around the woman's entire arm like a boa constrictor on a branch, and the two bounced their arms up and down, Daphne smiling like a child on Christmas morning, and Mustafa flapping his other tentacles gently against the ground.

"You are wasting time," a muffled robotic voice interjected. Charlie reached down into his pants pocket, pulling out his phone in surprise.

"Listen," Maria said. "We need to go east, and we have to do it as fast as we possibly can."

"East?" Daphne said.

"Yes. As far as we can go on your fastest plane."

"We're trying to save Earth," Sam said.

"Really?" Charlie said.

"Just directly east? No destination?" Daphne asked.

"Not east. They're going to Winnipeg," Mother said.

"What's wrong with my phone?" Charlie said.

Maria reached out and took the phone from Charlie, who seemed happy to hand it over. "Why Winnipeg?"

"There is no time for talk. You have to get there in two hours."

"Two hours to Winnipeg?" Daphne said. "That's not so easy."

When Charlie asked what would happen if they were late, Mother responded, "Everyone on the East Coast dies. You need to be flying, not asking stupid questions."

"I don't remember Siri being so snarky," Daphne said, furrowing her brow and looking at the phone with a scowl.

Maria was ready to get on her knees and beg. "Can you get us to Winnipeg in two hours?"

"Let me think . . ." Charlie looked off in the distance, scratching the bottom of his chin with his hand. "Well, there is that Citation X out there."

"Charlie, that's not our plane," Daphne said.

"I know, but it's the only one that has a chance, sweetheart. Top-of-the-line Citations can hit almost Mach 1. It's the fastest thing we've got."

"Can you fly it?" Maria said.

Daphne looked insulted. "Of course we can fly it."

"What are we waiting for, let's go!" Sam said, taking a step toward the door. Daphne and Charlie looked at him, but didn't budge.

"The FAA has grounded all air travel. No planes are allowed in the air as of a couple of hours ago," Charlie said.

"If you don't help us, millions of people will die," Maria said.

"So you are asking us to steal that airplane and fly it to Winnipeg in violation of the FAA, right this very moment?" Daphne asked.

"Exactly."

"To save Earth," Sam said.

"How are you going to save Earth?" Charlie asked.

"We're not. Mustafa is." Sam pointed at his brother, who seemed to straighten and puff himself out as all eyes focused on him.

"It's not a joke," Maria said. "This is really happening."

"On any other day, I'd think you were crazy," Daphne said.

"But there's Mr. Mustafa —*right there!*—standing in our lobby . . ." Charlie looked at his wife, and laughed.

"Yes. There's Mr. Mustafa," Daphne looked down at Mustafa, who gave her a crisp salute.

"You've seen the news. . . . It's not every day you get a chance to save the world," Charlie said.

Daphne sighed. "This breaks every rule in the book, and we might lose our business over it—*or worse*—but you've got a point. So be it! Let's go save the world, then. Let me just get my sunglasses."

The group exited the building, running across the tarmac toward a line of small jets arranged in a row. Charlie ran up to one of the larger planes and pulled a latch on the side. The stairs dropped, folding out of the side of the jet, and everyone rushed on board, taking various seats. Charlie made his way into the cockpit, and Daphne joined him. Almost as fast as the door was closed, the plane was moving.

The thrust of the engines pushed Maria back into the seat, and she felt the rumble of the wheels give way as the jet lifted from the ground. After they had been in the air for a few minutes, Maria felt the phone vibrate, and she reached down to see what had come through. Her face dropped.

"Oh no," she said, chest tightening. Mother had sent them a video.

It looked as if someone was recording from a rooftop. Concrete and brick buildings clustered together, satellite dishes and laundry lines spread across the tops of the buildings, the soft layer that added color to what would otherwise be a sea of dirty masonry. There were people in the streets. They were shouting and running. The sound of car horns could be heard. A baby was crying from somewhere nearby.

"Brazil," Maria whispered, as Mustafa and Sam crowded in to see what had left her shaking.

There was something off in the distance. It looked almost like a vertical brown wall, the color of dirt. Smoke and debris was thrown up as the wall moved, like a wave but in reverse. As it approached, buildings collapsed and fell into the wall, absorbed in an instant. The person filming was screaming, the shaking picture almost impossible to watch. Then the perspective shifted up as jet fighters streaked past, launching missile after missile at the vertical mountain. Nothing happened. The missiles simply vanished into the brown like the rest. There was a gigantic fireball that burst forth, struggling to expand, but rather than exploding outward, it collapsed back in on itself, sucked into the wall along with everything around it.

The destruction was suddenly much closer than it had appeared, and the camera panned down to the street, which was in chaos. Cars rammed each other, trying to push through to safety, but failing. There was nowhere to go. Row after row of buildings were torn and lifted up into the air, like bits of dust sucked into some huge vacuum cleaner. The edge of the town pulled up, and the person filming—a young man, from the sound of his voice—muttered a final, fervent prayer as the wall rushed toward the camera. Then the video stopped on a final frame of static, reddish brown.

The three stared at the last frame in the video in silence. The shock was visceral. All those people were now dead. Sam dropped his head into his hands.

"Did you see the explosion toward the end?" Maria finally said. "What do you think that was?"

"That was a nuclear weapon," Mother replied, speaking in the emotionless voice of the phone.

"They tried to nuke it? And nothing happened?"

"Conventional weapons will be useless against the Authority," Mother said. "You might as well be throwing rocks."

"I didn't think Brazil even had nukes."

"They are quite common, as far as I can tell," Mother replied. "Almost every country on this planet appears to have them."

Humans know how to split atoms? Mustafa signed. *I'm impressed.*

"See, not as stupid as you thought," Maria said.

There are many levels of stupid.

Maria frowned and looked up at the ceiling, taking a deep breath. Brazil had launched a nuclear weapon. They only would have done that as a last resort. And it hadn't worked? How was that possible? How could anything be immune to nuclear weapons? She turned her attention back to her purple companion. "Mustafa, in the van with Sanders, Mother said you were going to try to stop the Authority. What are you going to do?"

Mustafa flipped a tentacle around in the air, then dropped it back to the ground. *I don't know yet.*

"What strength do you have that a nuclear bomb doesn't?"

Charm and good looks?

Maria groaned. They were doomed.

Beyond her window the sky was perfectly blue, and civilization had been reduced to various dots in the landscape below. It was hard to imagine there could be so much destruction going on in a different part of the world. What would it look like when the Authority reached here? Would it be the same wall of force as on the video? How could anyone survive something like that?

"Maria," Sam said. "I'm so sorry. I never meant for any of this to happen."

Maria turned from the window. "It's not your fault, Sam."

"It is. If I had never come back, Earth would have been spared. Your grandmother and nephew wouldn't be in jail. Pepe wouldn't be in trouble. All of this is because of me."

Samples come back when it's time, Mustafa signed. *You had no choice, brother.*

"I should never have used the bracelet. I should just have been a regular human, like everyone else. Please forgive me, Maria," Sam said, falling out of his chair and kneeling in front of her. "Everything you love will be destroyed because of me."

Maria reached out, running her hand through Sam's hair. "You are as much a victim as anyone, Sam. You didn't even get to know your own parents. You were stolen from them before you were even born."

"No. If I were a victim, I'd be the one that was hurt, not your family. Not all those people in Brazil. Not this planet." Sam was shaking. "If only I had never met those cops. If only I had never met Sanders."

"Sam—"

"I should have brought the bracelet when they took me. I could have ended all of this. I was so *stupid.*" Sam's fists were balled, and his veins throbbed in his forearms.

"Sam, look at me."

Sam looked up, his eyes were on fire.

"That's not you." Maria held Sam's gaze for a long moment before he finally looked down. She gently prodded him on his shoulder. "Do you know what today is?"

Sam was silent, his teeth grit together.

Maria smiled. "It's the one-week anniversary of when we first met. Remember?"

The tension in Sam's body drained like the air out of a balloon, and his fists unclenched. He tried to say something but was unable. He looked up at Maria, his eyes wet with feeling. The rage was gone, replaced by something much softer. Maria reached down and took hold of his hand, squeezing it in both of hers.

A sound clip began playing on the phone. It was a deep male voice that Maria didn't recognize. "The Air Force has launched every plane against this thing," the voice said. "They sent everything. Even the B-2s. They're going to synchronize with the subs and ICBMs. They're going to hit it with every nuke we've got within the hour."

"What was that?" Maria asked.

"A clip from a conversation that John Sanders just had," Mother responded in her flat voice. "I thought you'd be interested to know."

"Who was the guy talking?"

"That was this country's Secretary of Defense."

"Will it work?" Daphne chimed in from the front. "The nukes?"

"No. It will not."

THIRTY-THREE

"We've got company," Charlie said in a gruff voice from the front of the plane.

Maria unbuckled her belt and approached the cockpit. There wasn't enough room for her to enter, so she stood at the door, hands placed on either side of it for stability, and leaned forward. Charlie turned toward her, concern written on his brow. He pointed a thick finger to the right of the cockpit, out the side window that Daphne was peering out. There was a gray fighter jet beside them, close enough that Maria could see the visor of the pilot as he glanced over at them.

"There's another behind us," Daphne said.

"This is a United States Air Force armed F-16," a voice broke through on the radio. "You are ordered to change course to Minot Air Force Base immediately."

"What should I do?" Charlie said.

"Can you ignore them?" Maria asked.

Daphne snorted. "Only if we want to get shot down."

"Would they do that?" Sam asked from behind Maria. He tried to squeeze his head into the cockpit to see for himself, and Maria adjusted to make room for him.

"Depends how bad they want us to change course," Daphne said.

"Do you think they know Mr. Mustafa is on board?" Charlie said.

Another F-16 suddenly soared up vertically across their path, just ahead of their plane. Maria gasped and bent down to try to follow the trajectory of the fighter.

"They call that maneuver a headbutt," Charlie offered.

"Repeat. This is a United States Air Force armed F-16. You have been intercepted. Acknowledge or rock your wings," the voice commanded over the radio.

Charlie moved the yoke gently to the side, rocking the wings.

The plane that had streaked upward across the path of the jet had leveled out and taken up a position just in front and to the right of the jet. It rocked its wings and flashed the landing lights off and on.

"That one wants us to follow," Daphne said, pointing at the F-16 dancing to the right.

Daphne flipped a switch to activate her radio. "We are unable to comply."

"The passengers on your aircraft are fugitives from the US government. You are ordered to alter course to Minot Air Force Base."

"I guess they know Mr. Mustafa is on board," Charlie muttered to himself. "I wonder how they figured it out."

"We're the only plane in the sky, and we took off from Las Vegas. They're not stupid, dear." Daphne said.

The F-16 to the right streaked ahead, performing a half-circle turn in front of the jet. On its return path, it launched a flare that streaked across the path of the aircraft.

"That's not good," Daphne said.

"A shot across our bow," Charlie said.

"You are ordered to alter course immediately. We have been authorized to engage should you refuse to comply with our instructions. This is your final warning."

"Oh shit," Daphne said.

Charlie glanced back at Maria. "I'm sorry, but we have to turn."

Maria looked out the window at the fighter pilot, a pit opening up in her stomach. Would the government really prefer to shoot them down rather than let them try to help? How could they be so nearsighted? She remembered her grandmother, now in prison. And Lucas too. Of all people, Lucas. And for what, revenge? There was no other reason. Why was it that all the petty, vindictive men found their way into power? Men like the cop who kicked Pepe. Or the one who tortured Sam. And John Sanders, of course. All they knew how to do was blow things up. And here they were again, with their F-16s, trying to interfere. When would they realize that everyone was on the same side?

When it was too damned late.

"Here we go!" Charlie said. "Now it's a party."

Maria refocused on the outside world and looked over. Now there was a fighter on the left side of the plane, but it wasn't an F-16.

"This is the Royal Canadian Air Force. We're here to escort you to Winnipeg," a voice came through on the radio.

"The Canadians?" Daphne said.

"That's a CF-188 Hornet," Charlie offered. "Look! There are four more . . . no, six more!"

"What are the Canadians doing in North Dakota?" Daphne said, leaning forward to get a better view past Charlie.

"I called them," the emotionless voice of Maria's phone announced. "I've been in touch with their Prime Minister, and we've had a long discussion about current world events."

"Is the extraterrestrial on board?" the Canadian fighter pilot asked.

Maria turned around, looking for Mustafa. He was still in his chair, his tentacles wrapped in loops around the back of the seat. What was he still doing back there? "Mustafa, come over here. We need the Canadians to see you."

Mustafa loosened one tentacle, then quickly threw it forward to brace against the side of the cabin. Three others joined it, creating what looked like a spider web across the walkway, the others remaining lashed down to the seats. Gingerly, Mustafa slowly moved his body from his seat, scooting it forward toward the cabin.

"What's wrong with Mustafa?" Maria said.

Sam laughed. "I think he's scared of flying."

Daphne turned around and covered her mouth as she watched Mustafa maneuver down the aisle. Maria felt a tentacle wrap around the bottom of her leg, a vice grip on her ankle.

"Mustafa, I'm not an anchor," she said.

It is not natural to travel like this. You are insane if you think this form of transportation makes any sense.

Maria rolled her eyes. "You're the one who jumps through portals."

That's completely different.

"Mustafa, don't worry," Sam said. "There's nothing to be afraid of."

We're in a pressurized tube, moving through an atmosphere at almost the speed of sound, and the only thing between us and instant death is the skill of the apelike humans who constructed this craft. I find plenty to be afraid of.

Mustafa grappled his way into the cockpit, making liberal use of all twelve tentacles to brace his body in case of the sudden catastrophic loss of pressure and altitude he seemed convinced was imminent. He squeezed in far enough to see, and then waved a spare tentacle through the window at the Canadian pilot, who saluted in response. Then, with a quickness that startled everyone, flew back to his seat, tucking himself in and pulling up all his tentacles so that the only piece of him visible from behind was the very top of his purple head.

The Canadian jets surrounded the plane, taking up a position behind the F-16s, which maintained their course. But the danger wasn't over.

"The American pilots have just received orders to destroy you," Mother announced.

Charlie jumped in his seat. Daphne cursed. Maria swallowed, then reached down and found Sam's hand in hers. Before anyone could say a word, there was an explosion from somewhere behind, and the shockwave jostled the plane.

"Whoa!" Charlie said, twisting around in his seat and trying to look behind him through the side window.

"What was that?" Sam said. "Are they shooting at us?"

"No!" Charlie said. "That was one of the F-16s! The Canadians . . . they attacked!"

"Really? The Canadians?" Daphne said, twisting toward the window on her side.

"Yes! Look, there they go!" Charlie exclaimed. The two remaining F-16s zoomed off, chased by a group of Canadian fighters. Two other Canadian units remained, taking up positions on either side of the jet in a protective escort.

"Time to put your fighter pilot hat back on, dear," Daphne said to her husband. "Get us to Winnipeg, and don't waste any time."

Charlie took the instructions to heart, and sent Sam and Maria back to their seats. Maria noticed the difference in how the plane handled immediately. Everything was faster and harder. The focus was on getting to the destination, with the comfort of the passengers being secondary. No one had told her to buckle her safety belt, but she had done it anyway and was glad, especially during one particularly rough moment during the descent. She looked over at Mustafa, whose anatomy didn't embrace the idea of seat belts, and saw that he had lashed himself to his seat with three or four tentacles that wrapped themselves around the base. She wasn't sure what it would look like if he felt queasy, given he didn't have a face to speak of, but she did note that the usual undulations in his tentacles had given way to a rigidity that was uncommon for him.

"Everything OK over there?" Maria asked, once they had touched down and were taxiing.

I don't think I like flying, Mustafa said, his tentacle flopping lifelessly back to the floor after he had finished signing.

The plane turned a corner and came to a stop. Daphne was up and by the door, releasing it and letting it drop. She exited, followed by Charlie. The others got up from their seats and made their way out of the cabin and down to the runway.

There was a short man there waiting for them, flanked by two soldiers in camouflage and machine guns. "Welcome to Canada. I'm Major Xavier Trembley, at your service."

"Thanks for taking care of us up there," Charlie added. "Reminded me of the old days."

Xavier tipped his head slightly and smiled.

"Whoa, what is that?" Maria said as her eyes landed upon what could only be described as a jet from a comic book. It was long and thin, with narrow wings that were pinched back. The front extended in a long tip that came to a very sharp point. The entire thing looked like an oversized dart more than an airplane. It was silver on the top and black underneath.

"That's your next ride," Xavier said.

Not again, Mustafa signed.

"You'll be fine," Sam said. "The last one was fun!"

"How do you know what he's saying?" Xavier asked, watching the exchange with curiosity.

"Sign language," Sam replied.

"But you're not signing back. So he can understand English?"

"He's pretty smart," Maria said. "He cleaned out a roulette table back in Las Vegas without any trouble."

"Seriously?" Xavier turned to Mustafa, clearly impressed. "You rock, little alien."

Is it good to rock? Mustafa asked.

Maria laughed. "Yes, it's very good to rock."

Mustafa's tentacles loosened up and began flapping out a soft rhythmic cadence on the ground.

"When he does that, he's happy," Maria said.

The Canadian watched Mustafa, nodding his head. "Excellent. We aim to please. I heard from the Americans that it's best not to piss him off."

"You could say that."

Xavier smiled, and his blue eyes lit up. He seemed much younger than his rank implied. "So he's actually a rocking, ass-kicking little alien then. I stand corrected."

Mustafa's undulations increased. It was obvious he enjoyed being complimented.

"Why did you say 'hey'?" Sam asked.

"I didn't."

"Just now, at the end of your sentence. You said 'hey.'"

"Sam, he's Canadian," Maria said, elbowing him. "That's how they talk."

"Oh," Sam looked at Maria, and then back to Xavier. "Sorry, hey."

"Sam!"

Xavier laughed. "You must be Sam."

Sam smiled.

"Should we get on the plane?" Maria asked.

"We have a little time." The Canadian's face became stern. "We have to wait for another party from your country to join us."

"We don't have a lot of time to waste."

"I'm aware of that. But America has just threatened us with nuclear war if we don't cooperate in this matter, so I'm afraid this part isn't negotiable."

———

It seemed they stood on the runway for an eternity, but in reality it was less than half an hour. A number of fast-moving fighter jets appeared over the horizon and landed with a crispness that wouldn't have been out of place on an aircraft carrier. There were four planes, each holding a pilot and a passenger. That made up a continent of eight US soldiers who approached Maria and her companions. When she recognized the man in the front, she had to suppress an involuntary gag reflex.

John Sanders stopped and studied Xavier. "I never thought I'd see the day when the Canadians would shoot down an American jet."

Xavier shrugged. His face was blank, although the corners of his mouth curled up slightly.

"You all are very lucky the Pentagon is so distracted by the Authority at the moment," Sanders said. "Otherwise, Canada would have a boot up its ass right now."

"Saved by the end of the world," Xavier responded. "Lucky us."

Sanders scowled and turned to Maria. "Hello again, Maria. You are quite a resourceful woman."

"How many innocent people died while the rest of us were standing around waiting for you?" Maria said.

Sanders shrugged. "It's OK. They weren't Americans."

Maria looked away. She wasn't going to waste her breath on the man.

"Come on, no time to waste with pleasantries," Xavier said, and began walking to the experimental aircraft nearby.

"How did you Canadians get your hands on a jet like that?" Sanders said, stopping for a moment to admire the aircraft.

Xavier smirked, but remained silent. He led them up a short flight of stairs, waving at them to follow as he stepped inside the metal dart.

Charlie tried to board behind Maria, but one of the US soldiers pressed a hand against his chest, restraining him. "No civilians, sir."

Maria turned, and made eye contact with Charlie and Daphne, thanking them both. They looked from her to the plane wistfully, then retreated to stand next to the two Canadian soldiers, watching from a distance. Daphne worked her arm around Charlie's waist and pulled herself close.

Where the Cessna Citation had been a model of luxury, with softened leather seats and polished wood accents, this new aircraft was all business. There wasn't a scrap of leather or wood to be seen anywhere. Instead, it was all gray metal, with webbed canvas seat buckles that felt like they had been lifted from some ancient World War I Jeep.

Maria struggled to get the buckle around herself, until she realized that it wasn't a seat belt, it was a complete body harness. She had to pass her arms through loops in the side, which then clicked down to a place between her legs on the chair. Xavier, who occupied the seat next to her, reached over and pulled the strap tight for her once she was done.

"I can barely move in this thing," she said.

"Yes, it's supposed to be like that," he said. He looked at

Sam, who sat on the other side of Maria. "If you enjoyed that last flight, you're going to love this one."

Sam smiled and nudged Mustafa with his foot. Mustafa wrapped tentacle after tentacle around the base of his seat, tightening himself down in a death grip to whatever was within range.

"You ready?" a voice shouted from the front. A thin man dressed in a gray flight suit stood at the door to the cockpit. He held a helmet tucked under his arm and scanned his passengers to make sure they were all fastened in. "Make sure to hold onto your gear. We don't want any loose firearms flying around the cabin when we hit Mach 5."

"Mach 5?" Maria said.

"Five times the speed of sound. This thing can haul some ass, as they say," Xavier replied.

"Is Mach 5 considered fast for an airplane?" Sam asked.

Xavier looked over, not sure if Sam was making a joke or not.

"Yes, Sam. It's fast," Maria said. She recognized the nervous feeling that fluttered in her stomach. It was the same feeling as when Lucas had insisted they ride the roller coaster. She hadn't wanted to do it, thought it was a horrible idea, and had done her best to try to talk her way out of it, yet there she sat, strapped in next to him in the front seat as the cars slowly made their way up to the first drop. She swallowed and wiped her palms on her thighs.

The pilot put his helmet on and fastened an oxygen hose in the front down to connect with his suit. He entered the cockpit and began flipping switches.

"Why does the pilot have to wear a helmet like that?" Maria asked.

"In case something goes wrong. Don't want him to pass out," Xavier said.

What about us? Are we going to pass out? Mustafa had loosened a tentacle, although he kept it close to the floor where he could quickly reattach it to something if needed.

"Calm down, Mustafa. It will be fun," Sam said.

The plane began moving, taxiing out. The engines pulsed. The sound was completely different than the previous jet. These engines were rough sounding and loud. The entire cabin was filled with a high-pitched whine that slowly increased in volume.

It looked to Maria like Mustafa wanted to say something, but instead he just tightened his tentacles down on themselves. A greenish tint seemed to have found its way into the purple coloring of his body.

Sam stared at his brother, laughing. "Mustafa is freaked out," he said.

The engines hit them in the back, and the plane lifted off. It flew at a steep angle, and the thrust kept coming long past the point when it seemed like it should have stopped. There were no windows on the side of the aircraft, so Maria had no idea how high up they were, but it felt high. She felt light-headed, and her hands and feet were freezing.

The plane leveled off for what felt like only a few minutes, then started descending. It wasn't the gradual descent of a commercial airliner, but more the plummeting freefall of a rock dropped from a clifftop. Now Maria understood the purpose behind the harness. She felt her entire body weight pressed up against the shoulder straps.

There was a hard impact, and they were on the ground. The bumps from the runway made their way through the wheels to her seat, and Maria could feel every crack the plane went over. She had been too preoccupied to realize it during the flight, but her whole backside was sore; the seats were only marginally softer than if they had been made of bricks.

The plane came to a stop, and the passengers began disentangling themselves from their safety harnesses. Mustafa slowly released himself, unfurling one tentacle after another.

"Welcome to Bangor," Xavier said.

"Bangor? Bangor, Maine?" Maria said.

"That's correct. This is as far east as we could get while being able to guarantee a safe landing."

"In other words, not flying straight into the Authority's path of destruction."

Xavier nodded.

"Were we even in the air for an hour?"

"Not even close," he laughed.

"It was fun, but still not as fast as opening a portal," Sam mumbled.

I will never ride in one of these again, Mustafa declared. He stretched, his tentacles straightening together, pushing his bulb up to a height Maria was not used to seeing it at.

Maria's phone vibrated. She pulled it free from her pocket. A strange sound emanated from it. It sounded like Mother was trying to say something, but the words were garbled, and at least two octaves too high to hear. It was a collection of squeaks, grunts, and other noises strung together in a sequence unlike anything Maria had ever heard.

"Something is wrong," Maria said, looking at the display. Had the plane ride somehow fried her speaker?

No, Mustafa said. *You just do not understand.*

"What?"

"Mother isn't speaking in English," Sam said.

Maria turned to Sam. "Do you know what she's saying?"

"No, but Mustafa does."

Maria held the phone out toward Mustafa, listening to the harsh alien language emanating from it. Mustafa didn't interrupt or ask for clarification. He simply sat, and listened. When it was over, he flapped a tentacle, squeaked once, and swayed back and forth.

"What the hell was that?" a gruff voice said. Sanders stood to the side, looking from Mustafa to Maria.

"It was a language you are too stupid to understand," Mother said. "I suspect this must be a familiar feeling for you."

Xavier laughed once, then straightened his face into one of perfect impassivity as Sanders spun on him, scowling darkly.

"It wasn't me that made the decision to allow you three to come all the way out here," Sanders said, turning back to Maria. His voice was raised, and spittle flew from his lips. "If I'd have had my way, you and Sam here would be tied up in small metal boxes right now, and that thing—" he pointed at Mustafa, "would be getting sliced up for someone's sushi dinner. If I even think that you're working behind my back, I'll put a bullet in each of your skulls so fast that your phone won't even have time to squawk a warning. You aren't running the show, and don't think for a moment that these Canadians will be able to do jack shit to save you if I decide to act on my words. You're on American soil now. Consider yourselves lucky to be alive. Do I make myself perfectly clear?"

"Perfectly," Maria spat.

Should I kill this man? He seems like a problem, Mustafa signed.

"What did he just say?" Sanders demanded.

"He says he understands you perfectly too," Maria replied.

"Excellent," Sanders said. "Then maybe we can all get along."

Are you sure? It would be so easy. You know he deserves it.

"Now what did he say?" Sanders said.

"He says let's get off the plane. He doesn't like flying."

Yes, that is true. But I still think we should kill him.

———

Two gleaming black SUVs sat waiting on the runway, and standing beside them, two men dressed in identical formal gray attire, complete with brimmed chauffeur caps.

"Hello, sir, I'm Marcus, and this is Lewis. We're here from Bangor Limo," one of the men said as Sanders approached.

"That's great, Marcus." Sanders turned around. "Johnson! Get a move on."

Johnson, the soldier who had driven the van back in Las Vegas jogged ahead. He quickly shook Marcus's outstretched hand.

"You got the keys?" Johnson said.

Marcus seemed confused. "I'm the driver, sir. Clients are not allowed to operate the vehicles."

"Do we look like your typical clients?" Johnson said, gesturing at the rest of the complement of US and Canadian Special Forces operatives who stood in a loose half circle around him.

"No, sir," Marcus replied. "But it's still company policy."

"We don't have time to argue, and you can stick your policies up your ass," Sanders said impatiently, moving to one of the SUVs. Lewis darted in front of him, opening the door for him so he could climb inside.

Marcus was about to say something, but then seemed to notice Mustafa. His eyes bulged in his head, and his mouth dropped open. Mustafa waved a tentacle his direction and moved toward Lewis, who suddenly forgot his job, instead staring at the purple creature standing in front of him, his face a mixture of shock and disbelief.

Mustafa walked up and unceremoniously let himself into the limo. Sam held the door for Maria, and the three were joined by a handful of commandos. The limo had sideways seating, with a long bench that extended the length of the vehicle. A minibar took up position across from them, colorful ambient lighting glowing from underneath the counter.

"We need to travel like this more often," one of the Canadian soldiers said.

"Where to, Chief?" Johnson said from the front. Marcus had given up any claim on the driver's seat as soon as he had set eyes on Mustafa. The man hadn't even come inside the limo, and stood outside with Lewis, watching as both of their rides were commandeered by the Special Forces operatives.

"Our orders are to head east. As far as we can get." Sanders sat in the passenger seat, his eyes scanning the horizon like a bird of prey searching for a mouse.

The limo pulled out, speeding off the runway and winding its way out and onto the freeway.

"How fast should I be driving?" Johnson asked.

"If somehow this actually ends up making a difference, every mile saves American lives," Sanders replied, looking at his watch. "You've got less than thirty minutes to work with." Johnson floored it, zooming around traffic. The limo behind followed suit.

Without seatbelts, it was hard not to be thrown about by the movements of the limo, and Maria braced herself.

"Why are you helping us?" Maria asked.

"I'm not helping you. I'm just following orders," Sanders replied, not bothering to turn his head to look back.

"The Canadians made a deal," Mother added. "The Prime Minister obviously went above this idiot's head in the chain of command and talked to someone with a brain."

When Sanders turned around, his eyes were burning coals. He didn't say anything, just stared at Maria, but he might as well have slapped her given the malice in that look. When he turned his head back to the front, he muttered something under his breath that made the driver look at him sideways with raised eyebrows.

"Holy crap," Maria whispered. She swallowed hard, turning her attention to the bar in front of her. She exhaled deeply, then reached out, taking hold of the neck of a champagne bottle. "I think I need a drink."

"Have you ever had champagne?" she said to Sam.

"No."

She began to undo the metal ties, but thought twice, and returned the bottle back where she had got it. She took hold of a whiskey bottle instead. "Actually, this is probably more appropriate . . ."

Maria reached out and took three glasses, giving one to Sam and another to Mustafa. She poured some of the brown liquid into each, then held hers out.

"You're supposed to clink the glasses together," she said, waiting for Sam and Mustafa to follow her lead. They reached out and touched their glasses to hers.

"To Earth," she said. She drank from her glass, and Sam did the same. Mustafa poured his over the top of his head.

"You're supposed to drink it, Mustafa," Maria said, laughing.

I just did.

"Oh. Well, then never mind."

———

"What are those flashes?" Sam said, ducking his head and peering out the front window.

"That, my friend, is what it looks like when Uncle Sam launches a shit ton of nukes at a single target," a US soldier replied.

The flashes were happening off in the distance, on the horizon. It reminded Maria of a thunderstorm, except the colors were different, less natural.

"It's pointless," Mother's mechanical voice declared. "I had the power to destroy worlds. Those puny explosions wouldn't have stopped me."

"What did stop you?"

"The Authority."

The soldier looked out toward the explosions, his eyes squinting and his lips pursed together. It was the face of a man not normally used to entertaining deep thoughts contemplating something much bigger than himself.

"This is far enough," Mother said. "You should get out of the vehicle, Mustafa."

Johnson heard what Mother said, and the car noticeably slowed. He turned around, looking through the open space that connected the driver's area to the back of the limo. "Stop here?"

"No," Sanders said. "I give the order when to stop."

"Stop now or die. Your choice," Sanders's own phone said.

Can I kill him now? Please? Mustafa signed.

After a moment of consideration, Maria shook her head from side to side in the negative.

"OK, fine," Sanders said. "Let's stop."

An unnatural wind had picked up and lashed Maria in the face with dust and debris. It was a cold wind, and harsh. She wrapped her arms around her torso and squinted toward the east. The ocean was out there, although she couldn't see it. The vertical wall of destruction she had seen on her phone came to mind. Would it be the same here? How could anyone stop something like that?

I think you should both stay here, Mustafa said.

"No way. I'm going with you," Sam replied.

"You can't talk us out of it," Maria added.

Very well. But stay behind me. Mustafa took off at a

medium pace. He moved due east, transferring his body from tentacle to tentacle in his unique, bobbing gait. Sam and Maria trudged along behind him, trying to shield their faces from the wind. One by one, starting with Xavier, the soldiers joined. They weren't used to staying behind in situations like this, and if the thought of walking head-on into certain destruction hadn't deterred them by this point in their careers, it certainly wasn't going to deter them now. Sanders brought up the rear.

As they progressed, the wind grew impossibly stronger, until it became hard to stand. Maria leaned forward and turned her head to the side. Her hair whipped about her face, blinding her. She could only look down and follow the purple blob in her peripheral vision. She felt a hand take hers and squeeze, and she squeezed back. Sam tried his best to get between her and the wind and managed to shield her from flying debris that would have struck her otherwise.

A spray of water hit her. She knew they weren't at the beach, but it was salty, and fresh. She spotted a seagull, flying backward. The bird was unable to overcome the wind, yet was stubborn enough to keep trying to fly east. There was a dull roar that seemed to come from all around her, and the earth itself felt as though it were trembling under some great force.

Maria managed to get a fistful of her hair and hold it back from flapping in her face. Raising her other hand to shield her, she squinted ahead. There was a harsh rumbling sound coming from directly ahead, almost as if a gigantic meat grinder was trying to process a mountain of stone. She gasped as she caught sight of what was making the noise. There was a tidal wave of rock and ocean bearing down on them, stretching across her entire line of vision.

Mustafa stood to the front. Most of his tentacles were placed wide, bracing himself against the wind. A lone tentacle stretched forward, as far as he could reach toward the wall of destruction.

A rock sailed past, narrowly missing Maria's shoulder. She heard a grunt from behind her, but didn't turn to look to see who had been hit. She couldn't take her eyes off Mustafa. She had expected him to do something . . . *anything*. But he wasn't. He was just standing there, a solitary purple speck in an ocean of brown.

Her clothes started to flap around her in a strange way, and her skin began to hurt. It felt almost like her body was preparing to be pulled apart. Like it wanted to be pulled apart.

Somehow, the wind managed to grow in ferocity, and she had to close her eyes. She leaned in, trying to avoid being toppled over. A hand somehow found hers. She held onto Sam and accepted what strength he was able to offer. The roar around her was deafening. *Lucas!* She had never gotten a chance to say goodbye, and now it was too late. She held her breath and tensed her muscles, bracing for impact. There was no doubt in her mind what would happen next.

This was how she would die.

There was as sharp squeal, and the wind ceased along with the thunderous noise, dropping away like the notes at the very end of a bombastic symphony. Maria looked up and saw Mustafa, his one tentacle extended east as far as it would go. It was the one with the missing tip, and once again, he bled from having been cut there. The incoming wall of force had just nicked him before it had dissipated. Towering over Mustafa's relatively diminutive figure stood the Authority, his golden body having materialized out of the air.

Maria gasped for air, a drowning woman who had suddenly found her head miraculously back above the waves.

Why have you come here? I instructed you to remain where you were, Mustafa signed toward where Sam and Maria stood.

I was unable to remain there. It is imperative that I speak with you, he continued, using a different set of tentacles. Maria realized that the Authority was communicating directly with Mustafa, who was trying to let the others know what was transpiring between them.

Very well.

Can you please speak so that the Earthlings may hear?

Why?

I desire for them to understand what transpires between us.

They are not sentient. They do not warrant our attention.

This is true. But I desire witnesses to the proceedings, and I have chosen these for that role. Mustafa gestured toward where Maria and Sam stood with one of his tentacles.

Certainly there are more fitting witnesses than these primitive organisms.

It is my choice. This is my right under Interstellar Law.

"So be it," the Authority said. Mustafa didn't have to translate for him anymore, as the statement materialized within the minds of everyone present.

I also desire that you translate for me as well. Not all of them understand my language. These words also appeared within the minds of all present, yet they did so in a way that unmistakably tied them to Mustafa. Somehow, the statements were attached to him in the same way that the color blue was attached to a memory of the sky: Mustafa's words and Mustafa were inseparable, as were the Authority's words and the Authority. In this way, their conversation could be held entirely by thought without there being the slightest possibility of confusion from any who listened in.

"Your physical body was almost repurposed. Your choice to come here was not well thought out," the Authority said.

"It was my belief that the Confederation could be trusted to protect a sentient life form, even in the path of a terraforming operation."

"Your faith was well founded. However, this is a delicate operation, and your presence here impedes my progress."

"My apologies, but I could not wait. I require an emergency hearing regarding my status."

"Your status will be decided in due course."

"It needs to happen now."

"The middle of a terraforming operation is not the appropriate time for a discussion like this. I do not have time to spare. Besides, your status does not fall under my purview."

"I insist." Mustafa straightened, raising his body slightly higher. He still stood roughly at knee level when compared to the Authority.

"As I said, your status is an internal affair that does not concern me. I will return you to the place where I found you, and you are instructed to wait with patience until my work here is done."

"You don't understand." Mustafa's tentacles twitched in a strange way. "I have received special dispensation from the Administration."

"What dispensation?"

"That you are to preside over an immediate emergency hearing regarding my status."

"I am not the arbiter of your status. This is not my role."

"It is now."

The Authority was silent. Had he been human, Maria was sure he would have placed his hands on his hips in this moment. There was a long pause before he responded. "I have received no such instructions. You realize the penalty for fabricating evidence in matters such as these is severe."

"I am quite aware of the penalties of falsifying information to the Authority. I am also aware that the Authority must act in accordance with its prime directives as set forth by the Confederation. Are you refusing to carry out your duties?"

"I am incapable of such a refusal."

"Then please double-check your logs and locate my dispensation. It was granted shortly after my asylum hearing, which you attended. I find it unusual that you have misplaced such an important transmission."

There was a short pause. Maria wished the Authority had a face. What was he thinking?

"I have no record of any such dispensation," the Authority declared. "And it is not in my nature to misplace transmissions."

"What is your explanation for your failure?"

"My explanation is that you have not been truthful in your representation of events. As I said, being guilty of such an act carries a severe penalty." The Authority grew in mass, towering even higher over his much smaller counterpart. An electric ripple could be felt passing through the air.

"Are you suggesting I have committed a crime?"

"I am."

Mustafa grew very still. "Formally?"

"Yes."

"And who decides guilt or innocence in these matters?"

"I do. I am law." The Authority took a step toward Mustafa, stretching out one of his golden hands. It was as long as Maria's forearm, and there was a disturbance in the air near his fingertips. "You are charged with falsifying information to the Authority of the Confederation. What have you to say in your defense?"

Mustafa slowly rubbed two tentacles together. "As you know, all dispensations are securely encrypted."

"That is true."

"And in the history of the Confederation, these protocols have never been compromised."

"I am quite aware of the historical record."

"Good. Then this is my defense." Mustafa rattled off an insanely long sequence of numbers.

"What is this number?"

"It is the internal reference code for my dispensation."

There was a short pause before the Authority spoke. "The identifier you have provided is correct in sequence, following in order immediately after my last recorded transmission from the Administration. However, I have not logged any such—"

"So the sequence is correct?"

"Yes."

"And the protocols to encrypt it are unbreakable?"

"Yes."

"Then it follows that my request is authentic."

"Perhaps the code has been compromised."

"But isn't that impossible?"

"It has never happened before."

"Then how do you explain the fact that I have been able to provide this identifier?"

The Authority was silent.

"The Confederation is made up of the most technologically advanced beings in the known Universe, and their cryptographic protocols are second to none. What outside race could ever hope to crack such a code?"

"Such a race with that capability does not exist in my records."

"And your records are extensive, are they not?"

"They compromise the combined knowledge of all worlds in the Confederation."

"And if a thing cannot be found there, it cannot be found anywhere, because by definition all that exists in the known Universe also exists in your records. So how can such a race exist? You are the Authority of the Confederation. Is it in your nature to be wrong?"

"It is my purpose to determine right from wrong and to uphold that which is lawful and true."

"Then how can I be accused of fabricating this code? I am a biological organism. The only computational capabilities I possess are my own meager brain and what limited technology these stick-wielding, non-sentient humans have to offer. Are you suggesting that the most secure cryptographic protocol in the known Universe has been cracked under these conditions?"

"I agree that the odds against that are astronomical."

"It makes no sense. If I *had* cracked the code, that would make me . . . what? A mathematical prodigy?"

"I see your point."

"Besides, it would take more than just a prodigy to crack such a code. I would say it would take at least a genius."

"I am not suggesting otherwise."

"Not just any genius, but a genius among geniuses, born of a race of geniuses." Mustafa slowly stretched out a tentacle in Maria's direction, then let it lay there pointing at her, the tip wagging ever so slightly.

"I believe we have established the difficulty of the task in question."

Mustafa paused, shifting his weight slightly. "I mean, certainly if I had done it, it would mean *at the bare minimum* that I was smarter than anyone else standing here," Mustafa waved a tentacle in the direction of the humans standing nearby. "Wouldn't you agree?"

"Undoubtedly, although I am unclear how this comparison—"

Mustafa's entire body seemed to puff outward. "In fact, we could go so far to say that I would have to be recognized as the single most intelligent creature in the known Universe . . . or possibly of all time. Would there ever have existed a smarter or more intelligent being than myself? Wouldn't that also make my kind superior to all others? Gods, even? Do we even have words to describe such elevated beings? You have the entire recorded history of the known Universe at your fingertips, and such a thing cannot be found anywhere in it. For this to have happened and for me to be the one to—"

Maria cleared her throat loudly, then coughed a few times. "Excuse me," she said meekly as she saw the Authority turn in her direction. "Apocalypse-dust in my throat . . . "

The tentacle pointed at Maria was withdrawn. "Of course, this is all just idle chatter. It is obvious that I am nothing more than a poor orphan who only seeks a home." Mustafa seemed to shrink back within himself, almost curling up at the Authority's feet. He crawled forward, rolling on the ground. Maria couldn't remember seeing a more pitiful display. Even Pepe, when confronted with a handful of hotdog treats, had shown more pride.

"Please see reason," Mustafa said. "You are a rational being. My people are incapable of subterfuge. Simple logic suggests that the identifier must be authentic, and that for some inexplicable reason there is a gap in your logs."

"Your arguments are sound. The identifier must be authentic." The Authority stepped back, lowering his hand. "It is unclear why I am unable to access the content of this directive. I will request clarification from the Administration and we will continue this conversation once they respond. In the meantime I will resume—"

"That is unacceptable." Mustafa sprung up from the ground in a smooth motion, advancing on the Authority.

The Authority was silent.

"Are you quite certain your systems are functioning appropriately?" Mustafa said.

"My systems are in perfect order."

"Then why are you refusing to follow the orders issued by the Administration?"

"I have refused no order. I simply—"

"We both agree that the order is authentic, so why are you trying to delay?"

"I am not. I—"

"The order is for an immediate emergency hearing. What part of that do you not understand?"

"I have not been able to verify the—"

"I am quite dissatisfied with your performance in this matter. I have filed a grievance with the Administration. I do not believe you are upholding the standards of your charter." Mustafa folded his tentacles across his body, a strange gesture of disapproval that was impossible to mistake.

"How have you filed a grievance? I detected no such transmission." The gold man seemed to grow taller, and leaned over Mustafa.

Mustafa quickly went red, white droplets covering the ground where he stood. "How dare you! First, you question the authenticity of an order sent by the Administration, and then you question my ability to communicate with that great body? How do you think I received their dispensation in the first place? Just because you failed to detect my transmission does not mean I did not send it. The arrogance!"

"Apologies. I was only stating the facts as I saw them." The Authority leaned back, giving Mustafa space.

Mustafa's color returned to its usual purple. "Has the Administration responded to your request about my dispensation yet?"

"They have not."

"What is taking them so long?"

"Their schedule is not under my control."

"Then I suggest we hold a provisional hearing, pending their response. It is my understanding this is an appropriate course of action according to precedent."

"I must advise you that should the Administration's response prove contrary to what you assert, the ramifications will be grave."

"Are you always this suspicious? Haven't I already proven my sincerity? I have full confidence in the Administration's confirmation of my statements."

"Very well. You may proceed."

Maria glanced over at Sam, who was unsuccessfully trying to hide a smile. She wanted to ask him what he thought was going on, but didn't dare interrupt.

"My world has been destroyed by an agent of the Confederation," Mustafa said. "I am the only surviving member of my species."

"This fact is not under dispute."

"I therefore claim the rights of a refugee as set forth in Interstellar Law, governed variously throughout sections 500 through 501."

"It appears to be within your rights to claim refugee status, although the determination of this status is not usually one I am tasked with making."

"Then make it provisionally. It is not up to either of us to question the Administration's wisdom in why they found this matter so critically important to place it upon your shoulders here in this barbaric corner of the Universe."

"This request is granted on a provisional basis."

Mustafa flapped a tentacle on the ground. Maria and Sam both noticed, and nudged each other. Neither knew why it was important, but they had become accustomed to reading Mustafa's body language, and tentacle flaps could only mean good things.

"Have you duly recorded my new status as a refugee with the Administration?"

"Of course."

"Excellent."

The Authority took a step back. "Now that this matter has been concluded, I must—"

"Wait! There's more."

"Only one matter may be handled at a time by special dispensation. Your status has been settled."

"I am not here for my status. I hereby approach you as a refugee, and the last surviving member of my species, and I seek an audience with the Authority of the Confederation."

The Authority stepped back toward Mustafa. "Your refugee status is acknowledged. Please continue."

"I hereby warrant that I represent an entire sentient race and ask for the Authority to recognize that I speak for my species in these matters, and not just for myself as an individual."

"It is recognized."

"Our species is without a home, and as a sentient race, we have the right to lay claim to suitable worlds not currently under the jurisdiction of any other sentient races. This falls under section 501.12.5."

"You have this right."

"I therefore claim this planet, being devoid of any native sentient races, as the new home world for my kind."

The Authority studied Mustafa. Maria couldn't be sure, but he might have slightly tilted his head. "I am terraforming this world in preparation of presenting it to a member planet of the Confederation that has recorded a request for a new territory."

"By being a refugee species, we claim first priority in territorial disputes," Mustafa said.

"The process has already begun. I have cleansed roughly six

percent of this world of its undesirable organic matter. A different planet would suit your species' needs more perfectly."

"Six percent? Holy Mother of God," one of the soldiers whispered.

"Section 501.12.8 gives endangered species the right to claim any home world not already populated by another sentient race. Under Interstellar Law, I desire to claim this planet for my species," Mustafa said. "Please check your logs for verification of my status and ability to make this claim."

"The logs clearly support your rights in this matter. Are you certain that this planet is the one you wish to claim?" The Authority said.

"I am."

"Very well. I have recorded it in the annals and have forwarded the notice to the Administration. Do you wish for me to continue cleansing it?"

"I do not. I am happy with it as is."

"Oh shit," Xavier said. "Did that little fellow just take ownership of the entire planet?"

"I think so," Maria said. She couldn't stop herself from smiling.

"Just a minute," Sanders said, stepping up next to Maria and facing the Authority. "This world belongs to us humans. You can't just come in here and decide that it belongs to some octopus because he asks for it. It's ours, goddammit. Ownership of this planet is not up for negotiation."

The Authority shifted, facing Sanders with his expressionless face. "The non-sentient beings present will silence themselves and avoid interrupting the proceedings further, or I will be forced to silence them myself." The warning was visceral, and Maria could feel the threat in her entire body even though it had not been directed at her. In that moment, she realized that the Authority had it within his power to rip every atom in her body apart and cast them to the ends of the Universe. She knew it because the Authority meant for her to know it, and the sudden impact of that revelation sent her fight-or-flight response into overdrive. Sanders felt it, too, and stepped back into a wall of tense, wide-eyed soldiers.

Mustafa undulated, swaying his bulb from side to side on his tentacles. He had begun to enjoy himself. "As the native sentient race to this planet, we would like to declare our friendship with the Administration and Interstellar Governance Body."

"As the Authority of the Confederation, I recognize your friendship and offer ours in return."

"As a friend of the Authority, and the great body of sentient races it represents, this planet would like to apply for admission into the Confederation. We understand that under section 502.1.1, this declaration must be accepted as long as the applying planet agrees to abide by Interstellar Law and submit to the Authority as final arbiter of disputes."

"You are correct in your interpretation of Interstellar Law. Do you accept these conditions?"

"Yes, we accept them."

"Then your request is granted," the Authority said. "This planet is now a provisional member of the Confederation of planets, with all due rights and privileges associated thereby."

"Wow, Earth is in the Confederation now!" Sam whispered. He hadn't let go of Maria's hand, and squeezed it for emphasis.

"As a member of the Confederacy," Mustafa said, "I ask for an Edict of Protection upon myself by the Authority, being the last surviving member of my race."

"Is there a credible threat upon your safety that has caused you to make this request?"

"Yes. The non-sentient beings upon this planet can frequently be hostile and unpredictable."

"Are you sure you do not wish for me to cleanse them for you?"

"Some of them amuse me. I believe the Edict will be sufficient protection."

"Very well. Your request is granted." A gold bracelet materialized around Mustafa's shortest tentacle, resting in the place once occupied by his silver one.

"Oh, fuck." Maria turned to see Sanders staring at Mustafa's bracelet from behind her. His expression betrayed his own greed for the bracelet, as well as his fear surrounding it. This was clearly not an outcome he had expected. One side of his face began to twitch, and he shifted nervously from side to side, staring at Mustafa and the Authority with the intensity of a starving dog watching a much larger animal eat.

Mustafa turned and held the bracelet aloft so that all could see it. Then he spun back to orient himself in the same position he had been in. "As a protected being, I request a declaration of my status to any other beings, sentient or not, who might come in contact with me on this world."

Maria had experienced a declaration from the Authority once before, in the hotel room in Las Vegas. Nonetheless, she was still taken aback by the sheer force of his message as it landed in her mind. The faces of the men around her registered their shock as well. There was a power in his words that could be felt physically, as if the brains of those listening absorbed a solid blow.

"Denizens of Earth, take notice," the Authority stated, broadcasting his message across the planet so that it landed in the awareness of all organic beings able to comprehend even a fraction of its impart. "An Edict of Protection has been granted to this being." The Authority didn't need to specify who the being was, as a complete understanding of Mustafa was transmitted as part of the knowledge. "He remains under the protection of the Confederacy, as does this planet. He is the representative of this planet to the Confederation, and his species holds position as the native sentient species of this world. Any threat against him or his position will be treated as a threat against the Confederation itself. Any hostile or subversive actions taken against him or his race will be treated as an act of war against the Confederation itself. You are hereby ordered to respect his authority in all matters and to protect his position as guardian of this planet."

A small fly had been buzzing around Mustafa's head, clearly interested in the unusual smell. It quickly flew away, recognizing Mustafa in its own way and realizing the threat to its existence. All beings on Earth, great and small, had been put on notice.

"Mustafa! You're like a king now!" Sam said enthusiastically, clearly excited about the developments.

And you are my worthy subjects, Mustafa said, flourishing a tentacle in an excellent imitation of a royal personage speaking to his people.

"Was this the plan all along?" Maria said.

Yes. Mother made me memorize the appropriate passages from Interstellar Law. The Authority likes it when you can state your case by citing specific statutes.

"You were very lucky to have . . . *remembered* that code when you did," Sam said, looking at his brother, then quickly glancing over at the Authority.

I told you I was good at math.

"Speaking of the consciousness of the nursemaid planetoid," the Authority said. "She is a fugitive and must be brought to justice."

Maria's phone buzzed, and Maria brought it out and held it toward Mustafa and the Authority. "Mustafa, guardian of Earth," Mother said. "I humbly seek asylum on this world."

"Your request is granted," Mustafa said.

"This being has declared war on the Confederation. I intend to destroy her. It is my duty under the charter granted to me by the Administration," the Authority said.

"Under Interstellar Law, member planets have the authority to grant asylum to those they feel are worthy. We reject the Authority's claim on this being."

The Authority stood, looking at Mustafa. Mustafa twitched his tentacles, standing his ground before the golden giant looming over him. Neither spoke for a long time.

"May I suggest a solution to our impasse?" Mustafa finally said. "I request a notice be filed with the Administration to allow them to weigh in on this dispute. Their wisdom would be welcome in properly interpreting the statutes."

The Authority was quiet for a moment, then replied. "That is an appropriate response under these circumstances. A notice has been sent to the Administration. I will place a temporary hold on pursuing justice on this being until guidance has been received."

"It is a logical course of action," Mustafa said. It was clear he was happy, as his tentacles thrashed on the ground like snakes.

"Have you any further business with me?" the Authority asked.

"That is all. Thank you for your assistance with these matters."

And then, as quickly as he had come, the Authority was gone. The sky was clear, and the sun was warm on Maria's skin. A gentle breeze carried the smell of the ocean with it, lifting her hair gently in its embrace and filling her lungs with hope.

THIRTY-FOUR

"You did that perfectly," Mother said. Her robotic voice was unable to express any emotion, so instead she forwarded a string of heart emojis in a text message. Maria held the phone up so Mustafa could see it, and received a happy squeak in response.

"Is he gone?" Sanders said, looking around warily, as if the Authority were going to pop back into existence in an attack from behind. "Was that it?" He looked around, trying to judge the lay of the land. Satisfied that the Authority wasn't anywhere to be seen, he turned his attention back to the three. His voice was merciless. "I want these two zip-tied and thrown in the car ASAP. And for the love of God, will somebody please put a bullet in that squid?"

Xavier moved fast, drawing a pistol from his waist and leveling it at Sanders. The US soldiers responded, raising their weapons, and the Canadians replied in turn.

"You dare draw on American troops while standing on our soil?" Sanders sputtered.

"Didn't you hear the declaration from the Authority?" Xavier said. "Any hostile actions against Mustafa will be treated as an act of war against the Confederation. Canada cannot allow that."

"You Canadians need to learn your place. You are our guests here, and if you're worried about triggering a war with an opponent that you can't face, that's exactly what is about to happen. Stand down."

"You all heard the declaration from the Authority," Sam said, addressing the soldiers around him. "Think about what you're doing. If you hurt Mustafa, then the Authority is going to come back and finish what he started. Is that what you want?"

"Trying to talk soldiers out of following their orders?" Sanders laughed. "Good luck with that." He turned to Xavier. "Tell your dogs to stand down. I won't ask you again."

Xavier glanced sideways at his men and returned his gaze to Sanders, his jaw set and his eyes firm.

"So you want to play a game of chicken with the world's only military superpower? Let's see what happens." Sanders took a step toward the nearest US soldier. The soldier kept his rifle level and his eyes on the Canadian troops in front of him, barely registering as Sanders drew the spare handgun from the holster on the soldier's belt.

Sanders held the weapon up, inspecting it with unabashed enthusiasm. "You know what I really like about these Glocks? There's no safety. Just point and shoot." Sanders turned, setting his hard eyes on Mustafa. He didn't need to speak his intentions, they were clear to all present.

Faster than anyone could react, Sam closed the distance between himself and the old soldier. With one hand he grabbed Sanders's wrist, keeping the firearm pointed to the sky. With his other he landed a devastating hook, smashing his fist across Sanders's jaw and knocking the man to the ground.

Sanders crawled backward, scooting himself away from

Sam. Without taking his wide eyes off his adversary, he patted frantically on the ground next to him.

"Looking for this?" Sam held the handgun up so Sanders could see it.

Sanders scrambled to his feet, his face flushed red. "Kill them!" he shouted. "Kill them all. That's an order."

You are no longer in charge, Mustafa said. Maria didn't need to translate for him. The message appeared in her consciousness, as well as in those of everyone else present. His normal purple color was tinged with red.

Mustafa made his way toward Sanders, taking his time as he crept forward. Sanders took a step back, looking for help from the sides. The US Special Forces team hesitated. Despite their training, they had seen and heard the exchange with the Authority, and had taken the warnings to heart. Sanders may be in command, but they were not going to risk a planetary war with a technologically superior adversary on his behalf. They had already seen what the Authority was capable of. Humanity would not survive the conflict.

I have not decided what to do with this world yet. I may let you humans live as you have been, or I may decide to clone myself and allow my own kind to be reborn on this planet in your place. . . . You will kneel when I speak to you.

"Like hell I will."

Mustafa flashed his bracelet and Sanders dropped to his knees, via force or acquiescence, it wasn't clear. Mustafa came up and extended a tentacle around the man's neck, tightening like a boa constrictor around its prey.

I wanted to kill you earlier, but my brother and Maria disagreed. But now seems like the ideal time. The tentacle around Sanders's neck tightened, and the man's face became red. *And after I'm done with you, perhaps I will do the same to every government official in this country, starting with your president.*

Sanders gasped for air and Maria stepped forward, only to be gently intercepted and tugged back by Sam.

Do you think you could stop me? I am under the direct protection of the Authority. Do you think your pathetic human weapons will do any good against me?

The assault rifles that the US Special Forces soldiers held at the ready were ripped from their hands, slamming to the ground. Some soldiers stepped back in shock. Others tried to pick their weapons back up but found they didn't have the strength to budge them.

I could destroy them too—your entire army!—and I could do it with a thought. It would be so easy . . . Mustafa's entire body flashed a deep shade of red, and he trembled slightly. He held Sanders there in his deadly grip, a predator toying with his helpless prey.

But I don't feel like spoiling this day by killing vermin, so this shall be your punishment instead. Mustafa pulled Sanders down so he was on all fours and climbed upon his back. A thick, white slime splattered from underneath his body, completely covering the man in long, sticky strands. The stench was overpowering, and Maria was forced to turn her head as Sanders began to retch.

"Did he just . . . ?" Xavier said, covering his nose.

"I think so," Maria coughed. "God, that stinks."

You are forbidden to clean yourself off for a period of twenty-one days, Mustafa said, climbing down and releasing Sanders from his grasp. It was the ultimate mark of shame. *If I find you have disobeyed my orders, I will flatten this continent and all who live upon it. Do you understand?*

Sanders cleared the slime from where it had gotten into his

eyes and tried to speak, but was unable to do so without heaving. He nodded once.

Now, be gone. And Sanders was gone. Mustafa's color faded, and he was soon purple again.

"Are you really going to level this continent?" Sam said.

Of course not, Mustafa signed. *I was just messing with that guy. He's kind of an asshole.*

Maria laughed. "What about the cloning and repopulating part?"

How many Mustafas do you think this planet can hold?

"I'd say one," Sam said.

"I'd have to agree with your brother. You are one of a kind, Mustafa," Maria added.

Then we can skip that part too. Mustafa flipped a tentacle once.

Maria rubbed the sides of her arms. "Let's get out of here. I've had enough drama for a day."

The three made their way back to the limos, followed by the Canadian soldiers and, at a distance, the Americans. The US soldiers had tried a second time to retrieve their weapons and, having been unsuccessful in even being able to budge them, had abandoned them where they lay.

"Allow me, your Grace," Sam said, opening a door for Mustafa and waving his hand in a convoluted imitation of what he believed was a formal gesture. Mustafa placed four tentacles on the top of his head, and slowly made his way through the open door, leaning back in an obvious caricature that Maria didn't understand, but still thought was hilarious.

"Those two are jokers, aren't they?" Xavier said, standing next to Maria and watching as Sam entered the limo, trying to duplicate Mustafa's gesture, but having difficulty since he didn't have enough arms and legs to work with compared to his brother.

"You should have seen them in Walmart," Maria said. "Oh my God."

THIRTY-FIVE

The drive was uneventful, and Maria heard not a single word spoken by any of the occupants of the limo the entire time. What percentage of Earth had the Authority said he had cleansed? Six? How many people had died in the process? This day would be remembered as the worst disaster in human history, yet somehow also the day of its salvation. Humanity had faced an unbeatable foe and had almost lost everything. It was a miracle any of them were alive. Maria had no doubt how close she had come to her own death. Her body had felt its very fibers being tugged at, ready to be pulled apart in an instant. Such a thing isn't easily forgotten. She glanced over at Mustafa, her eyes lingering on the gold band around his tentacle.

They slowly retraced their path, finally coming to a stop at the airport. As Maria exited the car, her body felt heavier than she remembered. She was tired, and at the same time, strangely relaxed. She was safe, and so was Earth. It was over.

Maria's phone rang.

"Hello?"

"Maria. It's Lita," Maria's grandmother said. "Where are you?"

"Somewhere in Maine. It's kind of a long story."

"Are you all right?"

"Yes."

"I wasn't sure if it was safe to call or not, but I had to tell you. I have amazing news!"

"What happened?"

Sam glanced at Mustafa, then returned his gaze to Maria. He was smiling in a way that indicated he already had an idea what the news might be.

"It's Lucas. He's cured! The Virgin has heard our prayers. It's a miracle!"

"What? He is? How?" Maria wasn't sure what to say. She wasn't sure she had heard her grandmother correctly. After all the tests, and all the doctors, was such a thing even possible?

"I don't know! But he's fine. And another thing . . . Maria, I'm not sure how to tell you this, but one minute I was in a horrible prison cell, and the next I was sitting at home, and there was Lucas, and he was cured!" More was said, but Maria couldn't understand it. Her grandmother was crying.

"Maria?" a young voice said on the other end of the line.

"Lucas? How are you, sweetie?"

"I'm great! Guess what I just did?"

"What?"

"I ran!"

"You did?"

"Yes! And I didn't fall!"

"You didn't?"

"And I don't have to wear my helmet anymore!"

"You don't? Lucas, that's wonderful!"

There was a moment of silence, before Maria's grandmother answered. "He just ran off, Maria! He ran! I haven't seen him run in so long."

"I can't believe it! That's amazing!"

"Yes. I'm going to go make a pound cake. I'm going to offer it to the statue of the Virgin in the front. I don't know how this happened, but I know she somehow had a hand in it, and I'm never going to forget what she has done for this family. I want you to thank her too."

"I will, Lita. Listen, I'll call you later. I have to check on something." Maria made her goodbyes, then hung up. She looked at Mustafa. She could tell he was happy by the way he moved.

"Mustafa, do you know anything about Lucas being cured?" Maria said.

Yes. I know a lot about it, actually. Mustafa may have said more but didn't have the chance. Maria had embraced him, squeezing his rubbery skin in as tight a grasp as she was able. She wanted to lift him up but found he was much heavier than he looked, and his extended tentacles made him extremely unwieldy. So instead she settled for squeezing and rocking the bulb of his body in her arms. Eventually, a tentacle worked its way up between where she held him, and gently pushed them apart.

It is not only Lucas. All the children are cured, Mustafa said.

"What do you mean?"

All children on this planet have been cured of their ailments.

"How is that possible? Don't you have to be close to them to do something like that?"

"The Authority is much more powerful than I was," Mother said. "The range of Mustafa's bracelet extends to a distance greater than the diameter of this planet. There is no place on Earth he is not able to reach."

"That's incredible! And you decided to use that power to cure childhood illness? And you did all of that just now, while we were riding in the car?" Maria said.

It was Sam's idea. He thought this would make you happy.

Mustafa rocked back and forth on his tentacles like a child sharing a precious secret.

"Sam!" Maria turned to the man who'd dragged her into this crazy adventure.

Sam grinned broadly, and his cheeks began to redden. "He's family. You don't give up on family."

Maria's mouth dropped. This man had just cured Lucas of an incurable, life-threatening illness. Not only Lucas; he had cured all children everywhere! Some women were courted with roses and chocolates. Others got lucky and had songs written for them. But this man had cured childhood illness on an entire planet, for her. Maria didn't give Sam time to answer but threw herself into his arms. The flame that had threatened to light so many times since that first day in the lobby of the Bell Rock Inn finally caught, and what started as a small spark quickly grew to a blistering flame as Maria kissed Sam, and he kissed her back with a passion and skill that surprised her. His arms encircled her waist and held her close, and the rest of the world melted away. She poured all her feeling into each press of her lips. Her gratitude for his appearance in her life. Her happiness that they had made it. Her excitement for their future together, and the humming chemistry that set her body alight. But most of all, she gave him her love. There was only Sam, his strong arms and soft lips, and the magic flaring between them.

Maria didn't know how long that kiss lasted; she only knew that after their lips finally parted she would never be without him again.

The Special Forces guys were cheering. Mustafa's tentacles were undulating in unison like twelve tails of a contented cat.

"Knock it off, you pervs," Maria said, blushing.

Come, it is time to go, Mustafa signed.

"Where?" Maria said.

To rescue Pepe.

Maria's body felt like it had become liquid, and together with Sam and Mustafa, twisted in a strange way she had only felt one time before. There was a popping sound, and the three of them vanished, disappearing into thin air. What remained where they once stood was now only a handful of fluttering leaves, and the strange scent of that purple creature whose name no being on Earth would ever be able to forget.

DID YOU LIKE THIS BOOK?

It's hard being an independent author. We don't have any marketing teams, publicists, or agents. It's just us, and our advertising budgets are usually made up of whatever we found behind the couch. We live and die by word of mouth from readers like you. If you enjoyed reading this book as much as I enjoyed writing it, then I think we make a pretty good team. Would it be too much if I asked (begged?) you for a review at the online bookseller of your choice? It's easy, you can do it in five minutes, and you'll be playing a not-insignificant role in helping to get my writing career up and running. Seriously, it's a *really* big deal. Thanks! :-)

ABOUT THE AUTHOR

Earik Beann is the author of *Pointe Patrol: How nine people (and a dog) saved their neighborhood from one of the most destructive fires in California's history*, and the sci-fi thriller *Killing Adam*. Previous to that, he wrote six technical books on esoteric subjects related to financial markets. He is a serial entrepreneur, and over the years he has been involved in many businesses, including software development, an online vitamin store, specialty pet products, a commodity pool, and a publishing house. His original love has always been writing, and *The Earthling's Brother* is his second published novel. He lives in California with his wife Laura, their Doberman, and two Tennessee barn cats.

Please visit Earik's website to learn more about his books, and join his newsletter to receive advance notice on new releases, discounts, freebies, and other goodies:

www.EarikBeann.com

The world runs on ARCs. Altered Reality Chips. Small implants behind the left ear that allow people to experience anything they could ever imagine. The network controls everything, from traffic, to food production, to law enforcement. Some proclaim it a Golden Age of humanity. Others have begun to see the cracks. Few realize that behind it all, living within every brain and able to control all aspects of society, there exists a being with an agenda all his own: the singularity called Adam, who believes he is God.

Jimmy Mahoney's brain can't accept an ARC. Not since his football injury from the days when the league was still offline. "ARC-incompatible" is what the doctors told him. Worse than being blind and deaf, he is a man struggling to cling to what's left of a society that he is no longer a part of. His wife spends twenty-three hours a day online, only coming off when her chip forcibly disconnects her so she can eat. Others are worse. Many have died, unwilling or unable to log off to take care of even their most basic needs.

After being unwittingly recruited by a rogue singularity to play a role in a war that he doesn't understand, Jimmy learns the truth about Adam and is thrown into a life-and-death struggle against the most powerful mathematical mind the world has ever known. But what can one man do against a being that exists everywhere and holds limitless power? How can one man, unable to even get online, find a way to save his wife, and the entire human race, from destruction?